HOW TO DATE A
DOUCHEBAG

THE FAILING HOURS

SARA NEY

First Edition: January 2017
Library of Congress Cataloging-in-Publication Data
How to Date a Douchebag: The Failing Hours – 1st ed
ISBN-13: 978-1386374404

Thank you, Internet, for providing the inspiration for the dating quotes at the beginning of each chapter. They're all based on *real* conversations, pick-up lines, come-ons, and texts between actual people.

For more information about Sara Ney and her books, visit:
https://www.facebook.com/saraneyauthor/

The douchebag is still single.
Go figure.

"My parents must have known
from the beginning that
I was going to be a sinner—
that's why they named me
after two books of the Bible.
Lord knows I'm no saint."
–Ezekiel Daniels

Violet

He isn't hard to spot.

    Big, solid, and imposing, Ezekiel Daniels might be sharing a library table with his friends, but his presence overwhelms the entire space like I imagine a tank in a driveway full of minivans would. Too big and out of place.

My attention is drawn *straight* to him.

I glance down at the tutoring schedule in my hand, cringing at the name printed in bold letters.

Ezekiel Daniels
Library, Student Services Center
9:30PM

The pit in my stomach clenches tighter and I glance at the guy again; that *has* to be him. It's obvious by the way he's impatiently staring around the room that he's waiting for someone. As if somehow sensing my scrutiny, the devil himself looks up, his moody, broody, menacing gaze scanning the perimeter of the room.

Searching.

Hunting.

His regard flickers over me, staring, expression completely unreadable. Void of any emotion, really, as he takes my full measure behind the library's circulation desk, the bookshelves offering me no shelter from his critical perusal.

He's so handsome I almost forget to breathe.

Black hair disheveled. Black brows drawn into angry slashes above remarkably light eyes, he's in desperate need of a shave.

And a tutor.

He slides a sheet of paper off the table and pinches it between two titan fingers; I know what's on it because it's identical to the one I'm holding. They should, but my feet don't propel me toward him to introduce myself, even though I know he's here for a tutoring session.

With me.

Nerves root me to the spot.

I watch as Ezekiel Daniels gestures wildly to his friends with dark furrowed brows, his lips forming angry words I cannot hear from here. One of his friends laughs, another shakes his head and leans back in his chair, bulky tattooed arms crossed, amused. The entire group has a palpable restlessness and air of boredom I wonder about, and horrified, I watch Ezekiel make a crude motion with his hands, miming a blow job with his mouth.

The entire table erupts into raucous laugher. Now they're so loud I can make out everything they're saying, and I strain, pretending to work while I listen. Watch when the friend hefts his big body out of that small chair and saunters across the room.

"What's your tutors name?" I hear the friend ask.

"Violet."

"Aww, how pretty."

So begins his leisurely shuffle across the library, weaving through the intricate labyrinth of tables, crosshairs set on a girl wearing a conservative black cardigan, pearls, and black glasses perched atop her brown, shiny hair.

She's studying, head bent, nose buried in a text book. I secretly applaud when moments later, she rebuffs him, sending him stalking back to his friends.

The behemoth with the tattooed arms tosses the paper at Ezekiel Daniels with a smirk, plopping down in stiff, desk chair.

"That's not her?" Ezekiel's booming voice carries over.

"Nope." His friend flips open a text book.

The unfeeling glower intensifies, and I watch a pair of full lips form another sentence, spouting my name, over and over, the low timber of his furious voice resonating across the cavernous room.

He does another scan of the library.

"It says her name is Violet. Where the fuck is she?"

He lifts himself to a stand. Catches my eye across the room.

When he raises his black brows and the corner of his mouth arrogantly, I back up until my butt hits the table behind me.

Ezekiel Daniels starts his own slow saunter toward the circulation desk—toward me—dragging his feet lazily along the hardwood floors, his lazy gate a thing of beauty.

Demands attention.

And it works, because I can't take my eyes off him.

Can't look away, not until he's finally standing in front of me, eyes blazing with ill humor. Cynicism.

"Is this where I find the tutor that was assigned to me?" he asks without preface, slapping his sheet of paper loudly on the counter with a smack. "I can't find her."

My eyes flicker down. See my name printed in bold, black letters.

"Y-Yes."

His eyebrows quirk again when I stutter, pleased with himself. "Do I make you nervous?"

"No."

"You sure about that?"

I fold my hands in front of me, resting them on the smooth wood, and ignore his question to ask one of my own, using my most authoritative tone.

"I-Is there something I-I can help you with?"

He scrutinizes me a few uncomfortable moments, unfriendly gaze sweeping up and down my torso before his beautifully sculpted lips part. "Is there a Violet available?"

Am I?

Am I available to this guy?

This is it, the moment I must make up my mind. Am I going to subject myself to him for the sake of my job? Let him chip away at my self-respect for what little money tutoring him will bring me? Am I going to force myself to sit the countless hours it may take to help him pass a class?

It's true that I need this job—but I don't know if I can bring myself to tutor Ezekiel Daniels.

Anyone can tell by looking at him that he isn't nice.

"*Well?*" he demands, pushing the sheet toward me. "Is she available?"

I raise my eyes, staring the devil in the eye.

"No. She's not."

"Don't look him in the eyes;
it's like looking at the sun,
but instead of burning
your retinas,
it makes you want to
sleep with him."

Zeke

"**A**re you listening to me, Mr. Daniels?"

I jerk my head toward the sound of my coach's voice, already aggravated to the point of distraction because he's determined to waste my time. His office is small, but so is he, and the cinderblock walls have faded to a dull blue, casting an eerie pallor over his skin.

The veins in Coach's neck strain as he fights to gain control of the impromptu meeting he's called me into. I'm not in the mood to listen.

With nothing to add, I keep my damn mouth shut, instead giving a terse nod.

"I said, are you listening to me, son?"

I want to remind him that I'm not his son—not even close. My own father doesn't even call me *son*.

Not that I'd want him to.

Jaw locked, teeth clenched. "Yes, sir."

"Now, I don't know where that chip on your shoulder comes from, and I'm not going to pretend to give a crap about what goes on when you leave here, but I'll be damned if I stand by and watch one of my boys self-destruct in my gym." His weathered skin stretches along with the grimly set line of his mouth.

He continues. "You think you're the first prick to come through this program thinking his shit don't stink? You're not, but you are the first prick to come with an attitude I can't seem to quit. You're also one sarcastic wisecrack away from getting a fist slammed through your pretty face. Even your own teammates don't like you. I can't have discord on my team."

My jaw ticks when I clench it, but having nothing to say in defense, I clamp my mouth shut.

He rankles on.

7

"What's it going to take to get through to you, Mr. Daniels?"

Nothing. You've got nothing that will fucking get through to me, old man.

He tips back in his old wooden desk chair and studies me, fingers clasped into a steeple. Balancing on the legs, Coach taps his chin with the tips.

It's on the verge of my tongue to tell him if he wants to get through to me, he can stop calling me *Mister* Daniels. Second, he can cut the bullshit and tell me the reason he pulled me into his office after practice.

After a long stretch of silence, he leans forward, the springs on his chair emitting a loud, scraping metallic sound, his arms coming to rest on the desktop. His hands glide over a sheaf of paper and he plucks one off the top.

"Tell ya what we're going to do." He pushes the paper toward me across the desk. "The director of Big Brothers Mentorship Program owes me a favor. You have any experience with kids, Daniels?"

I shake my head. "No."

"Do you know what Big Brothers is?"

"No, but I'm sure you're about to enlighten me," I retort, unable to stop myself. Crossing my arms, I adopt a defensive pose most people find intimidating.

Not Coach.

"Allow me to educate you, Mr. Daniels. It's a program designed to match a youngster with an older volunteer—such as yourself—that acts as a mentor. Hang out with the kid. Show him he's not alone. Be someone dependable that isn't going to bail. Typically, they're good kids from single-parent households, but not always. Sometimes the kids are left alone, deadbeat dads, that sort of thing. Sometimes their parents just don't care and they're left to fend for themselves. Know what that's like that, son?"

Yes. "No."

The sadist drones on, shuffling the stack on his desk. "There's an interview process I think you'd fail with flying colors, so we're cutting through the red tape and pulling some strings. You know why? Because you have potential to be successful and you're pissing it away by being a callous little asshole."

His chair creeks in the cellblock of an office. "Maybe what you need is to give a shit about someone other than yourself for a change. Maybe what you need is to meet a kid whose life is shittier than yours. Your pity party is over."

"I don't have time to volunteer, Coach," I grit out.

Coach grins up at me from his desk, the overhead lights reflecting off his thick glasses. "Too goddamn bad then, ain't it? You either take the volunteer hours, or you're off the team. I don't need a smoking gun on my hands. Trust me, we'd find a way to carry on without you."

He waits for my answer, and when I don't immediately respond, he presses. "Think you can handle that? Say, *Yes, Coach.*"

I nod tersely. "Yes, Coach."

"Good." Satisfied, he grabs a yellow No. 2 pencil and tosses it at me. "Fill that sheet out and take it with you. You meet your Little Brother tomorrow at their downtown office. Address is on the form."

Reluctantly, I snatch the pencil and paper off the desk but don't look at it.

"Don't be late. Don't fuck this up. Tomorrow afternoon you're going to see how the other half lives, got it son?" I nod. "Good. Now get the fuck out of my office."

I glower down at him.

His raspy chuckle hits my back when I turn toward the door. "And Mr. Daniels?"

I stop in my tracks but refuse to face him.

"I know it will be hard, but try not to be total prick to the kid."

9

Coach is a total asshole.

Not that I give a shit, because I'm an asshole, too. There isn't much I care about these days, so why would he think I'd care about some fucking kid? Especially one being forced on me?

My friends call me merciless; they claim cold blood runs through my veins, that I'm impossible to get close to.

But I like it that way; I like creating distance. No one needs me, and I need them even less. Happiness is a myth. Who needs it? This anger brewing inside me is more tangible than any happiness I've forgotten how to feel, never having been anything but alone.

It's suited me fine for fifteen years.

I'm still fuming when I waltz into the grocery store, grab a cart from the corral, and push it up and down each aisle with purpose, tossing food in without slowing my stride.

Steel-cut oats. Agave nectar. Walnuts.

I saunter to the nutrition and organics section, hands automatically reaching for the protein powder, gripping the black plastic container in one hand, and lobbing it in among the deli meat, bread, and bottles of water.

Turning the aisle and pushing the cart on the right side of the aisle, I skid to a halt, almost plowing into a little girl on her tiptoes, reaching toward a shelf. Her black curly hair is pulled tightly into two pigtails, her string-bean arms straining toward a box she'll never reach.

Even on the balls of her feet.

Plus, she's in my way.

"Dammit kid, I almost hit you," I growl. "You might want to pay more attention."

She ignores my warning.

"Can you get that down for me?" Her grubby little fingers wiggle toward a red box of sugar cones, forefinger pointing toward the top shelf. I note that her tiny digits are painted glittery blue, and there are bits of dirt encrusted under her nail beds.

"Should you be talking to strangers?" I scold down at her but pluck the box off the shelf anyway, gruffly shoving it toward her grasping hands. Glance around. Notice for the first time that she's unsupervised. "Jesus Christ kid, where are your parents?"

"At school."

"At *school?*"

"My dad works and my mom is in college."

"Who the hell are you with?"

The little squirt ignores me, tilting her head, narrowing her unblinking beady brown eyes at me. "You're saying bad words."

I'm not in the mood to play nice, so I narrow mine back. "I'm an adult. I can say whatever the hell I want."

"I'm telling." Her little mouth puckers disapprovingly and I can feel her silently judging me; I bet she's a real joy to have in class.

"Yeah, okay kid—you do that."

"Summer?" calls a loud feminine voice from somewhere around a corner. In a flurry of gray and white, the owner of that voice comes skidding around the corner, gasping for breath when she sees us.

"Oh my god, there you are!"

She falls to her knees.

Pulls the scrawny kid to her body in an embrace. "Oh my g-god," the woman repeats, stuttering. "Sweetie, you cannot just walk off like that! You scared me half to d-death. Didn't you hear me calling your name?"

The kid—Summer, apparently—holds her ground, trying to wiggle free. "I was getting ice cream cones and sprinkles."

"Summer." The woman pulls the little girl into an embrace. Takes a shaky breath. "Summer, when I-I couldn't find you, I thought someone had kidnapped you. I thought I was going to have a h-heart attack."

"I was right here, Vi," the kid squeaks out into the woman's
jacket, fighting to breathe through the struggle cuddle. "This boy
was getting my cones."

This *boy*?

I put my hands up. "Whoa kid, do *not* drag me down into the
gutter with you."

It's then that the woman senses my presence and looks up.
Up. Up, into my impassive, irritated eyes.

Our eyes lock and I'm startled to realize she's not as old as I
thought; she's a young woman, one that looks vaguely familiar.

Her eyes are a brilliant shade of hazel, widening with a flash
of panic and recognition at the sight of me, probably because I'm
casting an unfriendly frown down at her. I intimidate most people
and take pride in it.

Her lips part but no sound comes out, nothing but a startled
squeak. She recovers quickly, hugging the girl tighter and smoothing her hands down the girl's weak little forearms.

"W-Were y-you waiting with her long?"

When I realize she's speaking to me, a snort escapes my nose
and I ignore her question, instead pointing out the obvious.

"Lady, you make a shitty nanny. She could have been kidnapped."

Her head and shoulders dip, ashamed. "I know! B-Believe
me, I know."

The young woman's mouth clamps shut again, chin trembling. Taking a few deep breaths to compose herself, she swallows
nervously. "Thank you for helping her."

"*Helping*? That's funny. I'm no good Samaritan." I don't
want her thanks or to prolong this litany of mind-numbing chitchat.
"All I did was prevent her from toppling the display rack. She's
short as shit."

"Well th-thank you nonetheless." Another quick squeeze
around the little kid's shoulders and the young woman stands.

Petite, I gauge her height at around five foot five—tiny compared to my six feet. Wide hazel eyes. Thick blonde hair so pale it looks *white*, falling down over her shoulder in an intricate, wholesome braid. My gaze immediately falls to the neckline of her well-worn Iowa sweatshirt for an appraisal of her chest.

Flat.

Bummer, must suck.

I study her flushed face through narrowed, dubious eyes. "Do I know you?"

She swallows, glancing to the right. "I-I don't think so?"

I can't stand liars.

"I *do* know you. You live at the library."

An errant strand of hair that's not even in her face gets brushed aside. "I-I *work* at the library, yes. I also do some babysitting for enrolled students with daycare-aged ch-children and in Student Services."

She's fidgety as *fuck* and I wonder what her problem is.

Maybe she's flustered.

Or maybe she's on drugs.

I lean in closer to get a good look at her pupils—checking to see if they're dilated—and catch a whiff; she smells like virgin and what I imagine baby powder would if I knew what the hell it smelled like.

Lean closer still. "You should tell the *fucking* tutors there to show up for their *jobs*."

If it is possible for a human to turn a violent shade of pink from fingers to the roots of her blonde hair, this girl has managed it. Her hands fly to her face, palms pressed flat against her cheeks.

Takes a deep breath, clutches the little girl's hand. "I-I'll pass along the message." Pause. "We should get going."

"Yeah, you should go, because you're totally in my way." I give my cart a jostle, jerking it forward so they move and I can skirt around in what little room they're *not* taking up. Before I round the next aisle, I stab an accusing finger their way. "For the record, *Shitty Nanny*, that kid shouldn't be out in public; it should be in bed."

―――――――――――

I'm dumping the grocery bags onto the kitchen counter after the afternoon from hell, unceremoniously unloading the contents and tossing the brown paper bags. I rearrange the contents of a few cabinets to make room for the new shit and crack open a bottle of water while debating about dinner.

Lean chicken breast and broccoli. Vegetable stir-fry on brown rice. Choke down a bowl of oatmeal with nuts and berries.

Nothing sounds good.

Not after the piss afternoon I've had.

In the recesses of the hallway, I hear a door open and close, followed by silence. Moments later, the toilet flushes.

Jameson Clark, the girl my roommate Oz just started dating, saunters into the room. She's wearing tailored jeans, a fuzzy baby blue sweater. Glasses. The satisfied grin widening her lips is quickly replaced with a startled expression when she sees me scowling at her from the sink.

She doesn't like me.

Not that I give two shits, because I don't like her either.

Cautiously, James makes her way to the fridge, but hesitates before pulling it open.

"Hey, how's it going?" She tries to make small talk.

"Fine."

She gestures toward the fridge. "Do you mind if I ..."

I grunt. "Oh, by all means, please help yourself to our food and make yourself at home. You always do."

Instead of pulling open the fridge, she leans against the counter, studying me quizzically, like a puzzle she's been trying to piece together for months.

"You know I'm not the enemy, right?"

Bullshit.

"I don't know why you're trying to have a conversation with me right now. I'm not in the mood," I grit out between my teeth.

"Big shocker. You're such a grouch." James plucks an apple—one of *my* apples—out of the big bowl on the counter, and bites down, chewing. Swallows the first morsel. Takes another bite, filling the silence with the sound of her munching.

"I can tell something's bothering you, Zeke, and for all the growling you do around here, I know it can't be because of *me*."

James pops a leg out jauntily, propping it against the cabinet. My eyes are cast downward, drawn to the colorful blue toenails on her feet. They match her blue cardigan sweater.

She catches me looking at her toes and wiggles them with a smirk.

Dammit.

"I know we didn't get off to the best start, but I'd like you to feel comfortable around me. Maybe you could even consider me a friend."

Yeah, that's not going to happen.

I smile. "I know you think you're hot shit because you're fucking Sebastian Osborne, but believe me, you're not. I tolerate you because I have to, so you can cut the bullshit."

Her mouth falls open and my shoulders relax, having successfully squashed her interest in getting inside my head.

"Why are you *so* pissed?" she murmurs into the kitchen, more to herself than to me, wonderment tingeing her voice.

"Jesus Christ, why does everyone keep asking me that?"

It pisses me off even more.

"Zeke, even if nothing is bothering you, maybe you'd feel better talking to Sebastian—"

"You've been dating Oz for all of five minutes. Do us both a favor and stop trying to analyze me. I might be his friend, but I will never be yours." I stride to the door, grab my shit, and hike my backpack up onto my shoulders.

Jameson stares at my wake, wide-eyed and looking ...
A little hurt.

Well tough shit, I don't have time for this.

"I have an appointment at the library. I don't have time to girl talk with you right now, so please spare whatever delusions you have about us being buddies for someone else."

I yank open the door and don't give her a second look.

"You kids don't wait up."

"Look, I tried to like him but his dick tasted like failure and disappointment."

Violet

I cannot calm my racing heart.

As soon as I stepped over the threshold of the library for my shift, it started wildly beating. I know there's a chance I'll see Ezekiel Daniels tonight; he's been coming around lately, and now that I know he needs help with a bio class, it seems my luck avoiding him is about to run out.

With a sigh, I make a show of busying myself with the Student Services log-in binder, signing off on which students have come and gone, and enter staffer tutoring hours into the computer.

There's a hastily scribbled note stuck to the computer monitor in the back room that shouts:

VIOLET!!!!! ZEKE DANIELS WILL BE BACK TONIGHT. PLEASE <u>DO NOT</u> MISS THIS APPOINTMENT!! ANY PROBLEMS PLEASE TELL TRUDY ASAP!!!!

The shouty note is written in all caps in thick black marker.

Okay, messaged received: *do not miss this appointment.*

Got it.

I pluck the note from the desk to study the name almost illegibly scrawled there; it's the first time I've seen his nickname in writing.

Zeke.

"Zeke," I say. Roll it around in my mouth a few more times, testing out the Z on my tongue. Practicing so I don't trip on it. "Zeke or *Ezekiel* ... I can't decide which is worse," I mutter to the empty room.

I'm nervous to see him again, afraid of what he'll say when he sees me and finds out I'm the tutor who stood him up, then pretended not to know who he was at the grocery store.

With anyone else, I'd be honest. With anyone else, the truth would be *easy*.

But everyone else? They're usually nice.

The truth is, Zeke Daniels intimidates me. The truth is, I don't think I'll be able to concentrate while I'm working next to him, side by side. I'll be too worried about what he's thinking, what's going on behind that angry set of eyes. Worried about what sharp, biting comments are going to come out of his snarl.

Tick.

Tock.

Twenty minutes with nowhere to hide.

The clock on the wall counts the seconds, steady as the rhythm of my beating heart, which thumps wildly within my chest until the glass door to the library opens, propelled by a gust of wind.

Some new fallen leaves flutter in, the heavy doors slamming from the draft.

Along with them? Zeke Daniels.

He shuffles in, dark gray sweatpants hanging low on his hips, black *Iowa Wrestling* hoodie pulled up over his head, the university's bright yellow mascot screen-printed across the chest. Backpack slung over one shoulder, black athletic flip-flops, and a pair of black sunglasses perched on the bridge of his strong nose complete the overall ensemble.

He is utterly … *ridiculous.*

Unapproachable.

Daunting.

His arrogance knows no bounds; I can see it in his loose gait, the exaggerated swagger, and the too-casual way he's dragging his flip-flops across the cold, marble tile floor. It's noisy, irritating, and completely uncalled for.

In the moment, my mind drifts to his personal life, and I theorize that he listens to heavy metal music to sooth his foul temperament, drinks his coffee black—as black as his soul—and his liquor straight up. I imagine once he's had sex with someone, they're never invited back. I go one step further and theorize that they're never invited to spend the night at his place, either.

Zeke Daniels makes his way to a table at the far end of the room, near the periodicals, one out of the way with plenty of privacy.

Sets his bag down in one of the four wooden chairs. Flicks on the small study lamp. Plugs his laptop cord into the base and stands.

Turns.

Our eyes would have met then were it not for those ludicrous sunglasses. I choose the exact moment he lifts his gaze to look down at the ground. Busy myself with shuffling papers on the counter. Count to ten instead of chanting, *Please don't come over, please don't come over, please don't come over ...*

But luck isn't on my side because he most decidedly *does*.

Makes his way over like a predator at a pace so deliberate, I'm convinced he's doing it on purpose. As if he suspects I'm watching from under my long lashes, dreading his imminent arrival.

He basks in my discomfort.

The distance between us closes, his strides purposeful.

Twenty feet.

Fifteen.

Ten.

Eight.

Three.

His large hand reaches up, pushing down the hood of his sweatshirt, his fingertips pinching the earpiece of his sunglasses and pulling them off his face. My eyes follow the movements as he folds them closed, hanging them on the neckline of his hoodie.

His gaze lingers—those clear gray eyes famous around campus—and finds the shiny silver bellhop bell perched on the counter with the sign next to it that reads, *Ring for help.*

Ding.

The tip of his forefinger presses down on the small bell.

Ding.

He hits it again, despite me standing not three feet in front of him.

What an *ass.*

I conjure up a pleasant smile because it's my job, and what else is there to say but, "C-Can I help you?"

"Shitty Nanny," he deadpans by way of greeting, voice low and controlled. Humorless. "I'm here for a tutoring session with … shit. What was her name?" He pretends to think about it, tipping his head toward the ceiling.

Snaps his meaty fingers.

"Violet."

No salutation. No polite small talk. No direct mention of our run-in at the grocery store, although he does allude it with the lovely nickname he bestowed upon me.

I swallow, take a deep breath, and say, "I'm Violet."

The slashes above his eyes get severe. "*You're* Violet?"

"Yes."

Disbelief takes over his entire face before he schools his features. "You're my tutor?"

I stand a tad straighter behind the counter, bracing my hands on the Formica countertop, grateful for the support. My knees weaken. "Yes."

"You can't be."

"I can't?"

"Noooo," he drawls out. "Because I've seen you, what—how many times already?"

There's no use in denying it, so I simply say, "Two."

"Mother. Fucker." I flinch at his tone. "You were *here* the day I came looking for you. I saw you watching me." His eyes are accusing gray slits, deep voice rising, and I glance around, meeting several curious gazes. "Were you *hiding* from me?"

21

Yes.

My chin tilts. "I-I'm going to have to ask you to keep it down, please. People are staring."

"I don't give a shit what anyone thinks. Let them look." He leans in, upper torso bending over the countertop. "You stood me up."

My lips part, but no sound comes out. Not even a squeak. There's no good excuse for me having failed to do my job, and we both know it. Plus, I have a feeling he's not going to believe anything but the truth.

I pray Barbara doesn't come out of the back room to see what the fuss is, because then Mr. Daniels will tell her I bailed on him, which will look terrible since they're paying me to tutor him. I can't afford to get written up for standing up a student. It's part of my job, and my courage failed to help me do it.

"I know I stood you up, and I'm sorry."

Zeke runs his fingers through his short shorn hair. It's black as the night and glossy. "You knew my name when you ran into me at the grocery store, didn't you? You knew it was me." His sharp laugh is far from friendly. "No fucking wonder you looked like you were going to piss yourself that day."

Oh god. *He hates me.*

"I-I ..."

"*I-I,*" he stutters back at me, heatedly. "Spit it out V-V-Violet. Yes or no."

Wow. He goes for the jugular, doesn't he? Taking no prisoners, he nails me with a piercing stare, a battle of wills I will never win.

I don't even try.

Dropping my head, I'm unable to look into his angry, flashing eyes. "Yes. I knew who you were. Trust me, I-I feel terrible."

"*Trust* you." He laughs then, the long column of his thick neck tipped back. "Whatever, *dude.* Let's just get this over with."

"S-So you ... still want to have our session?"

Please say no, please say no, I silently plead.

"You obviously have no backbone in that spine of yours." He raises one dark, irritated brow in challenge. "Not up for it? Too bad. No fucking way am I letting you off the hook that easy."

I try not to cringe, but honestly? It's hard; he's sullen and broody and tenaciously confrontational.

This is a man who enjoys making people uncomfortable.

"Yes, of course I'm up for it. It's my job."

He narrows his unsettling blue-gray eyes before pulling the sunglasses down onto his eyes. "Grab your shit, Nanny. Let's go."

Stiffly, disappointed he's not going to cancel, I nod. "Okay. I'll get my stuff and meet you at your table."

In reply, he turns wordlessly on his heel, dodging and zigzagging slowly through the elaborate maze of library study tables, and I backtrack to Student Services to collect my things. Leaning back, I gape through the open doorway to survey his retreating form without being noticed.

Zeke Daniels is huge, built like a football player, all wide shoulders and solid muscle. Rigid edges and unyielding lines. Black onyx hair and eyes the color of gray sea glass. Intense eyebrows. High cheekbones. Square jaw. Coarse five o'clock shadow surrounding delectably sculpted lips.

He's outwardly beautiful.

It's the inside of him that could use some work.

"He is *just* a guy," I whisper, collecting my notebook, pen, and laptop. "He is just a guy, and it's only *one* session. It's only one hour. I can do this."

I can do this.

I tell myself again before heading over to meet him.

And again.

Until I almost believe it.

Zeke

I cannot believe this shit.

Making my way back to the study table, I seethe. Feel like a fucking idiot. Weaving past student after student, I meet the nameless faces of curiosity and obvious interest and glare, pissed off and irritated that that little *waif* got the best of me.

Made me look like a dumbass.

I only glance back once before yanking my chair out and taking a seat; Violet is hunched over a desk in the Student Services office. From here I can see her lips moving, deep breaths in and out, palms flat and arms braced above the table. Her long, light blonde hair hangs in a sheet around her fair skin, veiling her eyes.

As if she's made a decision, she straightens to her full height —which still isn't much, even on a tall day—squares her shoulders, and collects her things. Resolute.

She's cute, but that's the last thing on my mind. My eyes hit the biology textbook in front of me, determined to get this shitshow over with and end up with a decent grade.

When Violet joins me, her melodic voice carries. "Okay. So do you want to give me a little background on where you are in the class? I-I have most of the information but need a few details filled in for me …"

I watch as her slender hands arrange the writing utensils before us. Her fingers are pale, donning three thin, shiny gold rings.

She pushes the sleeves of her long-sleeved shirt to the elbows, revealing a wrist of matching bracelets. I quickly count four, each one with a small dangling charm, the metal *tinging* on the wooden tabletop when her wrist hits the surface.

It's annoying as *fuck*.

I refocus and make a dig. "Are those things going to be making noise the entire time?"

24

"What things?"

I direct my cool gaze to her wrist and raise my brows.

"My bracelets? Are they bothering you?"

"Yes."

"S-sorry." She pulls them off, one by one, and sets them aside, atop her small stack of books. They shine under the table lamp.

I take another dig. "I can't stand people who are unreliable, and that's you. Do you realize that?"

"N-no. I promise you I'm not unreliable."

"You stood me up for our first session. If that's not unreliable, what do you call it?"

Violet is quiet, pensive. "I'd call it ..." She clears her throat. "I'd call it intimidated. I was ... afraid to help you."

Afraid? I snort—actually *snort* through my nose. "Why?"

"Why?" she echoes.

"*Yes*, Violet, *why*. Christ, why would you be afraid to help me? It's not like I was going to *do* anything to you."

Her eyes widen, and she's trying to remain professional, remain composed, but she's nervous—I can see it in her eyes. She steels her resolve and straightens in her chair. "W-We got off on the wrong foot, and for that I ... I'm sorry."

"Fine." I tap my phone to check the time and Snapchat notifications. "Can we make the most of this time we have left? I'm failing bio and need this paper to bring up my grade."

A curt nod. "Yes, sorry."

That's another thing annoying the shit out of me. "Stop saying that."

"Saying what?"

"*Sorry*. Stop apologizing for everything, Jesus."

"Sor—" Violet bites down on her bottom lip, a nervous giggle unintentionally escaping her lips. "Shoot, I-I almost did it again, didn't I?"

Then.

She smiles.

My eyes, goddamn them, go to those curved glossy lips and rest there as she tries not to grin at me. Brilliant white teeth wink. Big, virginal doe eyes crinkle at the corners.

She's like a fairytale caricature. Like a pixie.

So endearing it almost makes me want to barf.

I look down at her hands, folded properly on the tabletop, fingers clutching the printer paper—*my* paper—her nails short and painted a light, pastel lavender. One of the nails has glitter on it. They're long and delicate fingers, fitting for someone so small, and I have no fucking idea why I'm even looking at them to begin with.

Pale skin. Unblemished.

Unscarred.

Untattooed.

Yet, I can see that those hands are capable, too, as they set the paper down and pluck a pencil off the table. Sturdy hands. Probably really hardworking.

"Just as a warning, I'll probably say it again," she confesses sheepishly, as if she can't help pointing out her flaws. "I do it a lot. I-I don't think I'll be able to help myself around yo—"

The pencil in her hand hovers over a sheet of paper with my name and information at the top of it. "Maybe I should get all the sorrys out before we start?"

Get all the sorrys out?

Jesus Christ, who the fuck is this chick?

"Knock yourself out," I rumble, leaning back in the chair and balancing on the back legs, crossing my arms as Violet takes a deep breath. "Go. Get it out."

"*Sorrysorrysorrysorry*," she expels in one long breath. Then, "Phew! That felt great!"

Even I, hard ass that I am, have to admit that was pretty darn cute; I nearly crack a smile.

Almost.

26

"Anyway, my apologies for before. I-I'm hoping we can start over."

"Yeah, whatever."

"All right. Okay. Now that *that's* out of the way." She clears her throat and proceeds, an air of efficiency taking over. She's more confident. "I guess we should begin. We have"—she glances back at the clock anchored to the wall—"roughly fifty minutes, g-give or take. Unless you want to work late?"

No way in hell am I staying any longer than I have to.

My *no* comes out sharper than intended.

And just like that, her gusto is gone.

Violet's lips part, and she emits a quiet, "I understand," before pushing a lock of hair behind her ears. Her fingers push the paperwork back and forth in front of her, and she folds down the right edge, running her nail along the crease restlessly, picking at it.

"Right. So why don't you tell me what you're stuck on and what you need help with."

Instead of telling her, I flip open a folder, expel my notes and project prospectus I've been struggling with, and push it toward her across the smooth surface of the table.

While she's perusing that, I flip open my textbook.

My index finger trails down the page, stopping at a passage I highlighted with an orange highlighter, the same passage I've had to read and reread at least a dozen times because I can't figure out how I'm supposed to write a paper based on what little information I've been finding.

There isn't adequate information to write an informed paper on my topic, and my grade depends on this essay.

Violet scans the prospectus, eyebrows scrunched up in confusion. "Have you chosen your topic?"

"Yup."

I thumb through the open folder, fish out and hand her another single sheet of notebook paper with handwritten notes. She takes it, reads it, then glances up.

"You're doing your research paper on *this*?"

I smirk. "What's wrong with it?"

She reads from the paper. "'Th-The biological and genetic, rather than moral, consequences of having a child with y-your first cousin?'" Pause. "*Um ...*" She sits up straight in her chair.

"Clever, isn't it?" I'm quite pleased with it myself.

Violet flushes. "W-What were your questions about it?"

"I guess I'm having a hard time finding facts to support my topic."

She hesitates, wrinkles her nose. "Facts like ... uh ... multi-factorial disorders?"

My brows rise, impressed. Apparently, the little stuttering wallflower really does know her shit about biology.

"Multifactorial disorders," I repeat. "Is that what it's called when a kid is jacked-up physically from all their parents' fucking?"

A wince. A blush. "M-more like *chromosomal* defects, but yeah, I'm assuming that's what you mean."

"So how do I put that in writing?"

"Have you googled the topic at all?"

Duh. Does she think I'm a fucking idiot? "*Obviously.*"

She's all business now. "What keywords did you use when you searched?"

"Inbreeding, banging cousins, fetal alcohol syndrome." The words rattle off the tip of my tongue, and judging by the look on her face, she's not impressed. "What's that appalled look for? Why is your face all red? Are those not accurate descriptions?"

"Th-Those are terrible keywords."

"Look, I seriously couldn't give a shit if someone is banging their cousin—first, second, or third. I just pulled the topic out of my ass for the sake of getting the essay done, and didn't want to be bored to tears writing it. So can we lose the whole scandalized virgin routine and move things along?"

I tap on the table with the end of my pen.

"Y-You're absolutely ..." Pause. "You're *certain* you want to continue researching *this* subject?" Violet's hesitation creeps into her voice. Her pale brows are bent, bottom lip jutted out in thought.

"Why? Does the topic make you uncomfortable?"

"No."

"Great, 'cause I doubt *you* have a better suggestion."

She bites down on her lower lip. "N-not off the top of my head, no, but I'm sure with a little effort, together we could come up with one."

She looks so hopeful and laughably naïve.

"Together?" For fuck's sake. "Aren't you the sweetest?" I scowl because quite honestly, I detest everything about this conversation. Being here with her. Needing a tutor. The thought of collaborating with her?

Petite, mousy, *stuttering* Violet and me?

No.

Hilarious in its absurdity.

I wouldn't have chosen her for help in a million fucking years.

I want to get the paper done, not write a love poem to science and biology.

But there *is* something I've been wondering. "So what's the deal with you and that kid?"

Her light brows rise. "S-Summer?"

"Do you nanny any other annoying kids that rudely knock shit over in the grocery store?"

Violet stops taking notes long enough to give her dainty, feminine shoulders a shrug. "She wasn't knocking anything over. She was curious and excited."

I stare, unconvinced.

She swallows. "I'm not her nanny; I'm her Thursday."

"Her Thursday. What does that mean?"

"Her mom i-is a student here, so as part of her tuition, Student Services provides a babysitter up to ten hours a week, free of charge, and I-I ..."

"Babysit her on Thursdays."

She nods. "Summer's parents are part of the assistance program for enrolled students with children. Her dad just finished an internship, and her mom has history and a lab Thursdays, so while she's in class, I-I hang with Summer."

"What the hell do you do for three hours with a four-year-old?"

"She's actually s-seven. Such a sweetie, the little doll face. We do arts and crafts. Do her homework. Go to the park."

Little sweetie. Doll face.

Christ almighty.

"The park?"

"Yeah, you know—the place with swings, sunshine, and slides? Jungle gyms. *Fun* stuff? You do know what fun is, don't you?"

I narrow my eyes—is she mocking me?

I wouldn't have pegged the waif as sarcastic or snarky, but looks are often deceiving. Suddenly latching onto a topic she's passionate about, she prattles on and on about the goddamn park like I give a shit.

"There's a really nice park down on State, right near the admin building, almost between campus and the downtown—"

I cut her off, impatient. "I'm not paying to hear about the location of the local park. I'm paying you to help me with biology."

She flushes, just like I expect her to. "Right. S—"

Sorry.

She catches herself just in time.

"You're seeing him again?
Girl, you're really enjoying
the month of DICKtember,
aren't you?"

Zeke

How I found myself at the park the next day—Thursday to be exact—I have no damn idea. I guess it had something to do with not having a single place to bring this freaking kid, the one I've been saddled with for the next few weeks.

Meeting at the Big Brothers Center, his ass is parked in a chair when I first walk in, chatting with some lady behind the desk like they've done it a hundred times.

All conversation stops when I shove through the door. I step up to the counter, fill out the paperwork attached to the clipboard, and catch the eye of the gray-haired receptionist behind the desk.

She rolls toward me in the desk chair, giving me the stink eye behind her thick purple glasses.

"You're late, and your little buddy has been waiting for eight minutes."

What is she, the volunteer police? Eight minutes is hardly a big deal.

I give her a one-shoulder shrug. "I had class."

"Try to be on time from now on or you'll get written up." She snatches the clipboard out of my hand, glances down at my scribbled responses, then asks, "And where will you and Kyle be spending your two hours today?"

Who the hell is Kyle? "Who's *Kyle?*"

The woman—Nancy, according to her nametag—tilts her head, bobbing her chin toward the back wall. The boy in the chair sits, feet dangling—he can't be more than ten or eleven years old—glaring from underneath the wide brim of an Oakland A's baseball cap.

I have to spend the next two hours with this kid?
Shit.
I try not to grimace, but fail.

32

"Well? I need an answer." She winks at the kid on the bench, even as her fingers hover above the keyboard on her desk, ready and waiting to input the location of my play date with my new Little Brother. "Where will you be taking Kyle?"

"*Where?*"

"Yes, Mr. Daniels." She annunciates impatiently. "*Where* will you be and what will you be doing with your little? Which activities?" She speaks carefully like I'm slow to understand. "We need to know *specific* information because of liability."

Nancy purses her lips and folds her arms. "This information was in the *informational* packet you signed off on when admitted to the program—reluctantly I might add. Now, you *signed* a release form stating you'd *read* the rules and regulations for our organization. Is that ringing any bells, Mr. Daniels?"

Right, I did do that.

Clearly I didn't fucking read any of it.

"I guess we'll ..." I look up into the mirror above Nancy, scowling when I catch a reflection of the little bastard, Kyle, rolling his eyes behind my back. "Is there a park nearby we can walk to so I don't have to put him in my truck? The one on ... State Street."

"Oh boy," Nancy mutters, affronted. She collects herself. "Greenfield Community Park, or Central County National?" Nancy's hands are back, hovering above the keyboard.

"There's a park called Central County National? Sounds like a prison," I deadpan.

"Well Mr. Daniels, there are a *number* of parks in the area, and those are two of them. If you're looking for a prison"—she looks me up and down again with pinched lips—"the nearest one is forty minutes north."

"Seven parks," interjects a smaller, youthful voice helpfully. "There are seven parks in the entire city."

"Right. Yeah. I'll take the Greenfield Community Park option, I guess."

"On State?" The older woman types it out. "Just to be clear."

Goddammit Nancy, who the hell cares?

"Sureeeee."

Nancy raises her head. "If you're meeting here, always log in your pick-up and drop-off time on the clipboard. If not, please email or text us your hours. Kyle knows the drill." She shoots him a smile and a wink. "You make sure to show the new guy the ropes, Kyle."

Another wink.

Kyle hops off the bench, and off we go.

"Looks like I'm stuck with you kid. Try not to be annoying."

The grubby kid in question doesn't respond.

Instead, he's busy moving farther toward the edge of the sidewalk to avoid me, putting as much distance between us as humanly possible on our walk to the park near the Big Brothers building. The kid—Kyle—balances on the curbs, walks on the grass, beneath trees, dodging and weaving his way in and out of yards along the way.

His scuffed up black sneakers offer zero tread when he takes another curb, barreling ahead by at least thirty paces like the hounds of hell are nipping at his heels—maybe they are, in the shape of ...

Me.

Closing in on Greenfield Community Park, the place Violet mentioned yesterday, I try to rein him in.

"Don't go running all over place. You should probably get back here."

He ignores me.

"I'm fucking talking to you, kid."

"I fucking heard you," he smarts back, his prepubescent voice cracking with false bravado that doesn't quite reach his posture. He adjusts the brim of his hat so he can ogle me better.

According to his file, Kyle Fowler is a fourth-grade latchkey kid who spends most of his time at the community center while his mom works. According to his file, he's quiet, respectful, and shows an aptitude for sports, his favorite being soccer.

Soccer? Gimme a break.

But according to my observations, Kyle Fowler is a wiseass punk with a chip on his shoulder bigger than mine and a foul mouth to go along with it.

I narrow my eyes. "Hey, watch your mouth."

He doesn't even blink. "You watch *your* mouth. I'm *eleven*."

I stop walking to cross my arms over my chest. "Look, if we're going to be stuck together for the next few months, the least we can do is try to get along."

To my own ears, I sound as disgruntled about it as he does.

His reply is one of loathing, followed by a grunt when he climbs onto the wooden picnic table and turns his back. "I don't need to get along with you, jerk. I got myself." He stabs a forefinger into his boney chest.

"Listen you little shit—"

He cuts me off. "I'm going to tell my mom you spent the entire time cussing at me, and then they're going to kick you out of the program." He flips me the bird.

"I swear to God, kid, if you don't knock it off I'm going to—"

"You're going to what? Tattle?"

My nostrils flare. What the hell is this kid's problem? "Why are you in this program if you hate it so much? How fucked up is it at your house?"

"I never said I hated it and it's none of your damn business." Kyle pauses before directing another glare my way. His small jaded eyes cast judgment at me over his shoulder. "I know why *you're* doing this. Someone is making you."

"Whatever." I check my phone for the time. "We have to kill an hour and forty-five minutes before I can take you back, so what do you want to do?"

He turns toward me, rolling his eyes from behind the lenses of his glasses. "Not sit in this lame park. Why did you bring me here? There ain't shit to do. Parks are for babies."

"I'm not taking some sloppy kid for a ride in my truck, so deal with it."

"I'm not dirty."

"Yeah right. I don't know where those hands have been."

Am I mistaking it, or did his shoulders slump? "My last big brother at least *fed* me when I was hungry."

"Do I look like I care if you're hungry?"

"No. You look like a giant butthole."

"That's because I *am* a giant butthole." Jesus Christ, did I just call myself a butthole? How low toward this kid's level am I going to sink?

I run a palm down my face and mentally count to five to regain patience.

As I'm doing that, Kyle pushes off the table and stalks toward the swings, dragging his tennis shoes through the rough wood chips. Instead of sitting in a swing, he grabs one by the seat and shoves it hard, sending it sailing through the air. The chains clang and hit the metal pole, creating an irritating echo in the otherwise quiet park.

"Knock that shit off," I call from my perch on the picnic table, irritated. "You're disrupting the peace."

Yeah—*my* peace.

He ignores me and his pale, scrawny arms give the seat another hard shove.

"Hey!" My voice booms. "I said knock that shit off."

I don't know why I even care—he's leaving me alone and wasting time like I told him to—but for some reason, the sound of the tinging metal is grating on my last nerve. Making me aggravated.

"Are you going to actually sit and swing on that thing, or just continue to annoy the hell out of me the whole time?" I bellow, deep voice filled with impatience.

Kyle shoots another scowl over his lanky shoulder, a storm cloud of resentment passing over his dark blue eyes before the bright rays of sun make his expression unreadable.

My jaw clenches out a labored sigh. This is harder than I thought it would be.

"Do you want me to come give you a *push*?" God, what am I saying? I don't think I've ever pushed anyone on a swing in my entire life. Plus, he's eleven; shouldn't he know how to pump it himself?

"*Screw. You.*" He releases the seat of the green swing, resuming his stomp through the wood chips toward the play set, kicking the toe of his tennis shoes into the splintered bed of chips along the way.

He's at the twisty slide when I check my phone again and groan. Only eight minutes have passed since the last time I checked.

I click open the Spotify app, a failed attempt to drown myself in music.

"You're not supposed to be on your phone during our activities," he shouts at me. "Maybe if you had read the manual, you would know that it's strictly prohibited unless absolutely necessary to promote the quality of our relationship."

"Oh yeah?" I shout back, closing out my apps and shoving the phone in my back pocket. "What else shouldn't I be doing?"

"What do you care? You've already broken like, five rules."

I have?

"Fine, smartass, which rules have I broken?"

Kyle stalks in my direction, scrawny arms swinging with the momentum of his stride. He stops in front of me, hands on the waistband of his black track pants. "Well for starters, you're not supposed to be swearing around kids. Everyone knows that."

"Would you get over it?" I cross my arms over my chest. "What else."

"You're supposed to tell my *mom* where you're taking me."

Jesus Christ. "Your mom?"

"Yes. And you're not supposed to be leaving me alone."

"What are you talking about? I'm right freaking here."

"Yeah, but you just let me wander around. You want me to get snatched?" He throws his arms up around and everywhere, waving them in every direction to indicate all the *wandering* around the park I've let him do, unattended. "You're supposed to be spending time with me."

"Kid, do you even *want* to be spending time with me? I'm an asshole, remember? Two minutes ago you called me a giant butthole."

Silence meets my question.

"Kid, for real?"

"My name is Kyle."

"Fine. *Kyle*. What do you want to do then? Ride bikes? Skateboard? 'Cause I'm telling you right now, I'm not going to be the one dreaming up shit for us to do."

"Skateboarding and riding bikes? Those are things you do at the park, and I just told you I hate it here."

"I don't have other ideas. Sorry."

Kyle fidgets with the zipper of his threadbare jacket. "Don't you have any cool friends we can hang out with?"

My mind immediately strays to Violet and Summer, who are probably doing something fun right now.

I shrug off the notion, aggravated that he can't just be happy swinging on the swings and climbing on the picnic tables and crap like a normal kid.

Why does he need to be entertained?

"Maybe next time, we'll see." Then, "Do you mind if I check the time, oh *Keeper of the Rules?*"

Kyle scoffs. "Whatever."

Ninety-seven more minutes with this kid. One hundred twenty-seven more until wrestling practice. Two hundred sixty-two minutes until I can slam my bedroom door on this shit day.

"We only have to tolerate each other for the next hour and thirty-seven minutes. Can you live with that?"

The kid stares me down, large brown eyes framed in a skinny face with pasty skin. A smattering of dark freckles across the bridge of his nose looks like dirt. His hair, unkempt and sticking up in different directions, gives him a wild air.

He inhales a breath. "You ..." Lets it out. "*Suck.*"

"I swear he gets as excited at
the sound of a condom wrapper
being opened as my dog does
when I'm opening a bag of food."

Violet

Zeke hasn't come back to the library in days. Not to study. Not for tutoring. Not for anything.

I can't say I'm surprised.

I can't say I'm disappointed.

I'm *relieved;* the whole week has been riddled with tension. Every time that door to the library swung open, I literally held my breath to see if Zeke Daniels was going to be standing there.

I know he's not done with his paper—not even close—so I can't imagine why he hasn't been back.

Unless he couldn't stand studying with me.

I wonder about it as little Summer and I walk toward a picnic area, hand in hand on our Thursday afternoon together. We easily find a table, and I set about the task of unzipping our backpacks, removing the books, paper, and craft supplies I brought along.

"How's your mom doing?" I ask, taking out a spiral drawing pad, holding it down when the wind kicks up.

"Good. She's tired but she only has one ... what's that called when you go to school?"

"Semester?"

"Yeah. One of those left. We're getting an apartment with Daddy or something so we can move out of Grandma and Grandpa's house when she graduates."

"An apartment! That's exciting!" I give her shoulders a squeeze. "Will you have your own room?"

She squeezes her tiny eyes shut. They pop open a second later, excited. "I think so!"

"Aw, that's great!"

And it is. Summer's Dad, Erick, just completed his degree and is interning at one of the huge corporations in the city, one of the largest employers in the county. He's thriving, Summer's mom

Jennifer is on her way to graduating, and their little family is finally going to be together.

"Hey," Summer interrupts my thoughts, poking me in the forearm with her pencil. "There's that boy."

I raise my head.

Give it a shake, fully expecting to see an actual little boy, but instead see Zeke Daniels and a child.

"W-what the heck is he doing here?" I wonder out loud apprehensively, tension growing in the pit of my stomach.

"Playing?" Summer suggests hopefully.

Except he's not.

Zeke strolls forward across the grass, brows furrowed toward the rambunctious kid literally running circles around him. His nose is in his cell phone.

"Would you knock that shit off?" I hear him loudly complain. "You're driving me *insane.*"

"You're the crabbiest human alive!" the kid shouts, climbing on a rock and jumping off, jabbing at the air ninja style. "You suck!"

When his feet hit the ground, the kid takes off running, shoes kicking up pieces of sand surrounding the slide.

"Grow up!" Zeke yells after him.

It's almost comical, and I bite back a laugh.

He halts in his tracks when he spots Summer and me at the picnic table, his eye roll visible from here.

"I am *not* following you," he says cantankerously, approaching the picnic table. I busy myself with rearranging the contents of Summer's tiny Barbie backpack so I don't have to look at him directly.

I hand her glittery princess stickers and a half-empty container of orange flavored Tic Tacs.

"I-I didn't think you were following me." I shoot him a wan, almost patronizing smile. "I'm hardly the kind of girl that inspires a guy like *you* to follow her around."

Oh god, what on earth possessed me to blurt *that* out?

Thank god Summer interrupts, pulling on my shirt sleeve.

"Vi, can I go play with that boy?" Summer asks, already half off the bench and on her way to little Zeke Junior, who's angrily stalking around the jungle gym.

Wow. The two of them are a fine match, and I have to wonder how Zeke Daniels was chosen when Big Brothers was reviewing their volunteer applications. Organizations like Big Brothers don't just take *anyone*. They have standards. Expectations.

I highly doubt Zeke meets any of them.

"Sure, sweetie." I call out after her, "Be careful. No running!"

Sigh.

Zeke gives me a peculiar look, eyes trailing my movements, especially when I flip my French braid over my shoulder. His light eyes settle on the pink silk flower stuck in the rubber band.

He shakes his head and stares off at the boy, now sitting on the ground in the sand with Summer. They're working together, molding a small pile into a hill and jamming sticks in the ground around it, like a castle with a wall.

Zeke's cell phone pings, and he palms it but doesn't check it.

"H-How is your biology paper coming?" I will my stutter to disappear, but it's not listening today. "A-Almost done?"

"It's coming."

I blink, trying to decide if there's an innuendo hidden in there somewhere.

"Do you want me to take a look at it before it's due?" I venture. "Proof it for you?"

"I'm sure it's fine."

"I'm sure it is, too, but let me know if you change your mind."

I glance toward the young boy, who's now gently helping Summer onto one of the swings. "We should get them over here and get Summer going. I know they're having fun playing, but she wanted to make her mom a birthday card."

I shout for them to rejoin us.

"We should probably just leave; he didn't want to come here, I had to force him."

"So why did you?"

"Because I don't care what he wants?"

I stare, shooting him my best skeptical look. I'm trying to wade through his bullshit, assuming it's waist deep, but don't call him on it.

"Besides," Zeke continues. "I don't know where else to take the little shit."

Ahh, now we're getting somewhere.

"What about the batting cages?"

He raises his brows. "Do I look like I play baseball?"

"No, but I-I bet you'd be good at it."

"Damn right I would."

Talk about an ego.

"Are you into sports?" He must be with a body like that. I ask as casually as I can, trying not to ogle him.

"Yes I'm into sports."

"W-Which ones?"

"Wrestling."

"You wrestle?"

"Yeah. Ever heard of it?"

The sarcasm is palpable and changes the tone of our conversation. Tension fills the air.

"Yes. I guess I didn't realize they had it at Iowa."

I didn't think it was possible for him to look shocked, but he does. "Are you being serious?"

"Yes. I guess athletics are the last thing on my mind."

I'm spared from his reply when the kids reluctantly join us, dragging their feet along the grass.

"The park is lame," the boy grumbles.

"Yeah!" Summer agrees, jumping on the kid's bandwagon.

"I heard you're not a fan of the park," I tease with an easy laugh, setting a piece of paper, pencils, and stickers in front of Summer so she can start on her project. "But maybe we can think of some other activities for the two of you to do together. How does that sound?"

"It's lame but *he* had no other place to take me."

"There are a million places to go!" I turn toward Zeke. "Let's discuss some more ideas."

"No."

Oh brother, what a grouch.

I ignore him, vowing to come up with a fun list later, and turn to the boy. "What's your name?"

"Kyle."

"Well Kyle, it's very nice to meet you. I'm Violet." I hold up a sheet of paper, offering it to him. "I know you're older, but do you want to craft? Your new friend is Summer, and she's making her mom a card."

Kyle scrambles onto the bench and eagerly snatches the paper out of my hand. "Sure! I can make one for my mom, too. And Summer's not the worst—for a girl."

I laugh again. "I'll consider that a compliment."

Zeke snorts. "A backhanded one."

Kyle looks up, confusion on his face. "What's a backhanded one?"

"A backhanded compliment is saying something nice and being rude at the same time."

"I wasn't being rude!"

I step in, spreading out some more paper to give the kids a broader selection, and to inhibit the argument brewing between a twenty-one-year-old guy and an eleven-year-old child.

"Paper? Crayons?" Zeke groans. "Ugh, seriously? Jesus. How long is this going to take?"

"I-is this not okay?" I pause. "Do you have somewhere to be? If he needs to get back …"

45

"I don't have to get back!" Kyle replies helpfully, already digging into the crayons.

"Fine." The storm across Zeke's face darkens as he crosses his bulky arms. "Make it snappy."

Zeke

"Hey Mom." Kyle bounds up to his mother two excruciatingly long hours later. Two painful, irritating hours spent watching him craft, color, and glue with Summer and Violet at the park.

"Hey kiddo. How was it?" She reaches for a lock of his brown hair, running her fingers through a short strand with a grin. "Is this glitter?"

"Yeah, we got into a glitter fight." Sheepishly, the kid hands her his drawing of a lion. "Here, I made this for the fridge."

While she studies the picture—a blue piece of construction paper covered in crayon and yellow, furry *balls*—I study her. Young, with frazzled brown hair, her black mascara is smudged under her eyes. Tired. Drained.

Kyle's mom extends a hand toward me, and I take it, pumping it up and down. "Hi, I'm Krystal, Kyle's mom."

Normally, when I shake anyone's hand, I squeeze it, but Krystal's fingers feel frail and weak. Cold as ice. The bones brittle as a bird's.

Exhausted.

She ruffles her son's mop of unkempt hair with hands that know a hard day's work. "Sorry I'm a little late, pal. I had to wait on Donna to take over my shift."

"Are you a nurse Mrs. Fowler?" I wonder out loud.

"It's *Jones*. Ms. I was never married." She frowns. "And no, I'm not a nurse. I'm a waitress at the truck stop off Old 90 and just worked a double. You must be the new Big." Krystal looks me up and down critically. "What did you say your name was?"

"Zeke Daniels."

She purses her lips my direction, checking me out again from head to toe. Krystal's shrewd brown eyes take in the sweat-stained hoodie I wore running, black puffy vest, mesh track pants that haven't been washed in over a week, and the two-hundred-dollar tennis shoes I'm wearing without socks.

Her penciled-on eyebrows rise before she glances down expectantly at her son, giving him a nudge with her elbow. "Well? How was it?"

"It was okay," I drone at the same time Kyle gushes, "It was so great, Mom! Zeke and I are already best friends." My brows shoot up into my hairline. "He's the *best* Big I've ever had!"

I scowl down at the little shit. "Laying it on a bit thick, aren't you?"

Kyle shrugs and his mom's disapproving gaze shoots back and forth between us; she knows one of us is bullshitting about the truth, but can't decide who.

Still, she says, "All right, so you're going to be his once-weekly." Krystal digs in her purse, producing her car keys. "I work every day, sometimes doubles, so I'm always running late."

Great.

"His dad isn't in the picture, so if you want to have him more than once a week, make sure you give *me* plenty of advanced notice. I know it's against the center's policies, but it would really help me out if you could take him more than a few hours, especially on Thursdays."

She is completely out of her fucking mind if she thinks *that* will ever happen.

"My number is …" she starts.

I stand with my arms crossed, leaning against the front counter.

"My number is …" Krystal repeats.

A pointy elbow jams me in the ribcage. "Zeke, get your phone out."

Fuck. My. Life.

"Hey Daniels. I heard you're a babysitter now," one of my team-mates calls out in the weight room just as I'm lifting a solid three hundred pounds above my head.

"That poor kid," someone else laughs.

I grunt, puffing out a breath of air, perspiration coating my upper lip, chest, back, and forehead. A bead of sweat slides down my temple as I build a wall, mentally blocking out the sound of Rex Gunderson's irritating voice.

"Does the kid have a hot mom?"

What the fuck?

I try raising my head, despite the amount of weight I'm currently bench pressing.

"Shake it off man, you're almost done. Six more." Sebastian Osborne—my teammate and roommate—glances down at me, mouth set in a hard line. "Shut the fuck up, Rex, he's in the middle of a set." Then to me he adds, "Five more."

Four.

Three.

Two.

One.

The metal bar hits the rack with a clatter at the same time the air leaves my body, a long, loud breath expelled from the exertion. I lay motionless, breathing in and out to catch lungfuls of air.

Flex my pec muscles. Raise my torso up, straddling the seat of the weight bench.

"I hear you're doing more than babysitting."

"Oh yeah?" I snap. "Where did you hear that?"

"My RA volunteers at the tourist information center next to some park. She saw you yesterday with some kids and a blonde chick."

"Well isn't she just a wealth of information."

"I see you're not denying it."

"Why would I? Your resident assistant already gave you the juicy details. I was at a park yesterday. *Riveting.*"

Gunderson laughs. "You babysitting for free, Daniels? I might have a job for you. My kid brother is eight."

"Don't you have anything to do Rex? Fill the water bottles? Fetch us some fresh towels?" Oz walks away from my spot on the bench and struts to the free weights. He stands in front of the racks, deliberating, before selecting two thirty-pound dumbbells and beginning reps of curls.

Violet clears her throat. "So, I-I know this is going to come out sounding awkward, but I told them I'd at least ask you."

"I thought I came to the library for peace and quiet so I can get this done, not chitchat."

She's here helping me again, but instead of getting down to business, she chooses *today* to be chatty. My bio paper is due in two weeks; desperation and determination to get the damn thing done are the only reasons I scheduled time to have her sitting across from me.

My pen hovers above the notebook open on the tabletop.

"I-I know, I know, but I told them—"

"Them who?"

"Summer and Kyle."

This get my attention. "What the hell do *they* want?"

Violet narrows those almond-shaped eyes at me, black lashes fluttering. Agitated. "They're children. Please be respectful."

"Fine. What do the darling children wish for you to ask me, pray tell?" I smirk. "That better?"

"Kyle and Summer were talking ..."

Fucking Kyle. That kid and his meddling.

"... and the kids were wondering ..."

Oh. The *kids* were wondering?

"... if we could do a play date on their next Thursday with the both of us. I-I promised I'd at least ask."

We sit silently while the words sink in.

She's asking me to do a play date.

Play. Date.

Me. With two kids.

Hysterical.

She forges on, because if there's one thing about Violet that I've discovered, it's that she will do anything for a little kid.

"Kyle assumed you'd say no."

"Kyle is a very bright young boy."

"You're not even going to think about it, are you?"

"Nope. Why should I?"

She takes a deep breath for courage and forges on. "Because, the kids want—"

"Oh! Oh!" I mock. "The *kids* want! Let me fall all over myself doing fun shit because some eleven-year-old is begging me to." I level her with a stare. "Tough. Shit. Kids don't always get what they *want*, Violet. It's called *life* and they're going to be bitterly disappointed throughout the rest of it."

She regards me then, quiet. Waiting.

Patient.

Always so goddamn patient.

It's unnerving and annoying.

Just like Jameson, Oz's girlfriend.

"I understand."

"You're not even going to try to change my mind?" I spit out, no longer able to stand her ambivalence. "You know, for the *kids*."

"No." Her soft voice is barely above a whisper. "It wasn't my intention to get you all worked up and m-mad about it. I'm so—"

"Don't fucking apologize. Can we just get this goddamn paper done so I can go home? I have a shit ton of other studying to do." I pinch the bridge of my nose with my thumb and forefinger.

Jesus Christ. She's looking at me like I just kicked her puppy, dejected and crestfallen, no doubt from my callous dismissal.

Well that's too damn bad, because I don't have time to think about her sensitive feelings. Or Summer's. Or Kyle's. So she can just take her sad eyes and downturned mouth and ...

Shaking my head, I ignore the knot forming in the bottom of my stomach, dismissing it as hunger pains. Yeah, that must be what it is; I haven't eaten in hours and normally don't go more than two hours between a snack or meal. Why else would my gut feel so shitty?

The silence at our table is deafening.

For the next thirty-five minutes, we do nothing but work side by side, taking notes and exchanging information for my paper. Violet doesn't smile. Doesn't laugh.

Doesn't stutter once, because she's not fucking *talking*.

Does nothing but edit my bio essay, that bright yellow highlighter gliding across my notebook in smooth strokes. Her indifference shows in the straight line of her normally smiling mouth. The hesitant replies to my scientific questions. The dulling twinkle in her now guarded eyes.

I follow them now as she reads my paper, scanning my carefully worded essay, following as her eyes trail along line after line, widening occasionally.

Smiling, too.

I can't stand it.

"What's so damn amusing?"

Inquiring minds want to know.

"Nothing."

"Bullshit. You're laughing at me. Give me the paper." I try to snatch it back but the little tease holds it far out of my reach.

"I wasn't laughing at you, Zeke." She sounds bashful. "I was surprised, is all, especially by this line here."

I lean in close as she holds it toward me, finger pointing to a sentence near the end of a paragraph.

"It's good. Insightful."

My jaw clenches and I cross my arms, moody. "I'm smart, you know, not a fucking idiot."

"I never implied that you weren't," she says quietly. Pauses. "But let's face it, it is a paper about people having babies with their cousins, and I-I wasn't expecting it to have so much intro-spection."

I raise a brow.

"Introspection is a *good* thing."

"Anything else?" I ask, now hungry for her praise.

"The whole thing is actually really ... good. I would tell you if it wasn't. I had Professor Dwyer my sophomore year and know how hard she grades."

She's not kidding; Dwyer is a tyrannical bitch.

I've had her for less than half a semester and already I can't stand her. Her class. Her TA, who is just as big a prick as she is.

"Anyway," Violet is saying, "I think she'll be pleasantly, um ... surprised? By your topic. It'll be a nice change of pace from all the other boring topics."

"What was your paper about when you had her?"

Violet squints, the corners of her eyes wrinkling in thought. Her pert nose twitches, reminding me of a rabbit. "Uh, let me think here for a second." Now she's closing her eyes, visualizing her paper, I'm sure. "I wanna say it was something on our environment and the effect it has on us getting cancer." She shoots me a sheep-ish look. "Snoozefest, I know."

"Sounds boring as shit."

Her hazel eyes widen. "Oh, excuse me Mr. First Cousin Birth Defect."

"Are you teasing me?"

She flushes. "I wouldn't dare poke the bear."

"I'm a bear now, huh?"

"That's what Summer called you after our little run-in at the grocery store." She scoffs. "Kids."

"Right. Kids." I glower. "I wonder what kind of bear."

53

"The kind that *eats* people."

When Violet checks the time and calls it quits on our session, we rise. She shuffles my printouts and slides them across the table toward me. I gather them up, shove them in my notebook, and stuff them in my backpack.

Curtly, her lips bend into a pleasant smile—a fake, manufactured, purely patronizing smile. One you'd give the smarmy guy hitting on you at the bar

"If you need anything else, or any additional help, you can email or call the help desk to make an appointment. If you can't get scheduled with me, we have staffers available Monday through Friday, from nine am to eight pm."

Her canned statement is professional, but lacks any real emotion.

Like me.

Shit.

"Come in and close the door behind you." Coach points to the chair in the corner of his office without lifting his head. The gray on his temples catch under the light, something I've never noticed about him before. "Sit."

I sit.

Shift in the shitty, uncomfortable chair.

He continues to take notes on his yellow notepad with the same red pencil he carries with him everywhere. Normally it's tucked behind his ear, out of the way, or in the breast pocket of his Iowa embroidered shirt. He uses it now to toil away at whatever match points, positions, and strategies he's dreaming up—something he's famous for in the Big Ten division.

Coach pauses long enough to lift a finger, raise it in the air, settle it on a cream envelope, and slide it across his beat-up wooden desk.

"Take this."

"What is it?"

"What the fuck does it look like?" He huffs impatiently. "It's an invitation."

I know he wants me to ask *What for?* so I don't.

Coach powers on, still scrolling across that yellow pad. "They have a fundraiser every year and it's coming up. I don't suppose Nancy told you."

"Nancy who?"

This time he does raise his head, blue eyes unblinking as he regards me. "Don't be coy Daniels, it doesn't suit you."

I rack my brain, trying to recall any Nancys I've met recently, but none come to mind.

"Nancy from the Center, where you're volunteering."

Oh, *that* Nancy. "That chick doesn't say dick to me, Coach."

"No, I don't suppose she would." He chuckles, low and deep.

Actually fucking chuckles.

Whose side is he on? "What does this have to do with me?"

"They have a fundraiser," Coach repeats. "It's in a couple weeks. We have no meet that weekend and I've excused you from practice, so I fully expect to see you there."

"See me there?"

"Yes. I take my wife, Linda; we buy a table, eat." He leans back in his old, rickety seat, the springs squeaking with every movement. Coach scratches his chin. "It's actually a really nice date night."

Coach is *married?* This is news to me.

"But Coach, a fundraising gala?"

"Yes. I'm sure with all your parents' money, you're quite familiar."

"Yeah, but—"

"Good, then it's settled."

"Yeah but Coach, I've literally only spent two days with the kid I'm mentoring. I just started the program."

"Well. There are two weeks until the gala. I'd say that's plenty of time to step up. Jump in with both feet, eh?"

I can see by his stalwart expression this subject is closed.

"I'll see you there. Make sure you're wearing a suit. I know you have one."

Yeah I have one; we're required to wear one when we travel to away matches.

"Are we done?" I huff, rising, hell bent on the brink of insubordination.

His reply is a dull chuckle.

"Yes, we're done."

"Oh, and Daniels?"

I turn.

"Feel free to bring a guest. In fact, I'd recommend it."

"I have this thing I'm being forced to do …"

"You mean besides bugging me while I'm at work and hanging out with Kyle?" she teases, interrupting me.

For a moment all I can do is stare at her, so surprised am I by her smartass comment. It's the last thing I expected.

"I-I'm sorry. I was kidding," she stutters.

"I know." I roll my eyes. "I can take a rash of shit when it's being handed to me."

Violet recovers, propping her elbows on the circulation desk and leaning forward. "Okay, so what is this thing you're being forced to do?"

"The Big Brothers program apparently has this *fundraiser* every year." I use air quotes and Violet cocks her head, confused, and narrows her eyes.

She frowns. "Why are you using air quotes?"

"Because it's lame?"

Her brows go up. "I-I don't think raising money for under-privileged children is *lame,* Zeke."

"Would it make you happy if I called it boring instead?"

"Slightly *better.*" She uses air quotes.

Whoa. Mousy Violet is showing her spine.

"I thought we could strike a deal; if you come to this thing with me, I'll bring Kyle on a play date with you and Summer."

"Why would you want to go to a big fundraising event with *me*? I heard it's formal."

"My coach expects me to show up with a date. He didn't come out and say it, but it was implied."

"I see."

"And if I invite some random chick," I continue. "There will be expectations."

"Oh." Her voice sounds oddly disheartened. "When is it?"

"The twenty-eighth. It's a Saturday, two weeks from this weekend."

"I guess I can look and get back to you."

"Can you check right *now*?"

"I-I suppose, but I don't have my phone on me."

"Come on Violet, we both know you want to come with me."

"I don't understand why you wouldn't rather just go by your-self. It's not like you enjoy anyone's company."

"That's partly true," I say with honesty. "But I figure we're in this kid thing together, since you're stuck with Summer and I'm stuck with Kyle, and none of my friends know any of the details cause it's none of their damn business, and there is no way I'm taking a wrestling groupie who only uses me for sex."

She stares at me, flabbergasted, so I continue.

"So if I have to go, I'm making you go with me."

"I-I don't know what to say; should I be flattered or insult-ed?"

I think about this, dole out the truth. "Probably a bit of both."

Violet's lips part.

No sound comes out.

Then, her lips press together in a thin line of displeasure. "And just so you know, I'm *not* stuck with Summer, and you're not *stuck* with Kyle."

I roll my eyes. "You know what I mean."

She crosses her arms and I swear to fucking God her nostrils flare. "No, I'm afraid I don't."

"Oh come the fuck *on* Violet. Summer is just a *job*."

"No, I assure you, she is not. She is a sweet, creative little girl who I've been watching for six months and I already love her like family. Like she's my little sister."

Now I'm the one pursing my lips and flaring *my* nostrils. "You know what I meant."

Those hazel eyes narrow. "Sadly I-I do know what you meant. Basically it was just *you* being *you*, but your delivery sucked."

"So did I blow my chances of you coming with me or not?"

"I-I don't know."

"What can I do to convince you?"

She considers my question. "To be honest with you, I-I think you get what you want way too often. The fundraiser is going to take all night, and a play date only lasts two hours, max, so I propose a trade: I'll go to the banquet if you agree to three play dates."

What the fuck? "What! No."

"All right." She turns her back on me, reaching into the metal returns cart and pulling out a stack, neatly setting them on the counter. Her hands move up and down the spines, aligning them in perfect symmetry.

I sigh so long and loud I catch a few people staring, and I glare.

"Fine. Two play dates."

She starts to giggle but catches it into a swallow. "*Four*."

"What the fuck? Your original offer was three." I scowl down at her, hard.

She shrugs.

"Fine," I relent, *generously*. "Two."

She busies herself again, returning to the task of removing books from the returns cart. One tidy stack after the next is placed on the counter, and for a few moments I watch her. Her pale fingers with those lavender nails that remind me of Easter. And flowers.

"Violet, quit ignoring me. It's fucking annoying."

She ignores me, but I know she's listening.

"Goddammit. You're not seriously going to make me go alone are you?"

She pauses to speak but keeps her back turned. "Alone? I suspect you'll be in a room *full* of people."

"You're supposed to be the sympathetic one here. You don't feel the least bit sorry for me, do you?"

"I-I don't think there's a single soul that feels sorry for you, Zeke Daniels." I catch the sly little smile stealing its way across her lips as she gives me a view of her profile; she knows she's got me by the balls.

Which is obviously horseshit.

"Fine. You win." I hastily blurt the words out in a panicked rush when she disappears into the office behind the circulation desk. "Three play dates."

Violet sticks her head out, blonde hair framing her face, interest lighting up her features. The extortionist is biting down on her lower lip, fighting a giant smile.

"Three." She nods. "Summer is going to be thrilled."

Awesome.

"We can start this Thursday I guess," I grumble.

She pauses, turns, then walks the short distance slowly back to stand in front of me, pale brows raised a fraction in surprise, the corner of her pink lips tipped *just so*.

"We can?"

"Don't act so fucking shocked, it's not a big deal."

That's a lie—it is a big deal, and Violet knows it.

I know it.

Something about her big, gentle eyes lighting up with satisfaction and delighted joy does something strange to the pit of my stomach.

For once, someone isn't pissed at me.

She's pleased.

It's a weird feeling. Foreign.

Violet walks to the circulation desk, plucks up a sheet of paper from the counter, scribbles on it, and returns with a handwritten line of numbers.

"What's this?"

"My cell." She hands the strip of paper over, hand extended. "So you can text me."

"Can't you just fucking put it in my phone like a normal person? What are we, twelve?"

The light in her eyes shines at the same time her upturned lips turn down. The small scrap of paper suspends between us, between her fingers, until the awkward tension in the air stifles me.

She's not going to lower her arm until I take it.

I snatch it out of her hand.

The small scrap of paper with her phone number sits on my desk, folded into thirds, in a neat little square.

It's been there for four days. Untouched.

Rising from my desk, I pluck it up, unfold it. The crumbly paper makes a crinkling sound and I smooth out the wrinkles on the edge of my desk before spreading it flat.

I stare down at Violet's neat, tidy handwriting. The loop on the V in her first name. The blue, fine-tipped marker lines, bold and crisp. I palm my phone, unlocking the screen, and scroll with my thumb over the green messenger icon. Click. Hit *compose* with a scowl.

Zeke: *We should talk about this Thursday. Figure out this play date crap.*

Her reply comes almost immediately.

Violet: *All right.*

I roll my eyes and huff at her unenthusiastic reply before tapping out mine.

Zeke: *Where do you think we should take the kids*
Violet: *Where would you like to take them?*
Zeke: *This wasn't my brilliant ducking idea so this is all on you.*
Violet: *LOL*
Zeke: *What's so funny?*
Violet: *You when you're trying to be badass but your phone autocorrects to ducking.*
Zeke: *Shit, I didn't even notice.*
Violet: *Okay, so, play date ... how about bowling?*
Zeke: *God no.*
Violet: *What about painting pottery at one of those fun studios—the kids would LOVE THAT.*
Zeke: *Are you fucking serious?*
Violet: *I'm trying to be helpful!*
Zeke: *It's a no.*
Zeke: *I said I'd play date; I never said I'd play nice.*
Violet: *Okay, how about the zoo?*

Zeke: *I would literally rather have my balls sliced off with a dull knife.*

It takes her four minutes to respond to that, and I smirk, imagining her face is bright red to the roots of that light blonde hair.

Violet: *It's warm enough outside for the zoo—we should try to take advantage while we can.*

Zeke: *No to the zoo. Next.*

Violet: *Um ...*

Zeke: *Try again, you're doing great so far.*

Violet: *They have dollar movies and dollar popcorn at the Cineplex on Tuesdays and Thursdays when they show old movies.*

Zeke: *Which theater does that?*

Violet: *The little one on Main. I think Fantastic Beasts is playing?*

Zeke: *Then afterward, you can go ahead and shoot me?*

Her next text takes an entire eight minutes.

Violet: *I'm going to be honest with you, even if it makes me uncomfortable talking about it—I think you should know these kids come from really low-income families and they get to go to the movies almost NEVER*

Zeke: *I'm not sitting through a flipping cartoon.*

Violet: *It's not a cartoon. It's kind of like Harry Potter.*

Zeke: *... which I have not seen.*

Violet: *I'm going to pretend you didn't just say that.*

Zeke: *Well have you seen the complete Star Wars trilogy?*

Violet: *Uh. NO.*

Violet: *Okay, what about a trampoline park?*

Zeke: *No offense Violet, but your ideas suck.*

Violet: *Really? I thought FOR SURE you were going to bite on that one ...*

Zeke: *Wait. Did you say trampoline park?*

Violet: *One just opened in the industrial park off McDermott.*

Zeke: *Fine.*

Her texts stop again. I wait a few minutes.

Violet: *Was that a YES to the trampoline park?*

Zeke: *If there are actual tramps there, then it was a yes.*

Violet: *Haha, very funny.*

Zeke: *I thought so.*

Violet: *That is EXCELLENT! They're going to be so excited!*

Zeke: *I too am thrilled beyond my wildest dreams, but not shouty caps thrilled.*

Violet: *Oh hey, Zeke?*

Zeke: *What.*

Violet: *Just a gentle reminder, don't forget to get permission from Kyle's mom.*

Zeke: *Peachy. I'll get right on that.*

"I'm having a hard time eating
this sandwich knowing how
many assholes my hands
were on last night."

Zeke

In the end, I didn't forget to message Kyle's mom. In fact, it was the one thing I didn't fuck up this week, and Krystal Jones was ecstatic that I was taking Kyle to do something he rarely gets to do.

Be a kid.

Have fun.

Play somewhere she normally can't afford to take him.

The conversation was awkward. Made me feel ... like an over-privileged asshole ... which I'll admit to being, through no fault of my own. I didn't choose to have wealthy parents, just like Kyle didn't choose to have a deadbeat, piece-of-shit absentee father. His mom works her ass off and they still have no money.

But whatever.

Not my problem.

Not *really*.

Instead of dwelling on it, I shift my focus to Violet, who's standing next to a tall blue trampoline, still wearing her fall coat.

I eyeball her skeptically. "Aren't you going to take off your shoes and shit and bounce? Let's go, chop chop."

"I haven't decided yet."

"Are you fucking serious right now?"

She's fiddling with the front of her jacket, nimble fingers tugging on the silver zipper pull, gently wrenching up.

I sigh. "Yes or no, Violet."

"I ..." She stops to take a deep breath and I know it's because she's determined not to stutter. "I don't think I'm planning on it."

"This was *your* idea. I'm not trampolining by myself with those cretins. Have you *seen* some of the little psychopaths they let loose out there?" She glances around me at the kids already jumping—a dozen little humans all riding that sugar high. "No fucking way are you abandoning me."

"Would you please, *please* watch your mouth in front of the kids?" she all but hisses.

I glance around to pinpoint the exact location of Summer and Kyle; they're a safe distance away, on the ground, untying their shoes and placing them in cubbies. Verdict: they're in no danger of any profanity that might come flying out of my mouth.

"Are you trying to change the subject?"

"No, Zeke, if I was trying to change the subject, I-I'd ask you to help me with my zipper. It's stuck." Her mouth tips down into a frown. "*I'm* stuck."

My eyes shoot from her pouty pink lips to her pink jacket, down to the slender fingers with those purple nails pinching the silver pull and tugging to no avail.

"Stop yanking on it, you'll make it worse," I demand, stepping the four paces into her personal space and closing my large fingers around hers, brushing them aside so I can access her zipper.

I bend my head to get a closer look at it, kneel in front of her to get a better look. A long strand of thread from the interior lining of her coat is caught in the track. It doesn't look like it's coming out any time soon, not without some actual time put into it; I'd need a scissors, better lighting, and about twenty minutes to fix it.

I hear an intake of breath above me, against the top of my head. Is she sniffing me? She must be—the hairs on the back of my neck are prickling.

Bizarre.

"Did you just *sniff* me?"

"No!" She gasps, horrified.

I snort, shaking off a shiver. "Yeah right. Don't lie."

Violet scoffs. "Not every girl wants to date you, you know. You're not that irresistible."

The way she says it makes me think I just might be—to her. Otherwise, why would she bring it up?

"Who said anything about dating?" I give a rueful laugh, fingers working the pink metal teeth on her jacket. "No girls want to *date* me."

I give the zipper another gentle tug as she laughs, warm breath tickling my ear as she leans to watch my progress.

I lift my head to meet her eyes. They're curious and close to my face, annoyingly … naïve.

"There's a big difference between a groupie wanting to fuck because I'm an athlete and someone who's seriously interested in dating, Violet. Only one of them ever happens to me."

I am *right* up in her face, still down on my knees, so damn close I can *feel* and smell her minty breath; my nostrils flare, involuntarily inhaling more of her.

I notice the distinctive colors in her eyes as she gazes down at me quizzically. Black mascara sets off soft hues of brown, gold, and blue. A stark onyx circle surrounds her vibrant irises. Her eyes are fucking magnificent.

There isn't a single freckle or blemish on her skin, and I curse myself for never noticing.

I'm definitely noticing now.

Dropping my hands from her coat, I rise to my full height, shoving them into the pockets of my jeans. "It's not coming open. Sorry."

"W-What do I do?"

"Clearly you have two options: jump with your jacket on, or pull the damn thing off over your head."

"I'm not jumping in my jacket; I'll die of heat stroke."

I smugly grin. "So you *are* going to jump with us."

Violet's wide eyes are directed at my grinning lips.

"Why are you staring at my mouth like that?"

Her teeth drag across her lower lip. "You just smiled."

"So? I smile."

Occasionally.

Fine. *Rarely.*

"It's …" She gives her head a shake. "Never mind."

"Tell me what you were going to say."

Her unblemished skin reddens. "It was nice. You should do it more."

"I'm not an asshole all the time you know; I *do* know how to smile." To prove it, I clamp down on my teeth and give her a toothy grin.

"You look like a hyena about to pounce on a gazelle."

"Uh, what the hell kind of metaphor is that?"

"Cheshire Cat?"

"Ha ha." Not funny.

"Crocodile?"

I snap my teeth together a few times, chomping down and advancing on her. She shoves at me with the palm of her hand, reaching for the hem of her jacket and pulling upward.

"It's just … you smile so rarely, it's like a Bigfoot sighting," she teases, yanking her coat. Lifts it up higher. "And you should—smile more, I mean."

Her hands grapple with the bottom of her jacket and she gives another tug—*tug*—inadvertently tugging her shirt along with it, baring her abs. The smooth pale expanse of her stomach and perky little bellybutton become exposed; my eyes are fastened to that indentation on her stomach and the cherry-colored birthmark slashing across her flesh.

Her jeans ride low in front, that tender skin dipping down into her waistline … into places I'm assuming no one but a doctor has ever been.

As she struggles, I catch a glimpse of Kyle's horrified expression at the sight of her bare stomach.

I react. "Stop! Jesus Violet, are you trying to give everyone a free show?"

"Why! W-What's happening? I can't see!" Her panicked voice is muffled, trapped in the prison of her jacket, unable to see.

"Your shirt is about to come off." I reach for the hem of her shirt, ignoring the spark from her skin when my fingers hastily pull the fabric over her flat stomach. "Let's try this again, shall we? I'll pull down while you pull up."

My knuckles graze the skin above her hips, tugging. Hurriedly, Violet yanks and pulls at the stubborn pink jacket, wiggling her way out until it's clear above her head.

Obviously, since she's wearing a V-neck shirt, I check out her rack.

Or lack thereof.

Beneath that tee are two discernable bumps, smooth but small, and *why the fuck am I all of a sudden staring at her tits?*

I rush through peeling off her jacket, and when she's free, the pale blonde hair surrounding her head sticks up in several directions. Adorable. Violet pats at it, smoothing away the flyaway strands, but even with her hair sticking out every which way, she looks flushed and happy and cute as all hell.

"I don't even want to know what I look like right now," she grumbles, stuffing her coat into Summer's cubby.

"Your hair is a rat's nest," I put in helpfully.

Summer, who appears at our side, rolls her eyes and shoots me a hostile glare. "You're not supposed to tell girls they look like rats."

"First of all, I said her *hair* is a rat's nest. I didn't say she looked like one—there's a big difference. Secondly, since when do five-year-old kids roll their eyes at grownups?"

"I'm seven."

"Whatever kid. If you keep doing that, your eyeballs are going to get lodged inside your skull—*permanently*."

Summer gasps. "No they won't!"

"Try it and find out," I intone cryptically.

The kid gives me another scowl so deep I have mad respect for her. "Nuh uh."

"Yuh huh." I raise my black brows. "It's true."

Violet clears her throat. "Okay you two, stop arguing." She digs into the back pocket of her jeans and produces a twenty-dollar bill, tries handing it to me. "Zeke, do you want to get our tickets?"

I stare down at the money then up into her compassionate hazel eyes. "You are *not* paying for the tickets. Like I'd ever let you pay for our shit." The idea is ludicrous.

I roll my eyes heavenward.

"You rolled your eyes!" Summer screeches, jumping up and down; she's hyper—to say the least—and her long dark pigtails bounce as she hops around us.

"I did not," I argue.

"Your eyes are going to be stuck up in your big, giant skull!"

Giant skull?

I glance at Violet. "Can you make her stop?"

Violet shrugs. "You started it."

With a grumble, I jerk my head toward Kyle. "Come on kid. Let's get the tickets and get bouncing so I can be done and get the hell out of here."

Ten minutes later, we're bouncing.

"I-I can't believe I suggested this." A pouting Violet boxes out in the corner of a red trampoline, legs spread and knees braced to steady herself. She's determined not to fall flat on her ass. "You were right. This was a shitty idea."

Nearby, Summer and Kyle are tiny jumping maniacs, hopping from trampoline to trampoline like frogs leaping on lily pads.

"Well," I gladly remind her, giving her a few quick bounces with the heels of my feet, causing her to lose her balance. She lands on her back with a flop as I lightly spring onto the net beneath us. "You *were* getting desperate for ideas I'd be willing to try."

She stares up at from the mesh, flat on her back. "You're right. I brought this on myself." Her arm goes out, palm extended. "Help me to my feet?"

I stare at her hand like it's a foreign object I've never seen and have no idea what to do with.

Must hesitate too long because she stutters, "N-Never mind," and tries to twist her body into an upright position. Only then do I react, my palm gripping her hand, pulling her to stand with too much force. She tips forward, bumping into me.

Beneath our stocking feet, the net bounces. We stand inches apart, so I have to bend my neck to look down at her. A little closer and she'd be flush against my chest.

I stare down at her pink lips, that crooked, amused smile.

"Zeke, watch what I can do!" A small, high-pitched voice calls out, giddy. I crane my neck to see Summer kicking her legs out haphazardly.

"What is she *doing*?" I mutter. "She's freaking out."

"She's showing off for you."

"That kid has zero skills."

"Just watch."

I point to Summer, gesturing to her erratic movements. "That's not even a thing, whatever that leg kick action is that she's doing."

Violet laughs. "She's having *fun*."

"She looks like a klutz."

She jabs me in the ribcage. "Tell her she's doing great."

"I'm not setting her up for failure by lying to her; that's not doing her any favors. This is real life, not mamby pamby land."

"Zeke watch me!" Summer shouts again, interrupting my speech. "Watch!" This time, she bounces and bounces and bounces, arms flapping like bird wings. "I'm flying!"

Her little feet have not left the ground.

"I don't know, you're not jumping high enough to be a bird." My hand scratches the five o'clock shadow on my cheeks and I mutter to Violet, "I'm still not impressed."

"Y-You're the worst!" Violet chastises, but still, she's smiling at me. "Can't you be nice?"

"Fine," I relent. Cupping my hands around my mouth to project my praises, I bellow, "Summer is the best jumper in the world! No, the universe! She's a bird, she's a plane, like a little godda—"

Violet grabs my arms, yanking my hands away from my mouth. "That's not what I meant and you know it. You can't shout swear words in a room full of kids."

"There are parents here, too."

"Never mind. Just start jumping," she says, uncharacteristically shoving my chest, pushing me. She laughs when I stumble, tripping onto another trampoline, almost falling flat on my ass.

I catch myself, bouncing back up to my feet like a boss.

"Someone isn't as light on their feet as they think they are," she teases, beginning a steady bounce.

Up and down ... up and down ... crossing her arms protectively across her chest, holding her rack like she's afraid they're going to be flopping around.

I smirk.

"I don't know why you're holding your chest like that. You have almost no boobs," I say it in an effort to be helpful, because seriously, the girl has no tits.

Judging by her flaming red cheeks, I've embarrassed the shit out her, and she presents me with her back. Slows her roll. Stops jumping all together and makes her way to the edge of the padded safety mat.

"Hey, where are you going?"

She ignores me.

I roll my eyes.

"Oh come on, don't get pissed." Jesus, why is everyone so damn sensitive all the time? "Can't you take a joke?"

She spins around, narrowing her eyes as she climbs backward down the ladder. "It's only a joke when other people find it funny."

"I couldn't sleep at all
last night because my roommate
had someone over.
It was a good hour of moans,
smacks, and what sounded like
someone running in flip-flops."

Zeke

"Hello?"

"Ezekiel?"

I scowl into the phone. "Jesus, no one calls me that. Who is this?"

"This is Krystal Jones. Kyle's mom."

Well, shit.

I glance down at the kid, who is half asleep in the passenger seat of my truck. We're on our way home from an arcade to meet his mom. "Oh. Hey Krystal. What's up?"

"I have a huge favor to ask, and I wouldn't be asking if I wasn't desperate ..."

"Lady, if you're propositioning me—"

"I need you to watch Kyle tonight, just a little longer. One of our second shifters called in sick and I really need the money from this shift but have no one to watch Kyle."

Uh, what does she think I am, a fucking babysitter?

"Ms. Jones ..."

"I just need an answer." It sounds like she's in a crowded diner, and I hear her glancing over her shoulder. Hear someone calling her name in the background. "Can you watch him?"

I squint over at her son. He's half out of it, head against the glass window, mouth falling open from exhaustion. Gross.

He better not drool on my damn seats.

"Uh ..."

"*Please.*"

Shit. Fuck. Shit.

"At my place or what?"

"Yes, if you could. I'm sorry. I don't even know if I trust you, but I'm desperate. I know it's against the mentor rules to even be asking you to babysit, but I need to keep my job. I need the hours."

The desperation in her voice has me squeezing my eyes shut and pinching the bridge of my nose between my thumb and forefinger.

"*Fuck*," I draw out.

Krystal inhales a breath. "Does that mean you'll do it?"

"Ugh. I'll do it if I have to." I hate myself, but I'll do it.

The call disconnects without any further instructions. Kyle peers at me through sleepy, hooded eyes. "Was that my mom?"

"Yup. Sorry dude, you're coming home with me."

He wrinkles his nose. "Do I have to?"

"Trust me, Kyle, I'm not thrilled about it either."

Heading toward my house, I give him another glance. He really does look tired, and for a brief moment, I wonder about his parents and life at home.

"Where's your dad, kid?"

"Where's *yours*?" Jesus, even half asleep the kid is a little smartass.

Still, it's a fair enough question. "My dad is … let's see, how do I put this so you understand? My dad is a bag of shit."

His eyes go wide. "Did he hit your mom?"

It's on the tip of my tongue to ask *Did your dad hit yours?* but I hold back—I'm not *that* insensitive.

Fine, I am. But still, I bit my tongue.

"No, my dad didn't hit my mom. In fact, they're still married."

"Does he buy you stuff?"

"Yes. He buys me stuff." Stuff I charge on his credit card.

"How can he be a bag of shit if he buys you stuff?"

I snort. "Kid, you have a lot to learn about life. Just because someone buys you stuff doesn't mean they actually care. Let's use my parents for example—they give me things so I won't bother them." I shoot him a frown. "You know, I'm kind of like you in a way; I was shuffled around when I was young while my parents worked. They worked night and day, starting their business and inventing stuff. Stuff that made them a lot of money. I had tons of babysitters, all that shit, just like you. Sometimes I think they forgot they even had a son."

"*My* mom doesn't forget about me," Kyle says with pride in his voice.

"No. She doesn't. She's working hard to keep a roof over your head. She's a good mom."

"Do your parents work a lot?"

"Kind of. They used to work day and night. Now my dad just works and my mom plays."

Why the fuck am I telling this to an eleven-year-old?

"Where do they go?"

I have no idea. No longer care. "Anywhere they want."

Any time. Any place. Any cost.

"Even on your birthday?"

"Yeah," I say gruffly. Quietly now, "Even on my birthday."

Birthdays. Christmas. Easter. Graduation. Move-in day my freshman year of college.

"But if they travel so much, where were you?"

"Nowhere, really."

Here.

There.

Wherever they stuck me.

Wherever they *weren't*.

Really, the only time I ever saw my parents was when their backsides were leaving while I cried. My mom used to hate when I cried. "It grates on my nerves," she'd say in an even tone. I think my clingy behavior made it easy for her to climb into the car without a backward glance or a wave goodbye.

No kiss. No hug.

Obviously I didn't realize when I was little that they were just fucking assholes, didn't realize it was nothing personal.

All I knew was that it crushed me.

My mother didn't do affection, even before success hit. She was too hurried for it. Always in motion, always on the go. Always moving a different direction. If I begged to be picked up as a toddler, I remember being shooed away, a burden.

I don't know why they bothered having me; my mother had no business having kids.

When my parents started making money—serious money—the DVDs they'd play to keep me out of their way became nannies and caregivers. Aunts and uncles and people they paid to watch over me that really didn't give a shit.

They were only in it for the money, too.

Then it really started rolling in, a windfall they earned when my father sold his first program to Microsoft. Bought stock in multiple dotcoms. Invested in several startups. This was back when I was very young, but I remember standing at the edge of the small kitchen listening to my mother cry with relief and joy. She cried about hard work and sacrifice. The long hours. The endless work days. The scrimping and saving, all on a bet that my father's ideas would pay off.

And they did, twenty-fold.

But of all the sacrifices they'd made—cheap dinners, shithole rentals with a garage my dad could use as an office, walking everywhere because the car had to be sold to buy computer parts ...

None were real sacrifices.

I was.

I was the real sacrifice.

Afterthought, burden—whatever you want to fucking call it, I was left behind after the big payday came.

My mom had always yearned to travel, even long before they had a pot to piss in. Exotic places. Dubai. Morocco. Iceland. China. She wanted pictures by the Taj Mahal and the great pyramids of Egypt.

Dad?

He couldn't have cared less.

SARA NEY

His passion was inventing and creating. Making something out of nothing. Technology out of thin air. His brain? Sharp and insightful.

Not insightful enough, it seems, because when it came to my beautiful mother, he was spineless. When she wanted to hit the road, charter private jets, and see the world?

He carried her purse and pulled her matching, newly minted designer luggage—only the best that her new money would buy.

"Who took care of you?" Kyle persists, his voice breaking into my thoughts.

"Some relatives." I don't tell Kyle they were paid to take care of me and only did it for the money. "Sometimes my parents' friends."

"That sucks."

Yeah. It did suck.

I was shuffled off to my grandparents the first time my folks jetted off. It was only going to be a week, so no harm in that, right? One week turned into several, several turned into weeks on end, and soon my grandparents had thrown their hands up and cried defeat. They implored their daughter to take her son along. "Ezekiel *cannot* miss school," my mother would say in this prissy, holier than thou voice, using any excuse to leave me at home.

The real reason: who could jet set with a young son desperate for their attention?

My mother has zero fucking maternal instincts.

My grandparents were older, retired, and not looking to raise a freaking kid. They'd done that already with my mom, who lived at home until she was twenty-two and had never been an easy child. My grandparents were tired.

In middle school I'd ended up with my Aunt Susan, her husband Vic, and their son Randall. I wish I could say things got better when I moved in with them, that I'd found a family unit who finally gave a shit, but that wasn't the case with them either.

Randall was a little dick.

78

A spiteful little prick if I ever met one.

Two years older than me, all I'd ever wanted to be was his friend. I honestly thought we were going to be like brothers when I moved in. What a fucking idiot I was.

Nobody hit me at their house.

But nobody hugged me either.

When Kyle and I arrive to my house there are no cars in the driveway. Not Oz's truck, not Jameson's Honda, not Elliot's fifteen-year-old Tahoe.

Which means I'm actually going to have to figure this Kyle shit out on my own, without any help.

Unless …

I pull the phone out of my pocket and compose a text.

Zeke: *Hey*

Violet: *Hey*

Zeke: *Are you still mad about the boob thing at the trampoline park?*

Violet: *No, I got over it. I realize you have no filter.*

Zeke: *If it's any consolation, they're still really great boobs.*

Violet: *Let's not say anything else about my boobs please.*

Zeke: *I kind of need a favor.*

Violet: *...*

Oh, I see—she's not going to make this easy, is she?

Zeke: *What are you doing right now?*

Violet: *Reading.*

Zeke: *What are you reading?*

Violet: *What do you want, Zeke? I know you're not just texting to be friendly. Ask me for the favor and get to the point.*

My brows shoot up; she's really being sassy. I like it.

Zeke: *Kyle is here. I need help.*

Violet: *Is everything okay?*

Zeke: *Well, yeah. I mean he's watching TV, but his mom has to stay at work and needed me to watch him. So he's on my couch.*

Violet: *Have you ever babysat a little kid before?*

Zeke: *That would be a no.*

Violet: *Yeah, I figured you'd say that.*

Zeke: *Yeah, so, he's here at my place ...*

Violet: *If everything is okay, then what's the problem?*

Freaking A, why can't she just volunteer to come help me? Why do I have to come out and ask? It's pretty obvious that's what I'm texting her for.

Zeke: *He's on the couch. Do I leave him there or what?*

Violet: *Does he look content? What's he doing?*

Zeke: *Watching TV. I don't know what the hell this show is called but there are two guys running around in superhero capes and blowing shit up, one is Captain Man. It's fucked up.*

Violet: *Is he laughing?*

Zeke: *Yeah.*

Violet: *Then you should be good :)*

Zeke: *I'll pay you.*

Violet: *Pay me to do what?*

Zeke: *Pay you to come save me.*

Violet: *From an eleven-year-old? LOL*

Zeke: *Yes, exactly. Any moment he's going to need something. Or realize his mom isn't coming back until late.*

Violet: *I guess I could stop by to check on you.*

Violet: *But only for a few minutes—this is your gig. I'm just coming to make sure you don't burn down your house with him inside it.*

Zeke: *Great. How does fifty bucks sound?*

Violet: *I just rolled my eyes—you don't have to pay me to stop by. Just tell me your address.*

Zeke: *2110 Downer*

Violet: *Putting on coat. See you in five.*

Violet removes her coat, draping it across the back of a chair near the door, and fluffs her white blonde hair. No matter how hard my brain tries not to notice her figure, my eyes can't help themselves: black leggings, black t-shirt, black Chucks.

She's slim and petite, fists propped on her hips.

"Where's the little guy at?"

My lips part, and I want to make a joke about *the little guy* being inside my pants, but don't want to be offensive after the whole trampoline park *boob* thing. Besides, my roommate Oz is the pervert, not me, and the last thing I want is for her to leave.

"In here." I point toward the living room. "The little shit passed out on me. I wasn't sure what to do with him."

"Aww, poor lil' guy. It only took eight minutes for me to get here!" Her hazel eyes narrow. "You didn't give him any beer, did you?" she jokes softly, tiptoeing to the couch.

Violet peers down at Kyle, bending at the waist to gaze affectionately as he snores soundly, then looks up at me. "I'm so sorry I said the beer thing. It was a joke."

"I'm an asshole, not an idiot—I got the joke. You're very funny." I shove my hand into my pockets, rooted to the carpet. "So? Do I leave him in here or what?"

Violet looks around, biting down on her lower lip. Her eyes light up. "Why don't we move him into your bedroom? Then he can get some decent sleep. I don't think you want him waking up when your roommates come home. He has school tomorrow."

Good point. "Okay, yeah. I'll toss him in bed."

That I can do.

I move to the couch, strategizing my plan for picking him up.

Bend at the knees, scoop up Kyle's limp, lifeless little body, support it in my arms—I free-weight more than this kid weighs.

Violet skirts around me, silently questioning which room is mine, and I nod with my head to the door at the end of the hall to the right. "That one," I mouth.

Violet sneaks past, turning the knob to my room and pushing gently on the door. Stands in the threshold, glancing around.

I made the bed this morning, so she rushes forward, pulling down the black bedspread, dragging it low enough for me to set Kyle down, completely dressed.

We stand side by side, staring down at him.

"His shoes," Violet mouths, pointing to the scuffed-up tennis shoes strapped to the squirt's feet. She then pantomimes that I should take them off.

Obediently, I kneel at the foot of the bed, untying one raggedy tennis shoe, then the other. Holding them in the palm of my massive hand, I give them a onceover: gray and black with red laces, the rubber at the bottom is peeling back from the plastic base. The laces have broken in a few spots, but were retied instead of replaced.

The toes of both are scuffed to shit.

His mom is right, the kid needs new shoes; these are horrible—no way they have any good arch support left. I disregard them, placing them carefully under my window sill, out of the way so Kyle doesn't trip if he wakes up and gets out of bed.

Behind me, Violet flips on a small desk lamp, her fascinated eyes roaming the room. She walks slowly to the bookshelf, browsing the stacks of novels about the Great Depression and American history. My collection of Game of Thrones Pop! Art and Star Wars stormtroopers. The Rubik's Cube I sometimes solve between study breaks. The vintage Firebird and Mustang model cars I put together last winter when everyone else went home to see their families for holiday break; they took me an entire month. I painted each piece by hand, assembling every teeny tiny little part myself.

God, what a pain in the ass that was.

Violet peeks over her shoulder at me, a secret smile tipping her mouth as her index finger skims the shelf.

I inwardly groan; Christ, all the shit on my shelf makes me look like a goddamn nerd.

She stops skimming when she reaches the one picture displayed, the one of me with my parents, taken when I was about six, right around when their business exploded.

We're standing in front of the garage of the red brick starter home my parents were renting and I'm holding the handlebars of a new bike.

It was my first bike and I remember begging my mom to take the picture. A few years ago I unearthed it at my grandparents' house and stole it, frame and all.

I don't know why.

How stupid.

Violet leans in for a better look, hands behind her back. She wants to pick it up to study it; I can tell by the way her fingers reach forward then quickly pull back.

When she's done snooping, she places a forefinger to her lips, gesturing for me to follow her out the door.

"Shhh." Her eyes crinkle at the corners.

I pull the door closed behind us, leaving it slightly ajar in case the kid should wake up and get scared or whatever.

"Did his mom say how long she has to work?" Violet's whispering though we're in no danger of waking Kyle.

"No. She didn't tell me dick—she was freaking out and hung up before I could ask any questions."

Violet nods. "Poor thing."

"I know, right? How did she think I was going to handle him all night? I have no idea what I'm doing, and all I wanted to do tonight was read and sleep. I'm fucking tired."

I trail behind her tinkling laugh all the way to the kitchen. "I didn't mean you when I said poor thing, I meant him. Poor thing, getting shuffled around. It's no fun."

Oh. She feels sorry for the squirt but not me?

Figures.

Then again, why would she? Violet has no idea I've done more uncharacteristic shit in the past three weeks than I've done in my entire goddamn life.

Volunteering. Hanging out with kids. Letting her browbeat me into more play dates.

Asking for help, like I did tonight.

"You want something to drink? A water or something?"

Jesus Christ, what am I doing? I don't want her to *stay*; I want her gone.

Let's go ahead and add that to the growing list of shit I normally wouldn't do: inviting a chick to stay and making her feel welcome by offering to quench her thirst. I know women—they're worse than mangy stray cats. You give them a taste of something once, and they keep coming back.

I like my privacy; I *want* my privacy.

I want Kyle gone.

I want my bed and to be in it by myself.

"Kyle is sleeping peacefully. There's no reason for me to stay. Are you sure you don't want me to leave?"

"Only if you want to; there's no rush."

"Where are your roommates?"

"No idea. Probably with Jameson." Mental groan.

"Who's Jameson?"

"The nerdy girl my roommate is dating." Then I hear myself add, "If you don't want water I can make you some hot chocolate or something. It's motherfucking cold out."

Shut up Zeke. For fuck's sake, shut up.

Violet smiles shyly, tripping up on her speech. "S-Sure, I can do a quick hot cocoa. That sounds toasty and delicious."

Toasty.

I have a girl in my house that says shit like *sounds toasty.*

Wonderful.

She lingers in the doorway of the kitchen while I open cabinet after cabinet, scavenging for hot chocolate mix. Crap, do we even have it? I'm positive I've seen Jameson drinking it every once in a while, especially when it gets cold out, because she's always getting fucking cold. I'm positive she has some here somewhere—that froofy shaved chocolate shit from Williams Sonoma, not the grocery store kind like normal human people buy.

The good, fancy shit.

I jerk open the lower cabinets, then the top. The cubby above the fridge and microwave, not really questioning why I'm so hell bent on locating it.

Finally, peering into the very last cabinet along the wall, I find what I'm looking for: a red and white peppermint-striped canister of hot cocoa, specifically, shaved chocolate. Fucking *hand-crafted*, it says on the metal container.

Directly next to it? A bag of square, vanilla *handcrafted* marshmallows—ooh la la. I grab those too.

Mug. Chocolate. Mallows.

Jackpot.

"You want regular milk, vanilla soy, or almond?" I ask over my shoulder, yanking open the fridge and bending at the waist to peer inside.

"You have all three?" She sounds surprised.

I glance over my shoulder.

"This is a house of athletes." I grunt. "We like variety and anything with protein in it.

She shoots me a shy smile. "Well in that case, I think I'll go with the soy."

"We have that 'cause Elliot is lactose intolerant." I root around, shifting shit around to free the carton of soy. "So we always have it."

"Oh! I don't want to use Elliot's stuff."

"Chill out, it's fine."

I don't mention that I'm the one doing all the grocery shopping, or that my roommates almost never pay me back for food, so technically, it's all my mine.

"Okay, if you're sure he isn't going to get upset, then I trust you."

I trust you.

Those three words have me standing there holding the milk, staring at her, weighing the words but just fucking *staring* at her like a moron because she said she *trusts* me.

Obviously she doesn't mean it in a deeper sense—it's fucking soy milk—but no one has ever said those words to me before.

Violet doesn't even know me. I doubt she even likes me—no one does. I'm not nice, and I'm not an idiot; I know what they say about me behind my back and the way girls look at me. They'll fuck me because of my body and because I'm a wrestler for Iowa, but that's where the desire ends.

My friends put up with my shit because they have to; I own the house they live in and I'm on their wrestling team. They're stuck with me until we graduate or I get kicked off the team because of my shitty attitude.

Sucks to be them, I guess.

Violet's large trusting gaze meets mine as I take her measure, still holding the milk. Her black leggings hug her slender thighs. Her black long-sleeved t-shirt is tight and pulls across her small chest. I can see the outline of a bra beneath the thin fabric, but continue traveling up her torso. Her long slender neck is checkered with red splotches.

Her blonde hair is a wild, sexy mess.

She isn't hating me right now; I can see it in her eyes.

I trust you.

I twist the top off the milk and pour the mug full, muttering "Fuck," when some spills over the side.

Her laugh is sweet. "Want help with anything?"

"I got it. You relax." What. The. Fuck. Am. I. Saying.

Robotically, I set the mug inside the microwave, hit the *quick minute* button twice. We stand there in an awkward silence for one hundred twenty seconds, the countdown on the clock taking a fucking eternity.

Thirty more seconds.

Twenty.

Eighteen.

"Thanks for the hot chocolate," Violet says when the microwave beeps and I yank the door open. Take the mug out, set it on the counter, and pull the top of the peppermint-striped canister.

I dig a spoon in and add three heaping scoops, hoping she likes her shit extra chocolatey. Stir it rapid fire, toss in a handful of marshmallows, and hand it to her.

"Thanks," she says again, sipping the white froth off the top. "Mmm, this is delicious."

I watch her tongue dart out and lick the melted chocolate off the lip of the cup, then the melted mallow. Watch to see if any of it clings to her top lip, wanting desperately to see her pink tongue dart out again.

Desperately?

Shit, I need to get laid. Or at least a blow job.

I'll definitely be jerking off later.

"Mind if I have a beer?" I ask, going back to the fridge, hand halting mid-reach for an amber ale. "Oh shit, that's right—I probably shouldn't have a beer because I have a kid in the house, should I?"

"Probably not a good idea."

I twist the top of a water bottle instead, leaning my hip against the kitchen counter as she takes a seat at the table.

"So," I begin. "What's with you doing shit for little kids all the time?"

Her light brown brows go up. "What do you mean?"

The cynical part of me—the part that appears most often—chuckles.

"Come on Violet, what's with you always doing shit for little kids? You know, babysitting and taking them to parks and being so patient. Was your childhood like, the goddamn Brady Bunch so you want everything to be magic and unicorns shitting rainbow dust all the time? I bet the Tooth Fairy came to your house, and all that other made-up bullshit." I pause to take a chug of water. "Did your parents kiss your blonde little ass growing up? Bet you never got into trouble."

She stretches out the silence, letting it grow heavy in my tiny green kitchen, expression going from shy and delighted to pensive and reflective.

"No actually, it was nothing like that at all."

I snort. "Yeah right."

"I wish it had been but ..." A small shrug. "My parents are gone."

"Gone? What do you mean gone? Like on vacation?" It isn't an unreasonable question; that's where my parents are—gone.

Violet shots me a peculiar look. "No. *Gone.*" Her voice is quiet, her features impassive. "They're *dead.* They died."

Well ...

Shit.

"When?"

"A long time ago. I was young. Four years old."

The halo of white blonde hair suddenly makes her look incredibly vulnerable now that I know yet another personal thing about her, something I didn't necessarily care to find out, but ...

Too late now.

Violet plays with the handle of her mug, running a finger up and down the polished white ceramic. Two hearts are painted on the mug with the initials J and S—two smudged, shitty-looking hearts my roommate Ozzy painted at one of those lame pottery painting places. Jameson made one, too, so it would be a matching set.

Puke.

"Anyway," Violet is saying. "It was a l-long time ago and hardly matters anymore. I've managed to move on."

"So, is that why you're always so quiet? Why you're so timid and shit?"

"Am I quiet? I hadn't realized."

My *yes* is vehement and curt.

She considers the question. "I suppose I am. I guess I haven't thought about it that way, but it probably stems from losing my parents so young. M-My ..." She inhales, taking a deep breath to steady her speech. "I wasn't raised by family, but my cousin says my stutter started after they died."

She lifts a hand from the mug, swiping it through her long hair, her lips tipping up. The bangles circling her wrists jingle.

"Not to bore you with details, but I withdrew into myself for a few years. I was that lonely little girl waiting day in and day out for them to come back."

Round hazel eyes lift to meet mine and we regard each other.

It occurs to me then that maybe we have something in common, and I can't remember the last time I made any parallels between someone else's personal history and mine. Can't remember the last time I connected with someone who had it worse growing up.

"Sorry to hear that." And I am; even though my parents aren't dead, I was a lonely little boy who spent most of his childhood waiting day in and day out for them to come back.

The mug of hot chocolate is suspended at her lips, the steam from the warm milk rising, and she blows on it before taking a sip. "Anyway. The Tooth Fairy made very few appearances when I was little. Magic and unicorns, on the other hand? *Totally* a thing."

Man she's fucking cute.

"I think you're trouble."

Her eyes gleam behind the cup. "Thank you."

"Thank *you*—for coming to rescue me."

She casts her gaze down to the tabletop. "I hardly think *you* need rescuing, Zeke."

My laugh is humorless. "You'd be surprised."

Violet shifts in her chair. "I bet you're full of surprises."

I shift on the balls of my feet. "Are you being coy with me?"

She's spared from a reply when the front door swings open, followed by a chorus of loud voices filling the entry hall of the house, signaling the return of two roommates, and one Jameson Clark.

Oz, Elliot, and James are laughing hysterically.

Elliot gasping for breath at something Oz just said, probably something perverted.

I lean to the right, staring out the kitchen to glimpse James brushing the cold from her sleeves. Removing her hat and mittens, shoving them both in her pockets. Peeling off her Thinsulate puffy coat and hanging it on a hook by the door.

That chick is always freezing cold; I know for fact it was *her* that cranked the thermostat instead of adding more blankets to her boyfriend's bed, as if sixty-five degrees isn't warm enough.

"… and then he looks up from the ground, right, and this girl is just staring down at him. And I yell, *Hey Gunderson, why don't you*—"

Sebastian Osborne's gruff voice comes to an abrupt halt when they round the corner, the entire trio stumbling into the doorway of the kitchen.

Three sets of round eyes, wide with shock.

"Holy shit." Oz laughs. "Are we in the right house?"

It's not every day I bring a girl home, but when I do, it's not to sit around making small talk, it's to screw. Also, it's certainly not usually a sweet, naive-looking girl wearing all her clothes and sipping a mug of hot chocolate.

Violet has chocolate and mallow on her upper lip.

Her blonde hair and rosy cheeks and pale skin are perfection.

She sets the mug on the table, runs a hand down her silky hair, flattening the errant strands nervously, and stands.

"Hi. You must be Zeke's roommates?"

"Unfortunately," I mutter under my breath.

"Yes. *Hi!*" Jameson pushes through the guys, shiny black ballet flats tapping against the wooden floor. She unwinds her gray scarf and extends her hand. "I'm Jameson. I don't actually live here, I'm Oz's girlfriend."

She throws him a thumb over her shoulder.

"I'm Violet." She's blushing furiously.

"You work at the library, don't you?" James asks with polite interest, eyes shining, shit-ass grin widening. She directs a few smiles my way, glowing with excitement over this new development, wheels turning in her diabolic girl brain.

Shit. I don't need *anyone* getting the wrong idea about what's happening here, least of all Jameson, who can't seem to mind her own business.

"Yes, at the circulation desk." Violet clears her throat. "Well, I-I'm actually the everything desk." Nervous laughter. "I-I tutor, I shelve books, I *babysit* ..."

"You're Zeke's babysitter?" Oz pipes up from behind his girlfriend. He taps her on the arm. "I knew it. That would explain her presence. Told you he needed a nanny."

"Shut up, Ozzy," I growl. "That's not what she meant."

My roommate rolls his eyes.

"How the hell are you putting up with him? You're a saint, aren't you?" Oz asks, pushing through so he can be front and center in the whole, fucked up conversation. "I'm Oz, and this handsome fellow is Elliot."

Elliot waves sheepishly, flipping shaggy brown bangs and pushing up his glasses. "Hey."

"So what are the two of you doing?" Oz wants to know. "Having a tea party?"

"Leaving!" I blurt out. "Violet was just leaving."

I don't know why I say it, don't know why I said it with so much *insistence* in my voice, but the words are out before I can curtail them or wipe away the wounded expression crossing Violet's face.

You could hear a pin drop it gets so quiet.

The whole damn house is silent.

I'd chance a look at her from under the brim of my ball cap, but I don't want to see whatever hurt I know is pasted on her face. Embarrassment. Humiliation. Shame.

Take your fucking pick.

Steaming hot, heavy mug still in her hand, she sets it quietly on the table. Stands ramrod straight. Fakes a smile. "I-I guess I-I was just *leaving*." Wipes her hands on the front of her leggings. "It was n-nice meeting you all."

Oh Jesus, the stuttering is my fucking fault.

"You don't have to go!" Jameson starts in with her special brand of nagging as Violet awkwardly skirts past, sleeve brushing my arm. "Don't listen to Zeke; he's a grouchy old bear."

Nonetheless, they let Violet pass.

"Shit. Hold up a second!" I follow her as far as the living room, hands half raised, palms up, beseeching. "What am I supposed to do about Kyle?"

She slides her tiny feet into her black Chuck Taylors, presenting me with her back. "He's sleeping Zeke. You'll be fine."

Everyone stands uncomfortably, giving us a wide berth, and I expect one of them to say something snarky. Instead they actually all look disappointed.

Well, they're about to become more disa-fucking-pointed because I have zero romantic interest in Violet. Do they honestly think I'd bang a chick like *that* and let her loiter around the house? She has *long-term commitment* stamped in the center of her goddamn forehead.

My taste in women is simple: one-night stands. Not someone you'd bring home to your parents.

Women with dark hair.

Blue eyes.

Disposable.

The door opens and Violet steps down into the cold winter weather, steaming breath rising in the dark, illuminated by the porch light I rush over to flip—don't want her tripping and killing herself on a rock or whatever.

"Hey, thanks for coming on such short notice." I prop the door open with my foot, leaning on the doorjamb.

She lifts a palm to acknowledge my statement but continues down the sidewalk to the street. An old tan sedan that must be at least ten years old is parked out near the curb, and I hear her keys jingling in the dark as she fumbles her way down the walk.

Jameson grabs Violet's jacket off the hook, shoulders past me, and jams her elbow into my gut before chasing her into the dark yard.

"Sooo ..." Oz can hardly contain his meddling. "What the hell was that all about—and what the hell is a *Kyle*?"

Elliot has cleared the room.

"Kyle is a kid I'm watching. He's sleeping in my bedroom." Oz opens his mouth to speak, but I stop him with a brisk, "Don't ask."

"But—"

"Just shut the fuck up for once, would you Oz?"

This is partly his fault.

"You know I can't do that man." He moves into the kitchen, picks up Violet's discarded hot chocolate, and sips from the mug. "Wow, this is good. Makes me feel all *toasty* inside."

Jeez, not him too.

He grips the mug in one hand, the counter in the other. Lifts the mug again and examines it with narrowed eyes. "You don't think that girl has any sexually transmitted diseases, do you? Before I go ham on this cocoa?"

He knows damn well what her name is, and he knows damn well she doesn't have any STDs.

I'm practically growling. "Are you fucking serious?"

He slurps from the cup. "As a heart attack." Lets out a loud, "*Ahhh*, this shit is good. Expensive, but good."

"She doesn't have any STDs asshole; why would you say that? And her name is Violet."

He quirks a brow. "I'm just treating her like all the other randoms you bring home. Don't get all bent out of shape. It's a fair question."

No, it's not, and he knows it. *And* he knows she is nothing like the randoms I occasionally bring home. Nothing.

"She's not like that—*if* you couldn't tell."

More slurping. "I didn't have the chance to make a fair assessment; you basically shoved her out the door and into the cold ten seconds after we got home." Slurp, slurp. "I bet she's crying into her Cheerios right now."

"Please, I highly doubt that."

"Dude, she was *stuttering*—what the hell were you doing to her? She was flipping out."

What the hell was I *doing* to her? Instead of defending myself to Sebastian Osborne, I roll my eyes.

"She always stutters."

His eyes get huge. "What do you mean, she *always* stutters?" He lowers his voice to a whisper. "Like, is she *deaf?*"

"No jackass, she's not fucking deaf! Jesus Christ, what kind of question is that? Don't be an asshole."

His hands go up in mock surrender. "Whoa, I was just asking. I mean, you can't just say someone has a stutter and not expect a litany of questions to follow."

Oh yes I fucking can.

But Oz isn't done, not by a long shot. "What are you doing with that girl, man? It's obvious you're not sleeping with her."

"Why is it obvious I'm not sleeping with her?"

He laughs. "Well, she doesn't look like your usual type."

She's not, but that doesn't stop me from asking, "And what is my usual type, smartass?"

We both know the answer to that one: big boobs, single, the end.

"Easy. Big boobs. In it for the D, and I don't mean *de*fense." Oz finishes the hot chocolate from the hand-painted heart mug with a long drag, setting it down next to the sink. "So, what the hell are you doing with that girl, Zeke?"

Why the hell is he asking me this? We don't have conversations like this, ones about sweet, naïve girls who drink hot cocoa instead of liquor, do nothing but nice things for people, and have kind hearts. We just don't. We talk about sports, and wrestling, and wrestling practice, so I don't know why he's butting into my business.

He's in a relationship, so that suddenly makes him an expert? Fuck.

That.

His bulky arms are crossed now, serious expression taking residence on his face. The overhead light in the kitchen makes the black tattoo sleeve on his arm more pronounced.

His dark eyes bore into me; he's expecting an answer.

"We're just … friends."

"Friends?" He looks confused. "I didn't know you did that."

"You didn't know I did *what*? Speak English."

He throws his hands up. "Friends. I didn't know you did friends, let alone friends with tits."

This isn't the right moment to point out that Violet doesn't have any tits, and it's not something I'd want to point out to him anyway—girlfriend or not, he's kind of a pervert.

"Fine. I use the term *friend* loosely," I concede.

Honestly, I don't know what the fuck I am actually doing with her. Am I attracted to her?

Maybe.

Okay, yes. I am.

And she's growing on me every second we spend together. Anything more than that? I have no interest in exploring what that attraction means.

I've never given much thought to what I wanted in a girlfriend, because I've never had any intention of having one. Dating. Being in a relationship.

Shit, I barely have a relationship with my parents, and we're related—so why am I thinking about Violet? Why am I letting her in my house? Inviting her to this fucking fundraiser?

"Violet." Oz chuckles. "Even her name sounds like fucking sunshine and shit."

It does. I begin rolling her name around in my head, playing it on a loop.

"James is going to be bummed," Oz speculates.

"Oh, well in that case, let me chase after her so I can propose." Like I care what Jameson Clark wants for my personal life.

Oz laughs at me. "I'm just saying, she'd love having another chick here to break up the testosterone."

I snort through my nose. "James has more testosterone than the three of us combined."

My roommate grins from ear to ear, pushing away from the counter and flexing. "I'm going to tell her you said that; coming from you, she's going to take that as a compliment."

"I'm sure she will."

The first thing I hear when Jameson returns to the house from chasing Violet down is the distant sound of the front door slamming shut. Then I hear two boots drop to the hardwood floor, one at a time. The pads of her feet trudging down the hallway.

Arm pushing into my room without knocking.

I put a finger to my lips, shushing her from my spot at the desk. I don't need her waking up Kyle, who's curled into a tiny, breathing ball that's been squirming every ten seconds.

Jameson's eyes widen when she sees him.

"Knock much?" I whisper-hiss. "It's not enough that you've infiltrated the house, now you're breaking and entering people's bedrooms?" I'm as quiet as I can possibly be through clenched teeth.

James stands indignantly at the foot of my bed, gazing down at Kyle. Whatever lecture she was about to deliver gets derailed by the sight of his slight, peacefully slumbering body.

Lucky little bastard.

She turns to face me, walking to stand beside me.

"Uh … *what* is going on with you lately?" Her low, easy laughter fills my bedroom. "Nice girls in the house. Volunteering. Now you're babysitting a little kid? What the hell is happening?"

"Would you get out of my room? The kid here is trying to sleep," I whisper frantically, raising a World War II history book, waving it in front of her face. "And I am trying to *read*."

"You can't kick me out," she whispers back. "Not until you hear what I have to say."

I glare at her, glare at her straight brown hair and bright blue eyes. She's wearing a boring gray t-shirt and the same damn pearl necklace she always has on, even when it's just a well-worn shirt.

"Technically I own this house, so I can kick you out if I want," I argue futilely.

Another annoying laugh in the dimly lit room as she crosses her arms, studying me. "You wouldn't do that."

"Oh really? And why is that?"

She ignores the question.

"Look, I didn't come in here to talk about me. We both know you and I have our own issues. I'm here to talk to you about why you just kicked Violet out of the house."

"That's a bit harsh, don't you think?"

"*I'm* the one who followed her out into the cold. She didn't even have her jacket on when she left, so yeah, you kicked her out."

I don't have to sit and listen to this bullshit. "Kicked her out? For the fucking record, Miss Know-it-All, I didn't *make* Violet leave, I said she was *about* to leave. She made the choice to go."

"Give me a break."

"Everyone being here freaked her out—I was doing her a favor."

"You announced that she was leaving. That's making her leave." Suddenly she gets serious. "You know what Zeke, all this time, I keep waiting for you to want more for yourself."

Jameson, oblivious to my nonverbal cues to get the hell out my room, lowers her voice and steps closer.

"What were you doing with her here, Zeke? What are you doing with *that* girl? She's seems really kind, and giving and gentle and—"

"Everything I'm not? Yeah, yeah, I get it. If that's what you were going to say, fucking say it."

Jameson slowly nods. "That's what I was going to say."

"Don't you think I know what I'm doing? Please."

James shakes her head. "No Zeke, I honestly don't think you do."

"Nothing. I am doing nothing with that girl." I snort, voice raising an octave. "Why do you even care?"

Jameson hasn't been around long, but she's already started meddling; every now and again she gets in our household business. Manages to insert herself where she's not wanted and raises my hackles, gets me riled up.

This is one of those moments; she's in my bedroom and in my business.

All up in my shit.

The last place I want anyone to be.

The worst part? She's not letting up. Won't stop talking and won't walk away. Jameson Clark is holding me hostage in my own freaking bedroom.

"If you like Violet even a little—and I suspect you do, because otherwise you never would have brought her here ..." Her voice is low. "If you like her even a teensy weensy bit Zeke, don't play games with her. She seems so sweet, and if you string her along ... I feel like it would ruin her."

"Ruin her?" *Why would I ruin her when I like her?*

"I don't know, maybe I shouldn't use the word ruin, it seems harsh—it's just she's bright and adorable and you tend to surround yourself with storm clouds."

"Wow James. Don't you think that's a little melodramatic? Even for you?"

She laughs quietly. "Oh Zeke, I've only said half of what I wanted to say, but I'm going to bite my tongue for now."

I look at her then, really look at her: earnest eyes, long shiny hair—she's not as plain and boring as she looks. If Jameson Clark had a sign around her neck, it would read *No bullshit.* She studies me, always doing weird shit like that. Analyzing people. Watching them.

Assessing.

She walks to the door, hesitating.

"You and I *both* know pushing Violet out tonight was a huge mistake, so don't bother denying it. In fact, I predict ..." She bites down on her lower lip in concentration. "I predict you lie in bed tonight once your little buddy there is gone, and for once in your life, you're going to feel shitty about the way you treated some-one."

I lean forward, hands braced on the armrest of my desk chair. Narrow my eyes.

"Oh yeah? And why would I do that?"

She smiles—one of those pitying, patronizing smiles that says she thinks she knows better.

I've seen her give that same smile to my roommate a hundred times.

"That's an easy one."

My brows go up; this oughta give me a good laugh.

"Because you *like* her. You just haven't figured it out yet."

#DOUCHEBAG

"That jawline could have
its way with me, but that's not
the problem. The problem
is I thought I was over him,
but he smells nice today."

Violet

"Got any homework?" His voice stops me from walking past his table. For once, Zeke Daniels is at the library of his own free will, not waiting be tutored, not with a group of his wrestling buddies.

Alone.

"Yes. I-I always have homework." I'm stumbling on my own stupid words and I hate myself for it.

Nonchalantly, like it's no big deal, Zeke leans back in his chair, arches his spine, extends his leg, and pushes out the chair across from him.

It slides two feet and stops.

I stare at it.

He stares at it. Raises a brow beneath the brim of his ball cap. Bends his neck and goes back to work.

"Sit. There's plenty of room," he rumbles. Offers me a tight smile. "We should probably talk."

Talk? *He wants to talk?*

"All right. Give me a minute."

I back away, mind working in overdrive, cataloging all the things he could possibly want to talk about, and I come up with the following: Kyle. Running me out of his house on Thursday. The fundraiser next week.

Taking a deep breath, I count to ten before gathering my backpack and laptop from the back office. Find my time sheet. Clock out.

Walking to his table feels like some weird, reverse walk of shame, my gaze trained on that pushed out wooden chair.

Act casual, I remind myself, *he is* just *a guy* ...

An insensitive guy.

Intimidating. Cold. Callous. Complicated. The moodiest, broodiest, douchebaggiest guy I have ever met.

From the looks of it, he wants for nothing; I've noticed his expensive clothing. Seen his current model pick-up truck, one with shiny silver chrome, kick plates, and detailing. Everything about him reeks of wealth and privilege, and yet, I sense that's not where his arrogance comes from.

I wouldn't even call it arrogance; it's more like resentment. He resents everyone that's happy.

When I join him, I see that he's cleared a space for me, and I set my things down. Stand next to the chair, unsure.

His dark head is bent, gray moody eyes shielded by the brim of his black ball cap. While his pen scratches across his paper in bold, hard strokes, my eyes do a quick scan of his broad shoulders and thick biceps.

His arms, bared from his short-sleeved tee, are peppered with a smattering of dark hair. For a brief moment, I allow my mind to wander, wondering what else on Zeke Daniels' body is covered with hair. What else on him is hard and solid and—

His head shoots up. "Where you just checking me out?"

"No!" *Oh god.*

"Good." He smirks. "Because as my tutor and official play date partner, that would be highly unprofessional, and I know how you like to put up boundaries."

Me? Put up boundaries? Hardly.

In fact, I have the opposite problem.

"I'm fucking with you Violet. You're the least closed-off person I know—well, besides Oz's new girlfriend, who can't seem to mind her own business."

Wow, he's uncharacteristically chatty today.

Uncharacteristically pleasant.

"Sit, please, you're making me nervous." He smiles, a quick flash of white making a brief appearance in the small space between his lips. My stare is rooted to that spot—*those teeth*—until he clears his throat and breaks my trance.

Once seated, I'm determined to get actual studying done. If Zeke wants to talk, he's going to be the one to broach the subject. Pry information out of me.

We only study in silence for *six* minutes before I glance up to find him wordlessly watching me, his piercing gray eyes straying when I reach up, push back a wavy lock of hair that's sticking to my lip gloss, and oh lord, he's staring at my mouth ... my lips.

I swallow.

He looks away before I do.

"Tell me something," he utters, surprising me.

"Tell you what?" I set down my pen, leaning back in my chair. "What do you want to know?"

"What's your major?" He throws his hands up before I can answer. "Wait, don't tell me. Elementary ed."

"Nope. Take another guess."

"Early childhood development."

"No." But I'm surprised he actually knows what that is.

"Hmmm." That mammoth hand rubs the stubble on his chiseled chin. "Pediatric nursing."

"Nope." My head lilts to the side on its own accord, and I narrow my eyes, staring him down, measuring his sincerity. Stare into those unsettlingly light, somber eyes.

"What makes you so sure my major is child related?"

"Well," he drawls out slowly. "Isn't it?"

I laugh. "Yes."

He leans back in his chair, a smug, satisfied set to his face. "I knew it."

"N-No need to get cocky," I say on a laugh. "You still haven't guessed."

"There's always a reason to get cocky. For me it's *getting out of bed in the morning.*"

We're both quiet after *that* comment, neither of us really knowing what to say. I don't trust myself to speak; I feel like I'm betraying myself by not asking about the other night, when he ran me out of his house and embarrassed me.

I know I should ask—it's been weighing on my mind since— but I'm not sure how, even after four days and three nights with nothing to do but think about it.

The thing is, I'm not sure he cares how it made me feel to be shuffled out of his house. How *embarrassed* I was.

How I cried all the way home.

"Hey Violet." Zeke taps the table with a pencil to get my attention.

"Hmmm?"

"Are we friends?" The yellow pencil is perched above his notebook and he goes back to scrawling in it, not making eye contact. The question slips out of his beautiful mouth so causally, like he's just asked me to pass the salt at the dinner table.

"Excuse me?"

"Are. We. Friends."

This is it. This is my opportunity.

Say it, Violet. Say the words: *my real friends would never have shamed me the way you did.*

Say them, Violet, *say the words.*

"*Are* we?" I ask quietly, hating myself for being such a coward, unable to say what I so desperately need to.

"You tell me." His low baritone is soft, cautious.

"I-I thought we were *starting* to become friends."

There. I said it.

"You *thought?*" I can see him getting cagey, the muscle in his jaw ticking. He's knows there's more to it than that, he just can't fill in the blanks by himself.

I set down my pen, clasping my hands on the tabletop in front of me. "Y-Yes. I *thought* we were friends, Zeke, but then when your *real* friends got home on Thursday night, you didn't want me around anymore. It made me feel ..."

My eyes close and I give my head a little shake. Can't meet his eyes, face flaming hot.

"It made me f-feel ..." I take a breath, breathing in through my nose; it's the only way I can steady my voice, control my speech.

When I steel myself, raise my eyes, and look at him, he's looking toward the bank of windows near the front of the library. Staring through them, mouth in a determined set, twisted at the corners. Not a frown exactly, but ...

I let the quiet engulf us, nothing but the sounds of the library surrounding us, realizing words are no longer necessary. I've said what I needed to say in the only way I know how—by saying nothing at all.

Still focused on the windows, he speaks.

"I wasn't thinking; I was reacting." He pauses. "It had nothing to do with you."

He doesn't apologize. He doesn't say he's sorry right then, but for now it's enough.

"All right."

He shifts his gaze. "Is it?"

No.

I cast my eyes downward, fixating on my notebook before glancing back up. His brows are furrowed unhappily.

"That's the trouble with you Violet. You're too fucking forgiving."

"Why is that a bad thing?"

"Because, when someone treats you like shit, you're not supposed to *let* them. Everyone fucking knows that."

His nostrils flare at me, eyes flash.

And before I can stop myself, the words are pouring out of my mouth, hushed but hurried. "F-Fine. How about this: no, I don't think we're friends, because I don't want friends who treat me like shit. Who act like afraid little boys. Who kick me out of their house after offering me a seat at their table. You're rude and stubborn a-and a total dick."

A bubble of laughter builds up inside me, and I fight it the entire way—but in the end, the laughter wins out.

"S-Sorry." I stifle a laugh. "I shouldn't be laughing."

"You don't sound sorry." He sounds disgruntled.

"That's because I'm not. Not at all."

"But you *just* called me a dickhead."

"And you know what?" I sigh, leaning back in my chair, folding my arms behind my head and clasping my hands. "It felt really good."

If I've surprised him by my candor, he doesn't show it. His face is an impassive mask. "Violet, what's your last name?"

"My last name?" The question is random, catching me off guard.

His response is a laugh so deep and amused, it sends a ripple up my spine. "If we're going to be friends, don't you think I should know your last name?"

"I-It's DeLuca"

"DeLuca? DeLuca." He squints at me. "Are you sure?"

"Uh, yeah?"

"Wait. Is that Italian?"

I nod.

"Because you don't *look* Italian. You're so pale."

Another laugh sputters out of me, and I have to put my head down on the tabletop to stop the noises coming out of my mouth. I can't even look at him; if I do, it will just make me laugh even harder.

"Now what are you laughing at?"

"Oh god. You." Tears run down the corners of my eyes, and I wipe them away. "Only you could call someone pale so honestly and make it sounds like an insult."

"Are you making fun of me, Violet *DeLuca*?"

"It's called teasing, Ezekiel Daniels." I stop, tilting my head to the side to study him. "Lamentations, Ezekiel, Daniel, Hosea …"

He watches me, unmoved. "Yeah, I get it—Ezekiel and Daniel are books of the bible."

"Are your parents religious?"

"No." He adjusts his black Iowa ball cap. "Well, I guess they must have been before they had me, but they aren't now."

"Are *you?*"

"*No.* It's just one fucked up, karmic joke. My parents must have known from the beginning that I was going to be a sinner— that's why it sounds like they named me after two books of the Bible. Lord knows I'm no saint."

His big body relaxes, sinking into his chair, slouching, still staring at me with those somber gray eyes. They're unflinching and so unhappy.

He changes the subject.

"You ready for the fundraiser next week?"

The casual mention of it has my stomach doing flips. To quell it, I dig out a water bottle from my backpack, twist off the top, and take a drink.

"I don't know. Are you going to be nice to me in public?"

I let the awkward silence between us grow uncomfortably long before clearing my throat. Tip my chin up.

"Zeke. I-I want an apology before I agree to go anywhere with you."

He frowns. "Violet …"

"You *owe* me one."

Removing his black baseball cap, he sets it on the table in front of him, running his fingers through his dark hair. The black slashes above his platinum eyes furrow in concentration.

"It was shitty. I knew as soon as I fucking let you leave it was wrong. Obviously I can't handle having girls in my house without acting like a jerkoff. I'm sorry."

I reach across the table and pat his hand. "There now, was that so hard?"

"Yes," he grumbles.

"Bet it made you feel better, didn't it?"

He refuses to answer, instead replacing his hat. Squeezes the brim and slouches down in his chair.

"So this fundraiser—anything I need to know?"

"Like what?"

"Like, I don't know … are we meeting anyone there? Are any of your friends going?"

"My friends wouldn't be caught *dead* in that place."

I laugh. "Oh, I'm sure that's not true." They can't all be hard asses with unyielding edges—like him.

"You're probably right," he concedes, disgruntled. "My roommate has turned into such a fucking pansy since he started dating his girlfriend. He'd totally go."

I smile. "So it's just going to be us?"

Zeke frowns. "No. My wrestling coach is going to be there with his wife, and probably a few other people in the program. Apparently Coach loves this kind of shit—who knew?"

"Why …" I have to clear my throat then, a stutter on the tip of my tongue. "Why is he making you go?"

There has to be something he's not telling me.

"Because he's a *dick*."

Another laugh threatens to spill out, and he shoots me a look.

"Someone's in a giggly mood today."

"Sorry."

His eyes bore into me, lips twitching. "I'm not."

8

#DOUCHEBAG

"I already saw this dick
in person and wasn't impressed,
so why the hell is he sending me
a picture of it, anyway?
I hate re-runs."

Zeke

For the first time in a few weeks, I don't drag Kyle to the kiddie park. Instead, I drag him to one across town—one with a skate park, a baseball diamond, and a basketball court.

"Hey kid. You any good at basketball?" I spy a basketball halfway across the old, fenced-in court.

There hasn't been a lot of upkeep at this place; the asphalt top needs resurfacing, and weeds grow like wild grass between the cracks. The court boundary lines need a fresh coat of paint, and don't get me started on the chain-link fencing that's seen better days.

Still, it's deserted, and as luck would have it, an old, faded basketball sits abandoned in one of the four corners.

I forgot to bring one.

Kyle shrugs his skinny shoulders. "We play it at school in gym class."

"You any good?"

Another shrug. "I'm pretty good. I can run circles around Tommy Bauer, so …" Another shrug.

"Wanna throw around some hoops? This park looks like it could use some action."

"Sure. I guess."

"Trot on over there and fetch that ball. I'm going to set my shit down on the bench." I look him up and down. "Want me to take your jacket so it's not in the way?"

"Sure. I guess." Off comes the gray, threadbare zip-up hoodie.

I really need to get this kid a new fucking sweatshirt, and obviously nothing but an Iowa wrestling hoodie will do. I make a mental note to grab one from the supply room where we get our sponsored apparel and shit. If they don't have kids sizes, I'll just grab him a men's small.

Kyle's lanky frame jogs back with the ball, holding it in his arms.

"You're supposed to be dribbling that thing," I joke.

"I'm saving up my energy for when I whoop your butt," he shoots back.

Little smartass.

He's a few feet away when he trips, and my steely gaze hits his feet. Those gray and read sneakers, worn to shit.

Back up to his face.

His big blue eyes are trained on me, and I force a grin.

"Want to make this interesting?"

He tilts his head. "What does that mean?"

A loud laugh escapes my throat, starting in my gut. "It's just an expression; it basically means, want to gamble on the game."

"Oh."

I can tell by his face he still doesn't have a fucking clue what I'm talking about.

"Betting is something I do with my friends. You wanna take a gamble? Winner takes all, loser pays up."

I snatch the ball out of his hands and dribble it once, continuing as he plops down on a park bench.

"A bet is something people do for fun. Like, let's say I bet you I can beat you to the fence. If we race and I win, you have to give me a soda."

His whole face lights up with understanding. "Oh yeah! A bet! We do that all the time at school!"

Cool.

"So, want to make a bet with me?"

"What kind?"

"I bet you can't make more baskets than me."

"Why are you betting me *that?* I'm just a kid."

Slowly, Kyle rises from the bench and walks toward me, stopping to bend and tie his shoddy, worn sneakers. I ogle them for the umpteenth time while he ties the laces.

Snap my fingers.

"Hey, on second thought. How about if you win, I have to buy you some new tennis shoes. Badass ones."

He gives me a dubious stare, the kind only a cocky eleven-year-old is capable of giving, but then, his shoulders slump.

"I'm never going to be able to beat *you*. You're huge."

Hmm, that's true.

"How about we start with a few pointers?" I dribble the ball, fumbling it between my hands, letting it bounce too high then letting it bounce away. It rolls across the asphalt, hitting the chain-link fence before stopping. "Dammit."

"Are you even any good at basketball?" Kyle's eyes narrow suspiciously.

"Hell yeah." I brag. "The best."

I jog to retrieve the wayward ball, trying to push it through my legs like they do in the pros. It hits the back of my knee and careens toward where Kyle stands by the bench.

"I thought you were a wrestler."

"I am, but I've always loved b-ball," I boast. "Played in *sixth* grade all the way through eighth."

I dribble again, aim at the backboard, which is just a large, square piece of plywood nailed to where the old backboard used to be—back when the park system actually put money into this shithole park.

I aim. Shoot.

And miss.

"Wow, you suck!" Kyle postures, chest puffed out confidently. "You're on!"

I put my fist out, and he bumps it. We both make them explode.

"Bring it!"

Seven days later, I'm in the kitchen cutting up fruit when Oz and Jameson walk into the kitchen, both of them standing in the doorway. James hangs back while Ozzy strolls in, yanks open the fridge, and retrieves two water bottles.

He cracks them both open, but keeps the tops on. "Jim and I are heading to a movie. You wanna come?"

"Can't." I shove a piece of apple in my mouth. Swallow. Chew. "Gotta take Kyle for new shoes."

"Who is Kyle?" Oz asks.

"My little brother." Shit. When did I start thinking of him as my little brother? I must be losing my edge.

"You have a little brother named Kyle?" Oz asks, confused. "I thought you were an only child."

"As if either of you know anything about me," I scoff. Then, shifting my eyes to the ceiling, sending up a prayer for patience, I add. "For fuck's sake, try to keep up. Kyle is the Little from the mentoring program I'm stuck doing for the rest of the semester. Remember? He was *literally* sleeping in this house two weeks ago."

Oz nods slowly. "Anddd ... now you're taking him shoe shopping?"

"That's what I said."

"For shoes." Pause. "Um, *why*?"

"He beat me at basketball." There's a duh inflection to my tone, and I turn my back to shove another piece of apple in my mouth. Chew. Swallow.

Oz and Jameson stare mutely, disbelief etched on both their slack-jawed faces.

"A little *kid* beat you at basketball?"

"Oh my god," I grind out, annoyed. "Yes."

I chance a look at them both; Oz is clueless, but Jameson ... *Jameson* is studying me through narrow eyes. Suspiciously.

114

In two seconds, she's going to be sniffing the air for my bull-shit.

My roommate prattles on, oblivious. "I still don't get why you're buying him shoes. Did he swindle you?"

"No. I lost a bet."

Oz laughs. "You bet a little kid he couldn't beat you at basketball? What an idiot. You're always losing bets." He steals a piece of watermelon from the cutting board. "Jesus, Zeke, how much money do you lose every year blowing bets with people?"

Enough.

I blow *enough.*

But Oz isn't done giving me crap. "Didn't you bet Gunderson he couldn't get that girl to go out with him? Then when he won, you had to pay him a hundred dollars, and he used it to buy a *textbook* he needed for his econ class."

Jameson crosses her arms, scrutinizing me. Her wide blue eyes rake me up and down, head to toe, blue irises boring down, hard.

She is so annoying.

"And what the hell was that gimmie bet with Erik Janz? How could you have bet that moron three hundred bucks on the Louisiana game? Everyfuckingbody knew Florida was going to get their asses handed to them, but you bet him they'd win anyway." He takes a chug of water. "Then what does he do with the money? Huh? Spends it on a new starter for his piece-of-shit car. Man are you a dope."

When he's done bitching at me and finally leaves the room, I look up to find Jameson still watching me, arms crossed, mouth twisted into a thoughtful expression.

"You know," she says slowly, taking a few steps forward. Advancing on me. Taps her chin with the tip of her forefinger. "I thought I had to watch my back around you—you know, right when I started dating Sebastian and started coming around. I thought it was only a matter of time before you hid in the bushes to jump me."

She gives an airy little laugh, pushing the black glasses perched on her nose farther up the bridge, leaning back against the counter to mimic my stance when I wish she would just leave.

"*Jump* you? Why the hell would you think that? I'm not a fucking psycho."

Her brows rise. "Well yeah, I know that now—deep down inside, you're just a big softie, aren't you? All talk and no show."

"Screw you, James."

Another lilty little laugh. "Only you would tell someone to screw themselves when they were trying to be nice."

I can't meet her eyes.

"Oh … my … *god*," she says breathily, drawing out the three words in a torturously slow preamble. "I know. I *know* why you do it."

Her words are slow and deliberate. She braces a hand on the counter

I make a *pfft* sound, yanking the fridge open and peering inside so I don't have to look at her face. She's aggravating the shit out of me.

"What is it you think you know, smartass?"

She snaps her fingers.

"Remember that bet with Oz? The one where you bet him five hundred dollars to kiss me in the library? You did it because you knew he was broke and needed money."

"You're crazy." I stare at the milk. "You've known me for all of two seconds."

She ignores me, chattering on, warming to the subject. "But you don't just make bets with anyone. You make bets with people who need help. It all makes sense now."

Jameson playfully pokes my bicep with a fingernail.

"You know this kind of makes you a philanthropist, don't you?" *Gasp.* "Holy crap, Zeke. You're … nice!"

"Shut up," I grumble. Why the fuck won't she just go away? "Are you done yet?"

"You're not even going to deny it!" She cackles, slapping her thigh with an open palm. "Don't worry Angry Daniels. I won't tell anyone your dirty little secret."

I feel her palm patting me on the bicep as she airily breezes from the room.

She sticks her head back in.

"No one would believe me anyway."

She winks.

For all her prim and proper ways, Jameson Clark really is a fucking smartass.

9

#DOUCHEBAG

"My sex life is driven by beer,
and spite."

Zeke

This fundraiser is packed.

Which is surprising given that it's not a huge organization we're here to raise money for. From the entryway, the moment we walk in, I immediately begin casing the joint. I don't know why I do it, but every time I walk into a room, I take note of the size, the exits, and the people in it.

So I stand here, Violet waiting patiently beside me.

Over in one corner, I spot Nancy from the Big Brother office, head thrown back and laughing at something a gray-haired dude is saying. She's about as dolled up as she can get: full-length mother-of-the-bride dress, hair curled, eye shadow so bright you could see it from the moon.

There's a band setting up, a small area sectioned off for dancing in the center of the room, and lining the perimeter, long banquet tables showcase the raffle and auction items. The moneymakers. Stars of the show.

The fundraiser isn't as formal as I'd expected; people are milling about, most of them with drinks in hand, in all styles of attire. Khakis. Dressy denim. Suits and ties. Floor-length numbers.

Stifled, I yank at the tie around my neck that seems to have gotten tighter on the ride here—like a noose.

My black suit coat stretches too snugly across my broad back and shoulder blades. The collar of my baby blue shirt buttoned too high and cutting off my air supply. Shoes too new and stiff to be even remotely comfortable.

Fucking Coach.

I wouldn't be here if he hadn't forced me to be.

And with Violet, no less.

Quiet Violet, waiting patiently next to me, near the coat check area, her calm demeanor only slightly quelling my resentment at being here. Always serene, always composed—if you don't count the random, nervous stuttering.

Her colorless blonde hair is down and arranged in loose curls down her back, a stark contrast against the dark-as-night dress coat she's wearing over her dress.

I know it's a dress because I checked out her pale bare legs when she was climbing into my truck, plum-colored heels boosting her height by several inches, the pastel nail polish she's always wearing playing peekaboo out of the tips of her shoes.

Cheeks pink. Lips dark burgundy. Lashes long and coated with black mascara.

Pretty. *Real* fucking pretty.

When she smiles up at me, skin positively *glowing*, flush with excitement, her teeth are straight and perfect, highlighted by her dark lips.

Violet bites down on that lower lip, probably chewing off her lipstick in the process, then beams up at me, hopeful and sunshiny and bright, like she's waiting to blow sunshine up my ass.

She looks happy, but I didn't come here to have fun and I didn't come here to fundraise. Or socialize. Or see people.

I'm here out of some twisted obligation.

"Daniels. *Son*," says the devil himself.

I turn to acknowledge Coach with a dispassionate dip of my head. He takes inventory of me, of my attire, and I take in his. Shoes, pants, shirt, eyes raking up my expensive paisley tie, his critical blue eyes are shrewd, shifting once I pass his inspection.

However, when he turns his attention on Violet?

His entire demeanor changes. Relaxes.

Softens.

"Want to introduce me to your beautiful date, Mr. Daniels?"

Nope.

I nod in her general direction. "Coach, this is Violet."

She blushes, nervously tucking an errant strand of hair behind her ears. Her shiny rhinestone earrings sparkle.

I wonder if she'll stutter when she has the chance to speak.

Coach grins down at her, his hulky physique towering over her. He casts a disappointed glance in my direction, mouth set into a hard line.

"Now, now," he chastises. "I know you were raised better than that, Mr. Daniels. Why don't you introduce her again? This time show some respect, eh?" He winks at Violet.

Fucking dickhead.

It takes every ounce of willpower I possess not to turn on my heels and crash back through the door we just strolled through to get in here. I'd do it too—I'd fucking bolt, with little thought to Violet's ability to keep pace.

I suck in a breath, tempted to loosen this fucking tie around my neck and yank it off completely. It's choking the shit out of me.

"Coach, this my tutor, Violet." Dammit, why the hell did I say that? Even *I* know I sounded like a fucking asshole, especially after the whole thing at my house with my roommates.

I take another drag of air, dialing down the angry a notch, and start over.

"Coach, this is my friend Violet, from school. Violet, this is Iowa's wrestling coach."

"Good to meet you, Mister ..." Violet's inflection rises at the end, waiting for him to supply his name.

"Just Coach will do fine, young lady." He smiles. My brows go up—this is the first fucking time I've ever seen the bastard smile.

I note that when Violet extends her hand, Coach gives it a gentle but firm shake.

He likes her.

Well, at least I did something right by bringing her.

"You kids heading to the bar for drinks?"

The bar? Now *that's* the shit I'm talking about.

"You're not drinking tonight, are you Mr. Daniels?"

I nod. "We have to hit the coat check first, but yeah. I'm going to need to be piss-ass drunk to make it through tonight," I joke crudely.

Coach shakes his head back and forth. "Daniels, the correct answer I'm looking for here is *No sir*, especially if you're driving this young lady home tonight."

Mother. Fucker. Is he here just to lord over me? Because he's off to a good start.

"No sir," I grumble, sounding a whole lot like a goddamn pussy.

"Good decision." He smacks me on the bicep, pleased. "My wife Linda and I are seated at table twelve if you kids are open to joining us."

"Th-That's," Violet stutters, then pauses. Takes a deep breath. "*That's* very kind of you to offer, Coach. I'm sure we'd love that, thank you."

We'd. *We*.

I'm not a religious person, but when Violet prettily accepts for both of us, I swear to God Coach smirks with satisfaction.

"Yeah, Coach. *Thanks*."

He smacks me on arm, taking a sip of his drink—probably to rub it in. "Good. Check your coats and grab something to wet your whistle. Find us when you get settled." The old fucker grins at Violet. "Young lady, it was nice meeting you."

I watch him walk away, whatever uncharitable thought I have interrupted by Violet clearing her throat.

"Should we check our coats? Or … did you want to put them at the table?"

"Check them. I want to avoid that table as long as I possibly can, no offense."

She nods, though I doubt she understands.

She has no idea that Coach is forcing me to volunteer with the Big Brothers Mentor Program—veritably blackmailing me. Has no idea I'm on the verge of losing my spot on the team because of my bad attitude. Has no idea that the wrestling team is the only family I have, and Jesus Christ do I sound like a whining little fuck.

I trail behind Violet as she gets in line for the coat check. She peels down the zipper on her black jacket, slowly shrugging it off her narrow shoulders.

Her *bare*, narrow shoulders.

I'm immediately drawn to the pale skin, her exposed collarbone like smooth porcelain. Her dress is dark plum and holds tight to what few curves she has, a rich velvet, ending mid-thigh.

I realize I'm staring when she smoothes a hand down the front and looks up at me, worried. "Is this okay? I wore it when I was in a friend's wedding last summer. I-It's the only thing I had that was dressy enough."

Like I care that she had to re-wear a dress. Do chicks actually give a crap about stuff like that?

"It's good."

And it is. She looks gorgeous.

I slide off my suit coat, take Violet's jacket, and hand them both over to the stalky high school kid behind the counter for a claim ticket. His eyes widen, surprised. Excited.

I realize he must follow university wrestling, must know who I am and be a fan.

See, the university does this whole huge marketing blitz in the fall to advertise their student athletes. Since wrestling is a powerhouse and a draw to the school, large banners hang on the field house, stadium, and gymnasium. They're basically the size of billboards.

And whose face do you think is plastered on one of them, live and in color?

That's right, yours truly, looking like the goddamn champion I am.

The kid plays it cool. "What's up, you checking your coats?"

"Two please."

"Uh." He clears his throat. "Are you Zeke Daniels?" He's still holding our coats, no attempts to hang them.

"Yeah."

Violet watches the whole exchange, a thoughtful expression sliding across her angelic face. It doesn't take a genius to figure out what's going through her mind: that I'm being a cocksucker and should be nice to the kid, should offer to sign something so he doesn't have to ask.

Probably not in those exact words.

And she'd be right. I should just offer because I know that's what he wants. But guess what? I'm not in the damn mood and don't fucking feel like signing anything.

"I …" The kid hesitates. "I, uh, have a poster in back if you, uh, could you sign it? I have a Sharpie, too."

"You have a poster in back?" That's creepy and weird.

"I knew Coach D was going to be here—he comes every year—and my buddy Scott heard you were a volunteer at the center. I was hoping you'd be here. Can I grab it for you to sign?"

Violet lays a palm on my forearm, and I can't help but glance down and stare at it a few seconds, completely thrown off by her gentle touch. "Isn't it wonderful that he's so excited to meet you, Zeke?"

She smiles, eyebrows rising a fraction … gives her head an encouraging little nod up and down until I hear myself saying, "Yes?"

The kid does a fist pump. "I've seen all your home games, and last week at Cornell?" His voice cracks with excitement. "Holy shit man, that pin on JJ Beldon was sick! Seriously sick! My friends and I lost our *minds*."

Violet nudges my arm gently with a smile on her face.

"Thanks?"

She pats my arm and—

Wait just one damn minute.

Is she … is Violet *coaching* me on how to be *nice*?

Her hand is still on my sleeve and I look down into her pretty, upturned face. Down at her bold, dark lips. Her huge eyes and long lashes. All that pale blonde hair.

She's a damn wet dream.

Fuck me.

"Yeah, get your poster, kid. I'll sign your shit."

I've never seen a kid move as fast as this one does, leaving our coats on the counter and sprinting through the back room, disappearing through a door.

"This is really nice of you," Violet says when he's gone.

The little faker thinks she can pull one over on me? I don't think so. "You're not fooling me with those innocent eyes and sexy lips. I know what you just did there."

"You do?"

"Yeah—you manipulated me into signing his shit."

Her chin goes up a notch. "I-I did no such thing."

"Liar."

She shoots me a sidelong glance, biting her lip. "Are you mad?"

"Nah. I was probably going to do it anyway."

When the kid comes flying back through the door with his poster, Violet is the one who takes the Sharpie from him and places it in my hand.

"I'll hold the poster while you sign it," she encourages quietly. I grunt, but like a good little solider, do as I'm told.

"Uh, what's your name?" I ask the kid, relenting.

"Brandon."

"You a wrestler?"

"Yeah. I can't afford tickets to come watch you guys in person, but I watch them all on YouTube after they've aired on cable."

Damn. His family can't afford tickets to come watch wrestling at the university? I thought they were only ten bucks or something. A pit of guilt forms in my stomach.

"Oh yeah? Every match, eh?" I ask him. "What's our record?"

"Nine titles. You've won twenty-three of the last thirty-seven national championships, and you're currently sitting at eighteen and oh for this season." He grins proudly, rattling off our stats.

He flips his bangs.

I look at him good and hard then—he does indeed look like a wrestler: not too tall, with broad shoulders. Brandon's shaggy hair probably gets in his eyes when he's down on the mat, not good if you're working up a sweat, and I wonder why no coach has ever told him to trim that shit up.

"You need a haircut," I blurt out harshly.

I feel Violet stiffen at my direct frankness.

Brandon raises his hands, raking his fingers through his hair. "*Uh ...*"

I roll my eyes at them both. "I *guarantee* if you cut it, you'll be quicker when you're down on the mats. Do you want to be great, or do you just want to be good?"

"I want to be a champion," he boasts.

I sign his poster with a sloppy scrawl, handing it back to him. "Then trim your fucking hair."

"Okay." Brandon nods. "Okay, yeah. I will."

"Good." I look him up and down again. "I'll work on getting some tickets for you and your friends to come to a few home games. Maybe you can come to a practice—no promises, but I'll ask."

Brandon's eyes bug out of his damn skull like I've just handed him a golden pair of wrestling shoes. "Holy shit, dude, for *real?*"

He's practically shouting.

"Don't get all fucking crazy on me—calm down. It's not a big a deal."

But I know it's a big deal to him—thanks to Kyle, I've seen what it's like to not have dick growing up. To not have enough money for a ten-dollar ticket to come watch a sport you love.

It's shitty. The kid shouldn't have to miss out.

"Yeah, yeah, I'm calming down!"

"Calm down, or I swear to God …"

Violet laughs—*laughs*—the soft chuckle starting in her shoulders before working its way out of her soft, plum lips.

I scowl. "What are you laughing at?"

"You trying to be *nice*."

"I'm not nice."

"That's why I said *trying*."

Her eyes are wrinkled at the corners but her teasing isn't mean—far from it. She's truly enjoying herself, enjoying whatever this banter is between us.

Then, in the background, I hear the beginning of the band tuning up.

"Well, Brandon, it's been real, but my date here and I are going to find our seats."

"Oh shit!" the kid enthuses. "Sorry! I forgot you weren't here for me."

I flip him the peace sign as I take Violet by the elbow, steering her toward the dining room. "Deuces, Brando."

"That was really nice of you," she says when I release her arm, the heat from her bare skin still warming my palm.

"Whatever."

"No, it was. His face lit up like a darn Christmas tree when you said you'd try to get him tickets to come see the team wrestle."

"Darn Christmas tree? What does a *darn* Christmas tree look like?" I tease.

"You know what I mean." She smacks me on the bicep, her hand resting there. Palm flattening on my upper arm. I look down at her hand, fingers long and delicate as they tap my arm while she talks.

A thin gold ring encircles her forefinger, and I stare at it for a beat. "He's probably texting all his friends right now. Can you actually get tickets? I bet it would make his whole year."

One more glance down at the hand she's forgotten to remove, her feather-light touch doing some really weird, fucked up shit to my insides—things that have *nothing* to do with sex.

I almost cover her hand with mine. *Almost.*

Instead, I involuntarily give my bicep a quick flex.

Damn—her hand flies off my sleeve, the spot instantly cold.

"Uh, yeah, it shouldn't be a problem. I'll ask Coach tonight at dinner. If not, I'll just bu—"

I clamp my mouth shut.

"Buy some?" she supplies.

My lips form a tight, straight line.

She tips her head at me, confused. "You'd do that if Coach can't get him tickets, wouldn't you? You'd buy them?"

I reach up, loosening my necktie. "Like I said, it's not a big deal." My nostrils flare impatiently; I'm over this entire conversation. "They're *ten* bucks."

Her eyes—those freaking doe eyes—do this odd upturned thing, her lashes pitch black against her snowy white skin, fluttering and brushing against her eyelids.

They look huge.

They look *euphoric.* Like my generous deeds are her *crack,* like the kind words have the ability to make her *high.*

Violet's lips twitch, a tiny dimple appearing in the corner of her mouth as they form the words, "Right. *Okay.*"

"Don't make this more than it is," I deadpan.

"I'm not," she lies.

"Yes you are. Don't romanticize me as someone who cares. Because I don't."

"I know, I'm not."

I give her a sidelong glance as we weave our way through the throng amongst the banquet tables, my hand finding the small of her back as I guide her along.

My gaze trails down to her perky ass.

"Yes you fucking are," I argue, fingertips lingering on the velvety material of her dress. "There's nothing noble about me buying some strange kid tickets to watch a few wrestling matches."

"Got it. No need to convince me." Violet gives her hair a flip so it falls down her back like a waterfall.

"I'm not going to argue with you," I maintain.

"I'm not arguing. You are." Her lilty laugh floats toward me, cheerful, like she's not afraid to make me mad by continuing to disagree.

Why can't I let this subject go? "You're being really unreasonable."

We've reached the table and before she can do it herself, I locate a chair for her and pull it out. She peeks up at me from under her lashes, sweetly. "Thank you."

"You're welcome," I grumble.

Violet

I'm finally beginning to understand what makes him tick.

Zeke Daniels is an enigma, hard with sharp edges and a compassionate interior he keeps so well hidden, no one would believe it existed if they weren't seeing it for themselves.

Well *I'm* seeing it now. I watch him at the table, listen as he begrudgingly beseeches his wrestling coach for a favor—not because he wants to, but because he promised Brandon he would try.

And he's doing it; he's actually following through.

"So, I didn't guarantee him anything," he's saying. "But if I could get my hands on a few—some for his, uh, friends. That would be good." His halted statements are amusing his coach, if the grin on his face is any indication.

He's enjoying Zeke's discomfort.

"I agree; getting them some tickets would be nice. Where does he attend school?"

Zeke shifts uncomfortably in his chair. "Uh, I didn't ask."

Coach sits back in his seat, folding his arms across his chest and taking Zeke's measure. I notice he does that a lot—observes and calculates before responding to anything.

There is nothing impulsive about Coach.

Both men continuously fiddle with their neckties. Zeke has loosened his three times since we sat down. His coach? Twice.

"Hmm," the man says, scratching the stubble on his chin. "It would have been nice to get the name of his school—we could invite the whole team to a meet."

"W-Why can't you?" I interrupt with a stutter.

Crap!

"Brandon is r-right over there. Why don't you just walk back over there and ask him where he goes to school?"

The kid is literally fifty feet away, watching our table like a hawk, like Zeke and Coach are demigods. In his circle, they probably are.

"Just go do it," I whisper, impatiently hissing through my lips.

Zeke stares me down. Practically growls my name. *"Violet."*

It's obvious he doesn't want to get up from the chair; he hates any kind of conversation. Hates talking to people.

Out of the corner of my eye, Coach watches us, eyes volleying back and forth between Zeke and me as our pseudo power struggle develops.

Zeke regards me warily. I see the conflict warring within him—not wanting to give in, but knowing he damn well should walk back over to Brandon and find out where he goes to school.

"Ugh," he rumbles loudly, pushing away from the table, shoving back his chair. *"Christ!"*

He sets it to rights before stalking toward the coat check on the other side of the room and I watch him zigzag through the crowd until he disappears, back toward the entrance of the hall.

I smile softly to myself, gloating down at my lap, not daring to look around the table.

No one has said a word.

I raise my head, watching the crowd for Zeke.

"So. Violet." Coach catches my eye, taking a long sip from his water glass, his wife Linda smiling warmly from across the table. Blonde, tan, and younger than I would have expected, she's been nothing but kind since we sat down. "That was interesting."

My blonde brows rise but I don't trust myself to speak and not stutter. *Oh?* My brows do the talking for me.

"He's one stubborn son of a bitch." Another drink of water. "I'm surprised he offered that kid tickets."

I nod. "I was surprised myself." Tuck a piece of hair behind my ear. "He, um, didn't want to come alone tonight."

I don't know why I'm telling these people this.

Coach barks out a laugh. "He didn't want to come at *all*." He studies me like he's been studying his wrestler all night, long and hard and critically, eyes blazing as intensely as Zeke's always are. "I doubt the only reason he invited you was so he didn't have to come *alone*. I doubt that very much."

Linda elbows him in the ribcage.

He takes that opportunity to purse his lips, leaning forward, resting his forearms on the white linen tablecloth. "He's complicated."

I nod. *Yes he is.*

"But, I suspect, so are you."

I nod. *Yes I am.*

Coach nods slowly, glancing up behind me.

Zeke has returned to the table, his massive frame yanking out a chair and plopping down in his seat, repositioning himself several times to get comfortable.

"Kennedy Williams High," he begrudgingly tells us. "He's a junior. There are eight kids on the team and not enough money for anything." His arms cross, grumbling. Always grumbling. "We should be having this fundraiser for *his* team, not—"

He stops himself.

"What were you about to say, Mr. Daniels?" his coach asks. "First you want to give the kid free tickets to one of our meets and now you want to fundraise for him? My, my, a bleeding heart now, are we?"

He's determined to raise Zeke's ire.

It works.

Obviously.

I mean, it's not hard to do. All a person has to do is sniff in his general direction and it pisses him off.

Poor thing; he's so high-strung.

"Tell you what," Coach says after a few awkwardly silent moments. "I'll get your kid tickets for two home matches for his entire team." He pauses. "Then I want *you* to give them a tour of the locker rooms afterward, introduce them to our team. Can you do that?"

"I'm not babysitting a group of teenagers."

Coach squints. Leans back. Nods.

"All right. Suit yourself."

He goes back to eating from the vegetable tray on our table, crunching loudly on a carrot and smiling. Knowing there is no way Zeke is going to—

"*Fine*," Zeke spits out, taking the bait. "Jesus."

I nibble my bottom lip, biting back a secret smile.

"So, I'm curious, do you have a boyfriend, Violet?" Linda asks. She's cutting up a tomato and bent on making small talk. Setting down her knife, she rests her chin in her hands, a pleasant expression on her face, like she genuinely wants to know if I have a boyfriend.

"No, she doesn't," Zeke answers for me, adjusting in his seat, wide shoulders brushing my slight ones.

I scowl, shifting my weight away. "H-How do you know?"

I'm capable of answering for myself.

For a moment, I wonder if he's embarrassed that I stutter.

What if he doesn't want me talking *at all*? I stare at the polished silverware and the water glass dripping with condensation.

Raise my head.

Coach, Linda, and the rest of our table watch me, expectantly.

I force a smile and shrug. "He's right. I don't."

"Well, no loss there," Linda jokes. "You're probably better off without one—the older they get, the harder they are to train."

"Hey!" Coach bellows jovially. "What's that supposed to mean? Can't a man catch a break?" He laughs, the rest of the table laughing along with him.

Linda gives him a tap on the arm. "You know I'm just teasing." Turns her attention back to me. "I should have had you sit over here with me so we could talk more. We have a nephew your age who's single, and gorgeous as he is *funny*."

Oh god, could this get any worse.

"She doesn't really have time for dating," Zeke responds.

"Yes I do."

"You do?"

I narrow my eyes at him. "Of course I-I have time to date."

Crook my finger to draw him in close—close enough that no one can overhear. Close enough that I can smell his aftershave … see the blue flecks in the corner of his stormy eyes … the new growth of five o'clock shadow at his jawline.

His nearness unnerves me. Jeez he smells heavenly. "You're being kind of overbearing."

He opens his mouth. "I am?"

"Can you dial it d-down?"

He pulls away to look at me. Draws himself back in to murmur, "I didn't realize I was being a dick."

I shrug, bare shoulders catching a chill from the AC unit above us, then shiver. His gray eyes track the movement, landing on my gooseflesh-covered collarbone. Stare at the column of my neck below my ear.

I lick my lips. "I thought I'd mention it as a courtesy."

"A courtesy?"

"Mm*hmm*." His eyes find my mouth when I hum. Hold there.

"Is this where I apologize?"

"Do you want to?"

His sculpted lips move so close to my ear I shiver—and this time, it's not from the air conditioning. It's from his warm breath on my neck, his nose brushing against my cheek.

My eyes slide shut when he whispers, "I'm wasn't trying to be a dick."

I nod, lids lifting, my gaze meeting Coach's stern eyes. He raises his brows and I give him a shaky, crooked smile as Zeke continues whispering in my ear.

"What do you suppose he thinks we're talking about?" Zeke asks.

"He probably thinks you're apologizing."

"No, he probably thinks we're flirting."

My neck tilts the slightest degree when I feel his lips graze my earlobe. "Would he be wrong?"

Zeke pulls away, slightly. Reclines back in his seat.

Slowly his head shakes back and forth. "No."

Maybe there *is* hope for him yet.

"Did I tell you you looked nice tonight?"

"Sort of." No, he hadn't told me I looked nice—he'd told me I looked *good*.

No mention of me looking nice. No mention of me looking pretty. He'd gone with 'good'.

"Did I at least tell you you looked *pretty?*" He's clutching the steering wheel, staring straight at the road, hanging a right at the stop sign, then left on my road.

"No." I laugh.

"I didn't?" He sounds puzzled. "What did I say?"

"Y-You said, 'You look good.'"

"*Good?*" He sounds disgusted. "Jesus fuck, I was kind of being an asshole tonight, wasn't I?"

"I think we muddled through it okay."

"Well, you did," he continues, almost to himself, as he pulls into my driveway. Puts the car in park and turns toward me. "You look nice. Pretty, I mean."

He turns his head toward the driver's side window, and I swear I catch him rolling his eyes in the mirrored reflection. At *himself.*

My mouth curves. "Thank you."

"Did you have fun tonight? I never did thank you for coming with me."

"I had a *lot* of fun. Thank you for the invitation." Oh god, I sound so formal. This is getting so awkward.

"Good, because … So anyway," he begins. "I got something for you."

He what? Did I hear that right? Did Zeke Daniels just say he *got* me something? Like what kind of something? What does that even mean?

"You did?" I'm shocked. "For *what*?"

"For *you*."

"You did?"

"Yes." His lip curls into what's probably supposed to be a grin, but in the dark, looks more like a sneer. "You suck at receiving gifts, do you know that?"

"A *gift*?"

"Are you going to repeat everything I say like I've just given you the shock of your life?"

I can see he's getting frustrated. Know it when he runs a hand through his thick black hair.

"I'm sorry I keep asking questions." I sit up straighter in my seat, interested. Curious. "What is it?"

Oops, there I go again.

In the dimly lit cab of his truck, with his face shrouded in shadows, Zeke lifts the center console, fishing out a small box. He holds it up in the palm of his hand, and I can see that it's a black and silver jewelry box.

"Just take it."

I falter when reaching for it.

"I-I can't b-believe you actually got me a gift." The wonder in my voice fills the cab of the truck. "I thought you were joking."

I'm not trying to be deliberately obtuse, but Zeke Daniels has truly stunned me.

"No."

"No, it's not a gift?"

"No, I—*Jesus* Violet, can't you just open the damn thing?"

I'm not *purposely* pressing him, but the questions just keep slipping past my lips before I can stop them.

It's a black, square box—one I'm very familiar with—and I hold my breath when I go to pry open the top, revealing the velvet jewelry pouch inside. I glance to find Zeke staring at me out of the darkness, expression unreadable.

Mouth in a firm line. Eyes hooded but impassive.

"Can you just fucking open it," he grunts, moody. "You're taking forever."

My heart beats a million miles an hour inside my chest, so hard I can almost hear it. I can see how impatient he's becoming by the way his eyes intently trail the movement my fingers make over the black bag.

"You're being really obnoxious, do you realize that?"

So antsy, this guy. *Like a child.*

"I think it's c-cute that you're excited."

Oh my god, did I actually just call him *cute*—and stutter while I did it? How freaking embarrassing.

"I meant to say *it's* cute when you're excited—not *you're* cute."

Stop talking, Violet!

But I don't. *Can't.* "I wish it wasn't so dark it here; I want to remember this moment." *Oh my god, why am I saying these things out loud?*

"Turn the damn light on then."

So I do. I reach up and flick the overhead lamp on, then stare down at the black velvet pouch, concentrating on the size and texture of it.

Of this *gift* from him.

I glance up at Zeke, and I think he's ...

Blushing.

Honest-to-god blushing.

Shakes his head and turns away, staring out the window into my dark neighborhood.

Biting down on my lower lip, I return to the task at hand, drawing at the gold strings on the black velvet bag. Pluck it open with nimble fingers. Dip inside, index finger and thumb hooking the delicate gold bangle I know will be inside. Slide it gently out until it's lying flat on my palm.

Lift it to my face to study it in the dim light.

It's a bracelet from tonight's silent auction.

Together, Linda and I had strolled the room, considering each auction item one at a time like we were actually considering buying them: "That would be fun!" Linda declared about a weekend waterpark getaway. "I'll wear my new suit!"

"Now what on earth would I do with all of that?" she'd asked when we walked past a barbequing set. "Guess I'll have to get a fancy new apron!"

Then, we'd come to the beauty and apparel items. Spa retreats. Nail salon vouchers. Scarves and handcrafted necklaces.

The bracelet.

My fingers go to the charm dangling from the thin band of gold, the stamped icon precisely as I knew it would be.

Two-sided disk, gold and silver, a sunflower bursting open on one side. The words *Everything happens for a reason* on the other.

I remember exactly what the auction description of the bracelet said, because Linda and I had studied it closely.

A surprising strength, this optimistic flower rises up from the ground, turning its petals toward the sun. It breathes life into all in its presence. Bright. Radiates happiness. Colorful petals and resilient roots. The sunflower gives others the encouragement to seek joy, even on the gloomiest days. Celebrate your power; it grows from that ever-positive light within you.

I remember what I said when I straightened after reading the blurb: "I wish I had the money to bid on it."

She must have told Zeke I'd fallen in love with it.

"I love it, Zeke." I breathe deeply. "I love it."

And I do.

Not only because I've never received a gift for absolutely no reason, but because it's so beautiful. It represents a part of my life I hope to embody: shiny, new, and full of symbolism. Like the rest of the bangles lining my wrist, this one too tells a piece of my story. Positive is how I live. Take the wheel. Zodiac. Guardian angel.

My eyes squeeze shut as I clasp the charm in a clenched fist, the metal warming to my touch; I saw the bids for this imitation gold trinket, saw how expensive it was.

It's not even *real* precious metal and it was going for an outrageous amount of money.

Before I can stop it from escaping, a single wet tear glides out the corner of my eye and down my cheek.

I wipe it away.

"Thank you."

Zeke grumbles in reply, the sound rumbling from his chest as he reaches up and flips off the overhead light.

My palm opens and I push the shiny new bracelet over my knuckles, easing it onto my wrist; I admire it alongside the others. They cling and clang and shine in the dim light suspended above us.

Then, before I actually think about what I'm doing, my body leans toward his big body, propelled by the heart pounding wildly inside my chest, until my lips encounter the bristly side of his cheek.

"Thank you," I whisper faintly into the shell of his ear, mouth stalling there. Brushing the skin of his lobe. Tip of my nose giving him a sniff, colliding with his temple.

Zeke stiffens from surprise—or because of the invasion of his personal space—but doesn't shrug away when my lips press to meet his jaw for another brief, spontaneous kiss.

I simply cannot help myself. I simply *cannot* move away.

He lowers his hands from the steering column of his truck, letting them fall heavily to his lap. Runs the tips of his fingers up and down the black fabric seam of his dress pants, up and over his thighs.

Zeke turns his head the slightest fraction of an inch, just enough so that our faces are inches apart.

His habitually harsh gaze roams my face, settling on my plum-stained lips, gray eyes softening, wrinkling at the corners.

"You're welcome, I guess," his bottomless voice rumbles, vibrating, breath all pepperminty.

I don't know who moves first, and I swear—this wasn't my intention. I don't mean to, but suddenly we're—

"Violet." He sighs the question of my name into my mouth as my eyelids slide closed, our lips touching. Briefly, hesitating. The barest whisper of contact sizzles in the space between the soft skin of his lower lip and mine. A long, charged quiver that lingers deep within my spine, compelling us *both* to fuse our mouths together.

Zeke Daniels shivers.

It's positively *electric*.

Chaste kisses. Kisses that make sweet … kissing sounds.

Once, twice. Again.

But then …

Our mouths open and it's not so chaste. Not so sweet. His tongue, my tongue. Tenderly. *Hungrily*. And oh god, his hands are in my hair, gently caressing and tugging at the silky strands lying in an artful blonde cascade over my shoulders. Rubbing them between the tips of his fingers.

He twists that strong torso at the waist so his giant palms are cupping my face, gentle thumbs stroking the tears of joy off of my flaming hot cheek as he kisses any sense I might have had left right out of me. So sweetly another tear escapes.

"The bracelet isn't a big deal," he whispers.

My eyes flutter open; his are squeezed closed, long lashes fanned flat against his skin, and I realize he's not talking to me; he's murmuring these things to himself.

"Violet." He *sighs*.

He sighs.

Zeke is ... He's *sighing* my name.

I want so badly to kiss his handsome, broody face all over. Kiss his deep frown lines away. Run my smooth cheek against his coarse, stubbly one. I want so badly for him to remove his hands from my face and put one between my legs, slip them between my inner thighs to the aching wet spot that's making me want to moan.

But he doesn't.

His hands stay properly above my waist, above my shoulders. Our mouths still welded together, Zeke's hands move from my hair to cradle my jawline.

Gray irises lower to meet hazel, foreheads pressed together, thumb pads slowly stroking the corner of my mouth.

No, not stroking. *Memorizing.* My mouth.

My lips.

The spell is broken when a light gets flipped on from the inside of my house.

The bathroom.

Which means at least one of my two roommates is awake.

Of course, he's the first to pull back. Pull away. Broad shoulders hitting the black leather driver's seat with a weighty thud. The massive palms that were just on my body are running up and over his face, first down, then up, and he tugs at his raven black hair 'til it's tousled.

Stares out the windshield.

And then, "The bracelet wasn't a big deal Violet."

Why does he keep saying that? Why isn't he looking at me? Not three minutes ago he was whispering my name ...

I'm so confused.

"I-It isn't?" My voice is so small, so small and *disappointed.* I finger the new bangle circling my pale wrist.

"*No.*"

No. *No.* He's always saying no, isn't he?

I slump in my seat, grasping for the forgotten jewelry box that's fallen onto the floor. Root around with my fingers to retrieve it from the mats, gather my purse.

"I-I guess I should go inside."

The yard is dark. With no streetlights, the neighborhood looks shady. My house is dark, save for that one glowing bulb on the east side of the tiny, ramshackle house.

It's apparent he's not going to walk me to my door. Our night is over and won't be repeated. I'm as certain of it as I'm sure of my own name.

My face is aflame from mortification, though I know I have *nothing* to be embarrassed about.

Deep breath, Vi. Deep. Breath.

"Thank you for the lovely evening and for the bracelet."

He nods in the dark.

Feeling slightly dejected, I clear my throat. "Good night, Zeke."

"Melinda, you up?"

I come through the back door, remove my dress coat, and hang it on the hook my roommate Melinda hammered into the wall herself.

"No, it's me. Mel's with Derek."

I'm not three feet inside the house when my roommate Winnie pounces, releasing the hold she has on the gauzy living room curtains, stepping away from the window.

The sneaky spy follows me down the dark, narrow hallway to my bedroom.

"Who on earth was *that*?" She doesn't hesitate to make herself at home, propping herself on the foot of my bed, fluffing a pillow to get comfortable. "Seriously, who was that guy?"

"His name is Zeke Daniels. We were at a fundraiser benefitting—"

"Bzzz! Time out." She makes a buzzer sound, holding her hands in the universal sign for 'time out' and tapping obnoxiously.

"Whoa, whoa, whoa, Vi, not so damn fast," she interrupts, her wide eyes enormous. "Zeke Daniels?" Her throat gives a little hum as she taps her chin. "Why does that name sound familiar?"

I raise a shoulder, not committed to answering. "He's an athlete. Wrestler. I've tutored him a few times, and he needed a favor, so I went with him to the—"

"Bzzz. Back up," she interrupts again. "You tutored him? When was this?" Suddenly, her phone is out and she's furiously tapping on the screen. "Z-E-K-E … ah, here it is." Long pause. "HOLY SHIT BALLS!"

She flips the phone and thrusts it in my direction. "*This* is the guy you were just kissing in that truck? This guy? Holy crap." Winnie shoves the phone directly in my face, displays a picture of Zeke in an Iowa wrestling one-piece, hands on his hips and scowl on his face. His name in the top left-hand corner, stats below. Weight, height. Record. Hometown.

Before she can yank the phone away, I catch a glimpse of wide shoulders, bulging biceps, and five o'clock shadow; he hadn't bothered to shave for the team picture.

I put myself in Winnie's shoes, see Zeke through her lenses. The handsome, frowning face, the black slashes above his dispassionate eyes.

"Wow. He's hot. Like, super hot. Just … wow. I'm speechless. Wow." She's looking at me like she's seeing me for the first time. "That is so unlike you, Vi."

My face is flaming hot because she's right; I don't go around kissing anyone, let alone guys that look like Zeke Daniels.

Winnie continues *tap tapping* on her phone, googling and Instagramming him, I'm sure. She's always doing that—scavenging for information.

143

"Oh wow," she says hesitantly. "Don't freak, but I found him on Campus Girl."

Campus Girl is a website run by college-aged women for women on college campuses around the world. You can search for your school, read articles—some of them helpful, some of them gossip—and submit information. Chat. Rate things like the cafeteria food, activities, student clubs.

And guys.

Winnie face is so buried in her phone it's actually glowing, the reflection from the small screen casting a blue pallor on her skin. "Yeesh. I don't know if I should read this out loud."

It's on the tip of my tongue to say I don't *want* her to, but curiosity wins out. I move near her on the bed, present her with my back so she can slide the zipper down the back of my dress.

The same dress I've worn to every special occasion in the past year, and thank god it still fits.

I remain quiet so Winnie will start reading the posts out loud.

"Someone wrote: Zeke Daniels is a sexist pig."

Yeah, I could see that.

Winnie goes on. "Zeke Daniels' number one talent, besides wrestling, is to hit it and quit it." She glances up. "Yikes."

"Zeke Daniels had sex with me at a party in the bathroom and didn't bother to wait for me to pull my pants up before walking out the door ... Zeke Daniels is a fucking prick." She looks up after that one. "Is that true?"

I shrug. No sense in denying it. "He's a little rough around the edges."

Her brow goes up, face back in her phone. "Zeke Daniels deserves a medal for biggest asshole on campus ... there is nothing nice about this guy ... Zeke Daniels is everything your mother warned you about, and then some ... don't bother ladies, he's not interested in commitment ... can someone say *issues* ..."

I cut her off before she can finish that last one. "Winnie, s-stop. Th-Th-that's e-enough."

She lowers the phone to her lap, looking abashed. "Shit. Sorry, Vi." Loud sigh. "What do you know about this guy? Is he safe?" Her bottom teeth nibble her top lip. "I mean, is this the kind of guy you've been hanging out with?"

"I-I wouldn't say we've been hanging out."

Not really.

"What would you call it then?" she wants to know.

"Studying mostly. Volunteering together." I begin ticking off all the things we've been doing the past few weeks. "Play dates. Homework. Tonight's fundraiser."

"Holy crap, Violet! Are you dating him? This guy is ridiculously good-looking."

My dress falls to the floor and I bend to scoop it up, not caring that she's seeing me in my strapless bra and underwear. She's seen me without clothes on a million times before; we've been roommates since her parents let her move out of the dorms sophomore year.

"Look at me Win." I raise my pale, sunless arms, running my palms along my narrow hips and stomach. "Do I look like the type of girl he would want to date? Do I s-*sound* like his t-type?" *Pfft.* "G-get real."

She straightens, sitting up. "What is that supposed to mean? Have you looked in the mirror lately? You're beautiful. If he isn't interested, then he's a freaking idiot—not that I'm telling you to date him, but if you wanted to, you could … not that I want you to."

"Good, because I'm not."

"I'm just saying you're freaking incredible."

"No, you're just saying that because you're family."

The family I created for myself when I got to school: Winnie, Melinda, and our friend Rory, who still lives in the dorms.

Winnie leans back, propping herself up by the elbows. Rolls her eyes toward the ceiling. "I just know how you are, okay? You're so … what's the word I'm looking for? Compassionate.

Not everyone has a broken wing that needs mending, Violet. May-be this guy isn't worthy of your special brand of caring."

But she's wrong.

He is.

She goes on. "I mean, he sounds like a total asshole. Please consider that before you sleep with this guy."

I slip out of my bra and replace it with a ratty old t-shirt, Winnie's deafening silence filling the room. Her eyebrows speak a thousand words.

I turn away.

"I hope next time you put the moves on him you know what you're getting yourself into. I don't mean to be a creeper, but dude, I was checking to see who was in the driveway when you guys pulled up. Totally was not expecting that giant truck to be parked there, and then the cab light went on, and I could see that it was you, and, well, I couldn't look away."

She rambles on. "I know it was you who kissed him first—he wasn't going to make a move on you. If you could have seen his face from where I saw it—you kissed the stuffing out of him, Vio-let. He was in complete and utter shock." She laughs, tipping her head back. Her shocking black hair hits my purple bedspread. "I about died. Died! Swear to God, if Melinda had been home …" Her head gives a shake.

I pad barefooted to my dresser and pull out a pair of yoga pants, stepping into them one leg at a time. "I assure you, I am in no danger of falling into anything with Zeke Daniels without thinking it through."

"I think you've missed my point, Violet," my roommate says. "Maybe you're in danger of … him falling into you. Because from where I stood, he didn't look that terribly awful."

I go to the closet and pull out a sweatshirt, slide it over my head. "He's not."

"Because everyone online makes him sound like a shitty hu-man being."

"He has his moments, trust me, but … mostly he has no filter. He's coming around—he's better with the kids."

Winnie hands me a pair of fuzzy socks from the drawer of my bedside table. "So what was it like? Kissing him?"

"I don't know."

She recoils, face scrunched up. "What do you mean, you don't know? Your lips were all over him—what was it like?"

I laugh, joining her on the bed. "It was …" I sigh. "Electric."

My roommate groans. "That's what I was afraid you'd say. Crap, I'm going to have to monitor this situation."

"There's nothing to monitor, but be my guest. And get off my bed, I'm tired."

Once Winnie finally goes back to her own room and I finally climb into bed, I lie atop the covers, twisting the new bangle on my wrist, the metal warmed by the heat of my skin.

In the dark, the pads of my fingers trace the etched sunflower, the beautiful words engraved in the metal.

"Everything happens for a reason," I murmur, marveling at how the heat from my body now radiates from the bracelet.

Everything happens for a reason.

I *know* this.

I've been learning it the hard way my entire life, one disappointment after the other, starting with the death of my parents—both of them—when I was young. I've had time to recover and grow and move on with my life, but—

I never do.

Never.

What I've done is adjust. Bend. Amend.

Change.

Learn to live without the things I once had.

That's what you do when you lose people you love.

They say that once someone dies, they're always with you in spirit; it's something I know to be true, because I feel my parents every second of every day. That doesn't mean it doesn't hurt. It only hurts *less.*

Their memories remain, but I have to work *so hard* to retrieve them, fragmented as they are. They're pieces I struggle to puzzle together, obscure and fleeting with every day and week and month and year that passes by.

I was so young when they died. So young.

They were so young when they died.

But I'm here.

I'm alive.

Lying in a bed, staring up at a ceiling I pay for with money I earn myself.

The death of my parents is what led to my stutter; I don't remember ever not having it, but my cousin Wendy does. I stayed with her family for a while when I was in elementary school, until they couldn't afford to keep me anymore. They just didn't have the money.

Wendy, who was ten when I went to stay with them, said one day I talked like a normal kid, and the next ... I didn't.

It used to be worse; I couldn't get through a sentence without getting my tongue tied on my words. I guess it was the trauma of being tucked in one night by your parents and having them disappear the next. When you're four, you don't understand the concept of death ... I mean, maybe some kids do, but I didn't.

I was sensitive, Wendy said. Retreated further into myself.

She was older, and kind. I slept on her bedroom floor; she and her sister—my cousin Beth—slept in the double bed. Together my aunt and uncle had four kids and couldn't afford one more, especially with my youngest cousin, Ryan, wheelchair bound with mounting medical bills they couldn't pay.

Eventually, I was able to start collecting a pension from the state, but that didn't come until later ... too many months later when I was already in the foster care system.

Then, as a final blow, my uncle was transferred out of state and I couldn't see them anymore. I've never been able to save enough money to visit them, and lord knows they can't afford to come see me.

I'm not a fool; I know I'm one of the lucky ones that went through the system and came out fighting for a better life. Quiet but strong, if you don't count my stutter.

One last parting gift from my parents.

One last memento from the trauma surrounding their deaths.

From the cops showing up at my house the night of their accident. A fluke. A freak accident. On their way home from a play, their premature, untimely deaths involved one strung-out addict who shouldn't have been behind the wheel, a speeding pick-up truck, and my parent's compact car. I vaguely remember my babysitter Becky—a teenage neighbor girl—freaking out when the cops came to the house ... the scramble to place me because our family was ... well, it was small.

And had just grown smaller still.

A few years ago I started collecting the bracelets. They're expensive, so I only have four, each one purchased with the money I make tutoring, working at the library, and babysitting kids like Summer, when I have enough spare cash to buy one, which isn't often.

Everything happens for a reason.

That one single bracelet circling my wrist, resting on my stomach when I finally settle my arm there.

The other four remain on my dresser.

I finger it, rubbing the sunflower disk with my thumb, smiling in the dark despite myself. Smiling despite Zeke Daniels and his reluctance to get close to another living human being.

That's fine.

I've been fighting for *better* my whole life.

One scared man-child isn't going to stop me from finding it.

149

Zeke

W hy did I give her that fucking bracelet?
      Jeez, now she's going to think I care and shit.
      I give my pillow a thwack, pounding it into a flat, downy mass, and readjust it under my head. Staring at the damn ceiling above my big, half-empty bed, arms behind my head.

I'm so fucking tired.

But I swear, every damn time I close my eyes, I see the *look* on Violet's face when she opened that box. Jesus, that face; those goddamn *doe eyes*—they gazed straight at me like I'd … like I'd healed an invisible wound I hadn't even known was there.

Those eyes are the reason for the bracelet.

In my *life* I've never seen eyes so damn wide and alive—they are going to haunt me for the rest of the night. Maybe longer. I caught a glimpse into her soul in that moment, which makes me sound like a fucking lunatic, but to hell with judging my own inner thoughts.

Violet just …

Just …

I can't even describe the moment, couldn't if you paid me.

Fucking Violet and her sappy, bleeding heart. This restless-ness is all her goddamn fault.

I thought she was normal.

I didn't realize she was hurting, too.

I roll this idea around in my mind, fluffing my pillow again so it's resting against my headboard, trying my damnedest to relax.

It doesn't work because I've realized Violet is broken.

Hurt. Damaged. Like me.

I punch my pillow angrily, frustration building—I can't even formulate my own fucking thoughts anymore.

Whatever, I'm not going to be around her long enough to find out what her problems are. She might be a friend, someone I'd take to fundraising dinner, but it's not like we will be hanging out any more after tonight, painting each other's toenails and sharing crybaby stories about our childhoods.

Especially since she stares straight through me, trying to figure me out. Sees through my bullshit.

I pound the pillow one last time, tossing one of the four onto the floor.

Violet might be quiet, might stutter, but she's no fool.

Maybe the fool here is me.

"You said too many real things
and now I need to crawl back
inside my protective fortress
of disdain, being an asshole,
and not giving a shit."

Zeke

Violet: *Hi ...*

I'm surprised to see a text from Violet when my phone pings; we haven't seen or spoken to each other since the fundraiser. Not because it's been weird, but because my training and traveling and tournament schedules have been fucking insane.

I had to cancel on Kyle this week to accommodate wrestling, and already feel kind of guilty about that.

We're entering town when Violet's second message pops into my notifications, the streetlights illuminating the inside of our bus. Around me, my teammates and coaches stir as we approach campus.

Violet: *I know it's been a week or wahtever but I just wanted to see how everything was doing. Summer was asking about play date, but no rush. I know you're busy and I won't hold you to the three but lets' I don't want to let them down/*
Zeke: *Okay.*

I stare at the text, reread her message a few times and can't think of any way to respond, mostly because there doesn't seem to be any point in her random text. Considering this is Violet we're talking about—organized, prompt, studious *Violet*—the run-on sentence, bad punctuation, and misspelled words throw me off.

I frown.

Violet: *I'm sorry, ignore that*

Too late for that, Vi.

Palming the phone in my hand, it glows again when the bus passes through security at the stadium, drives across the expansive mass of concrete, pulls up near the building. Stops.

We wait patiently as Daryl, the bus driver, does his quick cross-check, speaks with Coach at the front, and finally unlocks the folding door at the front.

We're home, and free to exit the bus.

Grabbing my shit from the overhead bin and the empty seat next to me, I follow behind my teammates as they're slowly herded forward, shuffling down the aisle, my wireless headphones still in place, heavy metal guitar riffs playing in my ears.

A few stadium personnel are already in the process of unloading our bags by the time I hop off the last step, dragging the black hood of my sweatshirt up over my head. Spot my duffle immediately. Swipe it off the ground and head toward my truck without a shower, head down, thumb brushing over Violet's text.

A few things occur to me then: I don't think she's ever been the one to text me first. It isn't much of a shock, since she's generally more reserved, the least pushy girl I've ever met.

I wonder what she's been up to since the fundraiser—since she kissed me in her driveway. That kiss kept me awake longer than it should have and had me watching Tumblr porn when I should have been sleeping, not jerking off my rod.

I wonder if this means I've actually missed having her around?

Or just that I like jerking it to porn gifs?

Or both?

Regardless, Violet is the only person that's texted me since we left for Ohio State; the team's been gone for thirty-six hours.

My thumbs tap out a reply.

Zeke: *The team just got back into town from an away meet in Ohio. Literally just pulled into the stadium, which is where we* *park our cars during away meets. What are you doing right now?*

I briefly wonder if she's drunk.

Violet: *What am I doing right now? Nothing because its wild and crazy Friday nigh, juts me myself and I.*

I yank the ball cap out of my backpack, sliding it on under my hoodie, twisting it left, then right, then squeezing the bill so it's tighter. My fingers work fast.

Zeke: *Violet, is everything*

Hit send. Oops.

Zeke: *Vi, is everything okay?*

Long pause.

Violet: *Do you want me to be honest?*
Violet: *No, it's not. Everythng i not okay.*

Movements in my peripheral catch my eye and I glance up, propping one foot on the running board of my truck. Oz is approaching with all his shit, duffle bags slung over his broad shoulders.

He raises his arms. "What the hell man? You couldn't wait five minutes?" His blue eyes narrow into suspicious slits. "You weren't gonna leave me here, were you?"

"Nah, just had a few texts messages that couldn't wait."

"Oh really—what kind of messages?"

My gray eyes flicker over him. "Dude, aren't you going to shower?"

"Aren't *you?*"

"I was going to hit it at home."

He pulls open the passenger side door, hefts his shit inside, and climbs in behind it. "Let me guess: you're texting Violet and don't want to waste another second fucking around inside the building. Aww, aren't you just the sweetest." He leans over the center console toward my door, bellowing, "Zekey has a girlfriend, Zekey has a girlfriend," like a fucking moron.

Jesus, why does he have to be so goddamn obnoxious?

I ignore him, but it's hard with the incessant shouting.

Not to mention, now he's grasping for my cell, wiggling his fingers. "Come on man, put the phone down and let's go. I told Jameson we'd—"

I throw up the middle finger. "Would you shut the fuck up for like, five more seconds? *Thanks.*"

His back plops against the seat and he starts buckling his seat belt like a good boy scout.

Zeke: *What's wrong Violet?*

Zeke: *Are you in some kind of trouble? Do you need me to come get you or something?*

Violet: *No, it's nothing like that. It's just, god—I'm so embarrassed I texted you. It's going to sound so dumb, but both my roommates are gone and I'm alone and I'm crying and can't see the keys on my phone*

Well that explains the shitty typemanship.

Zeke: *You can tell me what's wrong.*

Violet: *Today was the anniversary of parents' death, and I hate being here alone. There's this movie on and for some reason it just ... made me want to talk to a human and not sit here wallowing in front of the TV. And I feel so ...*
Violet: *I hate being alone.*

Well. Shit. Not what I was expecting.

Swallowing the lump in my throat, I climb into the driver's side of my truck but make no move to buckle my seat belt. No move to turn over the engine. No move to do anything but send her a reply.

Zeke: *I know what you mean. Is there*

My roommate's bitchy whine causes me to hit send too soon.

"Uh, hello, why are we still here?" Oz intones dully, rapping his knuckles against the window. "Are we just going to sit here all night, because if we are, I'll have James come get me."

"Dude." I take a calming breath so I don't explode. "Just— give me a minute, okay? I'm *thinking.*"

"*Dude*, what the hell is going on? Did you get some chick pregnant?" His bark of laughter dies when I look over, expression stony. "Shit. Did you?"

"No, Jesus Christ. It's Violet, she—"

It's not my place to spill her personal shit, so my lips clamp shut.

"Give me one more second to text her, all right numb-nuts? Just ... climb down out of my asshole so I can shoot her a note. She sounds like she needs some—"

Shit. I was about to say *She sounds like she needs some cheering up.* Good thing I caught myself, because seriously, the last thing I need is Oz asking me a shit ton of personal questions.

He raises his eyebrows when I tell him, "First we're running home—I call dibs on the shower. Then I'm running to Violet's place."

If Oz is shocked by this news, he—well shit, he's showing it.

The dumb fucker has his mouth hanging open, eyes wide as saucers. "It's Friday night, dude—aren't you coming out with us? Nothing crazy, just a few beers?"

"No."

My phone pings, and we both look into my lap, down to where my cell sits nestled between my legs.

"I'm going to her house to see if she's okay."

Violet

"Zeke! What are you doing here?"

He's standing on my front porch, hands stuffed in the pockets of a black quilted jacket. Jeans. Brown leather boots. Hair wet from a recent shower.

His wide shoulders slouch uncomfortably then shrug.

"I thought you could use some company." His mouth is set in a straight line, and if he hadn't just shown up voluntarily and un-announced, I wouldn't have believed he came willingly.

"You did?"

He shifts on the balls of his feet. "I thought we could go do something, uh … Fun."

Is he wincing?

Yes. He definitely is.

I pull back the storm door so he can step through, up into my tiny living room and into the house. Zeke Daniels is in my house, platinum eyes scanning the room. They take inventory of the twen-ty-year-old couch Winnie's parents bought us at Goodwill; it's gold and scratchy, but it's something to sit on. The dinged up cof-fee table we found on the curb last semester. There's a lamp in the corner, our only source of light in the room.

Winnie, Melinda, and I, we're like the Three Musketeers—or the Three Blind Mice, but poorer.

Zeke's large frame fills the doorway as he stands rooted to the spot, having not removed his boots. Unless he takes them off, he has nowhere to go, and from the looks of him, he has no desire to go stalking across our brown carpet.

"So," he begins. "Want to get the hell out of here?"

He doesn't have to ask me twice.

"Go do what you have to do to get ready; I'll keep the truck warm."

When he steps off the front steps, retreating to his giant black truck, I scurry to my bedroom. Yank open my closet, pull out a fresh pair of jeans. A solid black t-shirt; it's tight, hugs what little curves I actually have.

A silver necklace gets clasped around my throat, its delicate *V* dangling from a thin metal chain. Slide a few bangles on my wrist. Then I dash to the bathroom to check my reflection. Comb through my long, silky hair and decide to leave it the way it is. Add a few coats of black mascara. Pink lip gloss.

Eight minutes from start to finish, and I'm locking the door behind me, trudging down the front sidewalk toward Zeke's waiting figure.

Four seconds later I'm sliding in beside him. Toasty warm.

"Where are we going?"

He taps the steering wheel. "Where do you want to go? It's totally up to you."

I bite down on my lower lip, undecided. I remember giving him a list once before, remember him shooting down everything when trying to figure out which play dates would be fun for Summer and Kyle.

Nonetheless, there's one thing I've always wanted to do … and maybe he'd be willing to do it with me tonight, since this was his idea in the first place.

And he did tell me I could choose.

So I go for it.

"You know what would be really fun?"

His engine revs, obviously waiting for me to buckle up. "What?"

"I want to paint pottery."

Zeke's head hits the back of his seat, big palm combing through his wet onyx hair. "Please don't do this to me."

Giggle. "It's not going to be *horrible*. Besides, you said it was totally up to me, and this is what I chose—to paint pottery."

"*Fine.*"

"Do you know where it is?" He's taking a left at the stop sign, toward downtown.

"Yeah, I know where it is."

"You do? How?"

"My idiot roommate and his girlfriend came to this place for one of their dates. I had to pick shit up for them."

"Oh! That's nice of you."

"If you want to call it nice, knock yourself out."

"I've never done this before, so I'm pretty excited. I figure I have about twenty bucks to spend, so—"

"No."

"No?"

"This is my treat."

"Are you sure?"

Great, now he's irritated. "I invited you out, it's my treat."

"All right, but only if—"

"Violet, my mom might be absentee, but she always makes sure I act like a gentleman when she's around."

There's nothing else to say I guess, except, "Thank you Zeke."

It means a lot to me, more than he knows.

He might think this is a simple night out, at a place he can afford to take me, but to me, it's more. I hardly ever get to indulge in anything frivolous—every penny I earn goes toward books, tuition, and housing.

There just simply isn't ever enough to blow on … stuff. I don't go to the bars often because spending ten dollars on drinks is ten dollars I don't have to make rent or buy groceries.

Of course, I don't say this, because a guy like that wouldn't understand. Zeke Daniels doesn't look like he's seen struggle a single day in his privileged life. I don't fault him for this; it's merely an observation. He can't help having parents with the means to support him any more than I can help … *not*.

I shift in my seat.

"Crap." His gaze darkens, moves up and down over my torso. "Have you eaten anything yet?"

"No, but … I think you can eat food at this place. Sandwiches maybe?"

He grunts.

I stifle a smile, hiding it in the collar of my winter jacket. Watch out the window the rest of the way to the pottery place so he doesn't catch my grin.

"For the damn record," Zeke is saying as we walk into the place, "we are not painting matching *anything*. No mugs with hearts and shit, got it?"

Mugs with hearts and shit? What on earth is he talking about?

"Got it."

"And none of that holiday bullshit. No way are you getting me to paint a pumpkin plate or a holly jolly Santa Claus."

"What am I not getting you to paint?"

"A holly jolly San—" He sees me smirking. "Dammit Violet!"

"Paint whatever you want. I'm going to check out the plates and cups."

He trails along after me.

I remove a ceramic pitcher from the wooden shelf and hold it up. "Now what would I do with this?"

"Nothing."

"I could put flowers in it, or juice if I had people over." I set it back down. "*Hmmm.*"

A few feet down, Zeke takes a shot glass off the shelf. "What about this?"

My brows shoot up. "Do you do a lot of shots?"

His shoulders sag and he huffs, "No. Not really."

He puts the shot glass back. Takes down a flat paddle with a slight curve at the end. "What the hell is this thing?"

I glance over. "I think that's a spoon rest. For the stove."

"That's fucking dumb."

Ignoring him, I meander over to the glasses and goblets. "Hey, what about this mug? This is fun." It's huge and has plenty of surface for painting.

Zeke makes his way over. "I *said* I didn't want to paint matching mugs."

"So go paint something else." I flip the heavy cup over to check the price. Eighteen dollars, plus the studio fee.

Ouch.

I bite my lower lip, debating, not wanting to spend twenty-five dollars of his money.

"Fine," he complains again. "But there *is* nothing else."

I chuckle. "Then paint a mug."

Long silence. "Okay, grab me one." Pause. "Please."

I grab two and head back to the table where a cute brunette girl who looks like a high school student has us set up with brushes, water, and paper towels.

She's been watching us walk around the entire time we've been here, both intrigued and surprised by the sight of the massive Iowa wrestler. He's a stark contrast to the colorful and bright surroundings, and stands out like a sore thumb in all black.

I guess we both do, because I'm wearing black, too, to match my earlier mood.

"What are you going to paint on yours?" I ask Zeke. All we have left to do is choose our paint colors.

"No fucking clue. What about you?"

"Hmm. I don't know. Maybe something purple? Or … my initials?"

"What about your initials in purple? Add some flowers and shit."

"Hey, that's a great idea!" I beam up at him. "You know, you could paint something having to do with wrestling. What about painting it black and yellow?"

"That's not a bad idea." He's definitely warming up to the idea of being here. Together, we collect our paint—black and bright yellow for him, lavender for me. Lime green. Dark purple.

We take our seats and work in silence … at least for the next fifteen minutes.

Until, "So, do you want to tell me about them?"

"Who?"

"Your parents. What were they like?"

I sit back in the uncomfortable wooden chair, pausing with my paintbrush in the air, a blob of lavender dripping off the end. "From what I remember, they were fun. My dad was shy and kind of a huge book nerd, and my mom was this beautiful, fairylike …" I swallow. "She was blonde. Beautiful."

Zeke nods, cleaning his brush in a jar of water. Blots it dry on the paper towel.

"Anyway, they were young when they had me, but really in love. They met in a law library where my dad worked, just out of college, just barely. He wanted to be a lawyer." I resume painting my mug, focusing on the curved leaves I'm making around the handle. "My mom was still a student, but she was only taking one or two classes because they had me so soon after they got married. My aunt told me she wanted to be a teacher."

"I'm …" Zeke starts. "I bet she would have been a good teacher, just like you."

"I'm not going to be a teacher. I'm going to be a Social Worker."

"I know, but you love kids. You must get that from her."

"Yes." I don't know how to broach this next part, so I just blurt it out. "What about your parents Zeke? You hardly mention your family."

His brush pauses too, but he doesn't look up. "There's not a lot to tell. I've always been more of an afterthought."

"What does that mean?"

His cold gray eyes look into mine. "It means they don't give a shit."

"How can that be?" I whisper as the festive and upbeat top forty music beats through the sound system above us. It's loud, but I know he can hear me. I know he's considering the question.

"They're selfish, that's why."

"Where are they?"

"They travel. I don't know, Violet. They don't tell me where they're going." He dabs at the mug with his brush.

"Do you have any brothers or sisters?"

Dab, dab, dab. "Nope. Just me."

"I already told you I'm an only child. Sometimes I wonder how my life would be different if I had a sister. Or a brother, you know? To share this burden. So I wouldn't be alone."

God, now I sound like a one-person pity party. "Thank *god* I have my friends." I'm smiling as I say it.

"Speaking of which, what's up with your roommates?"

I look up. "What do you mean, what's up with my roommates?"

"Are they around a lot or what?"

"Yes and no. We all work a lot. None of us really go out because—not to sound pathetic or whatever—but that costs money none of us have. Although"—I dip my brush in the water jar and tap it against the edge—"we are going out tomorrow night to the bar where Melinda's boyfriend works since neither of them could be around tonight, and honestly, it's been forever since we've done anything fun."

"Fun?"

He says the word out loud; it's the one word he's picked out of my entire diatribe, his paintbrush slashing through the air toward me, tracing the small silver V on the necklace hanging at my throat.

"*V.*"

I raise my fingers, grasping the small silver letter dangling around my neck.

"My aunt gave it to me when I was little, for my fifth birthday, the last one I celebrated at home." I swallow. "The V is for Violet."

He snickers quietly, tipping his head back. "Or V for virgin."

"That too, I guess," I say quietly, embarrassed, even though I gave up my virginity two years ago.

"You don't think that's funny?"

"If I was actually a virgin I'd probably be embarrassed by it."

"You're right—that's private. I shouldn't be joking about it."

Nope, he shouldn't be.

My right brow rises, and I dip my chin in a nod. Smile to myself, running the brush along my mug.

"My roommate Oz is the pervert, not me." He sighs warily. The air between us is riddled with a prickle of tense energy. "I'm sorry."

My head dips again, but I peek up at him under my long lashes.

"I am Violet. That was fucking rude."

"Let's just drop it, okay?" The last thing I want to do is sit here and talk about my virgin status—or lack thereof.

Zeke

"That looks like a bumblebee." Her words are wrapped in a delighted laugh.

I glance down at my ceramic mug, the one I've slapped a big I on (for Iowa), along with some crudely painted yellow and black stripes.

She's right. It's starting to look like a giant fucking bumblebee, and not even a skillfully painted one.

"Shut up, Violet!"

"I'm sorry! It's so cute though! I can't wait to see what it looks like once it's fired and shiny from the kiln."

"What the hell is a kiln?" And what does she mean, *once it's fired*?

"A kiln bakes the paint onto the ceramic. Then it will be nice and shiny when it's done." She continues stroking light purple onto her cup, delicately drawn on flowers and polka dots. It's pretty fucking adorable, way sweeter than my shitty Iowa mug.

"You mean I have to wait to see what it looks like finished?"

She looks up, surprised, brush paused in the air. "Is that what you're all worked up about? You're excited to see it and don't want to wait?"

"Well yeah! I want to see it!" Duh.

"Zeke Daniels, I can't believe it! You're excited about your mug?"

"Fuck yeah!"

We both laugh and it feels good, way fucking better than being pissed off, which takes considerably more effort.

"Hey." I give her hand a little poke with the tip of my paintbrush, leaving a little blob of yellow on her wrist. "I just realized something."

Those big hazel eyes gaze at me, long black lashes fluttering, the angelic blonde hair shining. Man she's beautiful, glossy lips parting, causing me to shift restlessly in my seat.

Jesus. *No.*

I shake my head. Shake it again.

Clear my throat. "Do you realize you haven't stuttered since we've been here?"

"Really?"

"Yeah, really." I smear black paint on my mug. "Why do you think that is?"

Violet's mouth opens, then closes, like a cute little fish gasping for air. "I don't know? I-I …" Her pert nose wrinkles. "Shoot!"

"Dammit," I groan. "I'm really sorry I mentioned it."

"N-No, it's okay. How long have we been here, an hour and a half? That's a long time for me." She looks proud. Beaming.

"Must be because you're comfortable around me, huh?" I wink—actually fucking wink—teasing. "I don't make you nervous anymore."

"Actually, yes i-it probably means you don't make me nervous anymore." Her pink lips are still glossy and bent into a bashful smile.

"Are you serious?"

"Yes, of course."

"But *no one* feels comfortable with me."

"I do."

"*Why?*" I stare at her like she's bat-shit crazy. She must be.

"Don't take this the wrong way, but … mostly I think it's your size."

"Uh, how would I take *that* the wrong way?"

"I-I just figured you prefer to come off as intimidating. I was intimidated at first, but now I just find it comforting."

"Uh, the next words out of your mouth better not be *like a giant teddy bear.*"

"Those are not my next words. I didn't say snuggly, I said

comforting."

I lean forward in my chair. It creaks. "You don't think I'm snuggly?"

Her forehead creases. "Have you ever snuggled in a cozy blanket?"

I snort. "Of course not."

"Have you ever snuggled a cute little furry animal?"

I scoff *and* roll my eyes. "No."

"Have you ever snuggled someone watching a movie, or when they were upset?"

"Uh, big fat *no*."

"I rest my case." She grins, satisfied. "Comforting, not snuggly—though for the record, you're missing out."

"Whatever. I could be both if I *wanted* to be." Deciding my mug is finished, I push it into the center of the table and shift around the small stack of containers and supplies impeding my view of hers. "C'mon, c'mon, let's see it. Let's see your masterpiece."

"I'm still working on it," she whispers.

I get the feeling she isn't talking about her mug.

Violet finishes her project; it turns out a whole hell of a lot better than mine. Hers is neatly designed and intricately detailed, light lavender with little flowers painted all around a dark purple monogram of her initials, the letters curling and intertwining. Mine on the other hand?

Looks like a steaming pile of dog shit.

I won't get into specifics, but a three-year-old could have done a better job.

I scowl at the damn thing.

"We never got anything to eat. You hungry?"

Violet bobs her head up and down. "I could go for something to eat, yeah."

"We could grab something on our way back to your place?"

"Sure, sounds good."

Together, we clean up our messes, toss our paper towels in the trash, throw our brushes in the water, wipe up the black paint surrounding my fucked up mug. When I tip the stupid thing over to write my name in pencil on the bottom, the yellow smudges and gets on the end of my sleeve.

Awesome.

But, despite that, I can't help noticing that Violet looks cheerful. Chipper.

Chipper, Zeke? *Really?*

Christ, that's something my grandpa used to say when he was alive. Whatever, Violet looks happy. A thousand times happier than she did when I arrived on her doorstep tonight.

When she's loaded back in my truck and we're headed back toward campus, I stop at a fast-food burger joint and buy us both hamburgers. We eat them in silence, sitting in the parking lot.

"Thanks Zeke." She takes another bite of her sandwich and chews. Swallows. "For tonight, and for … *this*." She holds the half-eaten burger up in the dark, the wrapper making crinkling sounds.

"No problem."

And it wasn't, I realize. For the first time in a long time, I'm not completely put out by going out of my way for someone else. Maybe because my participation in this outing was of my own free will, wasn't forced. In any case, seeing her happy makes me not quite so … something.

I don't know what the fuck I'm feeling, but it's not irritation.

Or annoyance.

Or anger.

It's more like …

I glance over at her in the dark, nothing but the glowing lights of the restaurant filling the cab. Illuminating the soft, delicate planes of her face. The glossy strands of her hair.

She catches me watching and smiles.

I …

Smile back.

11

#DOUCHEBAG

"You can't have your cake
and stick your dick in it, too."

Violet

hould I invite him in?

*S*He's just sitting there, watching me, and I know I have to decide before I hop out of his truck if I'm inviting him in or not. Zeke is removing his seat belt, hands fiddling with the keys in the ignition, and I know now is the time to make a move.

Or not.

Not *that* kind of move, god no—I'm not that kind of girl.

I wonder if he'd come in if I invited him to watch a movie. Wonder if it would be totally awkward, or not a big deal.

I blow out a frustrated puff of air, frustrated with myself for having no experience with guys like Zeke Daniels. He has experience written all over him, like he's been around the block a time or two then jogged around another lap.

I glance over.

"Do you want to come in?" I've never been this bold and can't believe I'm asking—and asking *him* of all people. Winnie would *kill* me. "Maybe watch a movie or something?"

His head turns, and he stares at me for a few of the longest seconds I've ever counted, eyes flickering up and down my person.

The heart inside my chest races. My temperature rises. Palms get damp.

"Sure."

"R-Really?" I blurt out, shocked.

"I have nothing else going on." His hands motion around the interior of the truck. "Do you?"

"Nothing but calling it a day early, maybe reading."

His head tilts in thought. "What's your genre? I know you saw mine."

"Um." My face gets even redder. "New adult romance."

"What the hell is *new* adult romance?"

Oh god.

"I-It's characters that are over the age of eighteen?"

"So, like, love stories and shit."

"Yes. Exactly like love stories and shit." I laugh.

His head nods toward the house. "So when we go inside, are you going to force me to watch chick flicks?"

"I actually didn't think about what I was going to force you to watch, but now that you mentioned it, the idea does have merit."

His brows lift. "The idea has *merit*?"

I push open the passenger door, nudging it with my shoe. "Are you coming or not?"

"Yeah, yeah, I'm comin'."

He follows me into the house, removing his big brown boots at the door, setting them off to the side on the mat. His coat follows, draped on the back of the couch.

Zeke Daniels standing in the middle of my living room, surveying the space, deliberating on where to sit—couch or recliner, couch or recliner.

He's massive.

He chooses the couch, dead center, legs spread.

Finds the remote, clicks on the television.

He looks … content.

"Uh, want anything to drink?"

He cranes his neck toward where I'm puttering in the galley kitchen. "Sure, if you have water, I'll take a bottle or two."

Or two?

I hear him flipping through the channels, the audio changing every few seconds.

"Is this a Netflix and chill thing, or just Netflix?" he calls from the living room, laughter in his voice.

"U-Um, we have Prime, so j-just that."

Oh my god, this was such a bad idea. I'm in way over my head with this one.

"You're no fun, Pixie," he replies, and I hear more action from the TV.

Pixie? Did he just give me a nickname?

I try my hand at a joke when I walk back into the living room, carrying three bottles of water that took me way too much time to retrieve from the fridge.

"If you want to get crazy, you can always practice snuggling with me. I'll let you hold the blanket."

He blinks.

Blinks again.

I smile.

He scowls.

But he also doesn't reject the idea.

I take this as a good sign and plop down next to him on the couch, reach behind me to grab a blanket, and settle in. "Anything on, or should we pick a DVD?"

"I found a few things. *The Walking Dead*, a few new releases. *True Blood*, and, uh … *Outlander*."

I cannot keep the astonishment out of my voice. "I'm sorry, did you just say you're willing to watch *Outlander*?"

It's based on a historical romance novel set in the highlands of Scotland; the main character time travels back to the 1700s and falls in love with a strapping Scott. It's one of my favorite books, and I've been wanting to binge watch the series.

"*Yes.*" He's practically glowering with indignation. "I *know* when you were in my bedroom you were scoping out all my European history books and shit—don't act like you weren't."

"I totally was, I'm just surprised you'd want to watch Outlander. I'd love to watch it if *you* want to."

He squints at me. "That depends; what episode are you on?"

"The episode right before she marries the Scotsman? I think."

"What! That's as far as you got?" I've never seen him so animated. "You're an entire two seasons behind! You're only at *The Garrison Commander* episode? *Ugh.*"

Seriously, I can't believe I'm sitting here listening to him go on about this. He's truly disgusted with me.

It's hilarious. *He's* hilarious.

Not *ha ha* funny, but oddly playful in his own way.

An enigma.

"Hey now, don't get all crazy guilt-tripping me. I don't have a lot of free time to watch TV!"

Both of us are laughing now, and the grin on his face—I want to kiss it off of him. Grab his face and kiss it all over. He's adorable.

So handsome.

Straight white teeth, square jawline completely covered in five o'clock shadow—he's stunning. And that smile?

Guh. Where does he always hide it?

It's a crime against humanity.

"Fine, we'll start at the wedding." His beefy arm rises, clicking the remote toward the television, flying through the menu selection until he arrives at Outlander. Chooses season one. Chooses episode: *The Wedding.*

Click, click, click goes the remote.

"Obviously I watch a lot of TV." He chuckles. "This ain't my first rodeo."

"That's surprising. When do you have time with your busy social schedule?"

"My busy *social* schedule? Goddamn you're cute." He gives me a sidelong glance, still pointing the remote control at the TV. "I don't know if you've noticed, but I'm the last person people think of when they hear the word *social.*"

"I-I—"

"Don't worry, you didn't just insult me. Let's just watch the show, although, I should warn you—spoiler alert!—there's some tits and ass."

"T-Tits and *ass*?" I repeat, blushing. I mean, what's worse than stuttering out the word *tits* in front of a handsome boy? Nothing.

Nothing is worse.

"Nudity," he clarifies. "You okay with that?"

"Okay with nudity? Sure."

Zeke

I have a hard-on.

Not the soft, chubby promise of one or the tingling stirrings—this is a raging boner.

My grip on Violet's plaid blanket tightens when the Scotsman Jamie Frasier and his wife Claire begin *fucking* on screen. She's on top, riding him—you know, because he's a *virgin*—in a chair, sinking down onto his erection, and I can't fucking take it anymore.

I chance a glance at Violet; I've never seen her face so flush, and I've embarrassed her plenty in the few weeks we've been hanging out.

"I-Is it hot in here?" she mutters under her breath, fanning herself by yanking on the collar of her black t-shirt.

"Yeah it's fucking hot in here." And getting warmer with every passing second.

"Should I open a window?" I volunteer, half off the couch and walking to the bank of windows at the front of the room before she can reply. I adjust the stiff dick in my pants, easing it to the side of my thigh before unlatching the lock and sliding my hands under the frame, pulling upward.

I crack the window a good nine inches—the length of my throbbing cock—wipe a set of sweaty palms over my pants, and yank my shirt down over my crotch.

Violet misses me gimping it back to the couch because her eyes are glued to the horny Highlanders *banging* on the television, in high def and Technicolor.

I ease myself back down, and despite the rising temperature in the room, grapple for the blanket and spread it across my lap, adding a throw pillow on top like a teenage boy afraid to be caught whacking it by his mother.

Normally I wouldn't give a shit if some chick saw my boner, but this is Violet—I don't want her to feel violated or whatever. I want her to feel safe with me, not like I'm going to fucking jump her with my giant cock.

On screen, Claire Frasier has just spread herself wide on the bed, and the Highland ginger Jamie is slowly scaling lower on her body. Nipples pointy and wet from his mouth. Head tipped back. Lips parted, sounds coming out of them both while he goes down on her.

This was such a bad idea.

I fucking *knew* the wedding episode had sex in it; I just didn't remember it being this graphic.

The actress's tits are *right* fucking *there.*

"Do you want to turn this off and watch something else?" I hear myself croak out, realizing just then that when I sat down on the couch, I grossly miscalculated the distance between us. Instead of giving her inches of berth, our legs and thighs and hips are touching.

"No," comes Violet's soft whisper. "It's okay."

"No?"

I shift in my seat, the heat from her denim-clad thigh only making the tension worse.

"No. We're good."

I know I shouldn't react—I do—and yet, when Violet's soft hand finds mine beneath the blanket and slides into mine, and *fits* … I move, body inching closer like a magnet is drawing me nearer.

Our fingers entwine, her other hand runs along the top of my thigh, patting it, seemingly unaware of the raging war inside my underwear, my body losing an intense battle with itself.

Fucking traitor.

She innocently lays her head on my shoulder.

The blonde hair on the top of her head tickles my nose, sending an odd twitch straight from my spine to my already pulsing dick. The little terror strains against the fabric of my jeans.

"*This* is snuggling," she informs me just as Claire Frasier has an orgasm not ten feet in front of us. Violet's pretty face tips up so she can look into my eyes.

Her body leans, fingers finding the bulk of my bicep and landing there, all the while clutching my other hand. It must be uncomfortable.

So I move.

Shift my body, slide my newly free hand around her narrow waist, pulling her in.

I groan, head hitting the back of the couch, counting *one, two, three, four* in a piss-poor attempt at some semblance of self control.

Four.

That's as high as my brain can count because I stop breathing when her smooth lips find the pulse in my throat. Give it the tiniest, barest whisper of a kiss.

Soft, exploratory kisses, up and down the column of my thick neck, gentle nuzzles beneath my ear. "You're not so bad at it," Violet says, lips just inches from mine.

Whoa, what the fuck.

There is no fucking way she's trying to seduce me right now. No. Way. She's too naïve and gentle. In my gut, I know she's just being affectionate. No way is she trying to get laid.

So what the hell is she doing, kissing the side of my neck and whispering flirty shit into my ear? She might as well be whispering lines from a porno. My brain works in overtime, trying to sort it out but coming up with nothing.

I sit ramrod straight, afraid to move. Not wanting to lead her on, or worse yet—take advantage.

Is this what being noble feels like?

If it is, being noble fucking sucks.

Am I attracted to Violet? *Yes.*

Do I want to bang Violet? *Yes.*

Would I screw her if she threw herself at me? *Yes.*

Her head hits my shoulder again, whole body relaxes into me, vibrant and warm. Buzzing. The hum of electricity circling is deafening, and when she tips her face to smile up at me?

I lower mine.

Give in, just this once.

Lips grazing.

Again.

Again. And again.

Faint. Tantalizing.

Small, teasing kisses I didn't know I was capable of.

Kisses that leave bruises? *Those* have always been more my speed. Girls that bite and spank and like to be told what to do? That's what I'm used to. Girls who make all the moves, are aggressive, who don't expect anything in return but an orgasm— *those* girls don't want to be friends.

My lips rest on hers, and I inhale her clean skin and perfume. Lift my hand to stroke the side of her face, caressing her smooth porcelain skin with the pad of my calloused thumb. With hands that might not have known hard work, but have worked hard. Hours upon hours of training and breaking my back for the wrestling team. Early mornings and late nights. Long road trips. Short weekends. Sacrificing a personal life to sink every spare moment into my team, until I'm left gasping for breath, because they're all I've got.

But *Violet* is with me now.

I'm not sure what the hell it all means, or what the hell I'm doing here with her, but I know how good it fucking feels with her mouth pressed against mine. With her fingers running the length of my thigh, intentionally or not, driving a hot zip of friction to my groin.

I groan into her mouth, dragging a hand from her face, straight down her arm. It hits her hip, kneading the flesh above the waistline of her jeans. Squeezes. Fingers the fabric of her hemline and curls, tugging.

She presses closer with a little hum, small breasts brushing my chest, our breaths mingling.

We can't get enough of each other. Violet's hands are in my hair, gliding along my shoulders, gripping, feeling, memorizing every hard line of my upper torso. Touching me like she's never felt a man's pecs before, never felt their arms or chest or muscles.

Touching me like …

Like I'm …

Shit. The way I'm touching *her*.

I want to *fuck* her so bad now I can hardly think straight.

My hand roams her slender form, large hand running up and down her thigh. In between her legs and under her shirt.

Up her flat stomach.

There's nothing special about her bare torso; it's not like I haven't had my hand up a girl's shirt before. But this is Violet's heat, Violet's skin, and she's letting me run the open part of my hand toward the curve of her breasts.

I arrive at her bra; it's so small I can fit my entire hand over the sheer cup. No underwire. Textured, I finger the lace and slide my hand all the way inside. Fingers toying with her breast, thumb flicking her nipple.

Violet moans. So unexpectedly long and *loud*, I play with her again. Her tits are small, sure, but when I effortlessly glide my palm over the palest, silkiest skin I've ever felt, the size isn't even registering in my brain as inadequate.

She feels perfect. Unspoiled.

On the television, there's shouting and arguing as the Highlanders engage in battle, but I barely hear any of it.

Our tongues roll, hers tentative at first. That's fine, I don't need her trying to devour me; we can build to that.

My hands slide out from under her bra, tracking toward the waistline of her pants. Dip down into her waistband, back and forth over her hips with just enough room to roam.

She sucks in a breath.

Holds it.

I smile into her mouth, teeth nipping at her bottom lip, fumbling to find the button on her jeans, feeling around the denim belt loops blindly, like Helen Keller on steroids.

"Zeke, please stop."

I freeze. Stop. Fingers motionless at the fly of her pants. Lowering my hand slowly, I pull away from her body, eyes seeking her wide hazel irises. Face flushed, her parted lips plump from being thoroughly sucked and kissed.

"I'm sorry, but we have to stop."

I lean forward on the couch, resting those coarse palms on my knees, running them up and down my thighs before raising them to my head, running them through my hair.

"It's fine, Violet."

"I-I thought m-maybe I could do this, but I can't."

Can't?

That—that right there is what sets me off.

"Do this with *me*, or with anyone?" The words slip out of my mouth, already knowing the answer.

She doesn't want to do this with me, and why the hell is that bothering me so much? I'm not fucking good enough? Too angry, too dark, too forward?

"This has nothing to do with you."

"Whatever. I said it's fine." My jaw is clenched. I work it back and forth to loosen it, certain I must look like a psychopath.

She's struggling to tug her shirt down, straightening the hemline, pulling it over her waistband. "Y-you don't sound fine ..."

I laugh, the sound slightly maniacal. "Trust me. I was *fine* before you came alone, and I'll be *fine* long after you're gone." I stand abruptly, snatching up my jacket then tugging on my boots.

"Why are you getting so upset?" One hand rakes over that pink mouth, tips of her fingers stoking her swollen lips.

"I'm not," I grind out, unconvincing.

"I-I just didn't want things to go too far."

"Too far? We've been making out for like, five minutes. Don't flatter yourself."

Her face turns bright red. "But you were unzipping my pants …"

"So? What did you think I was going to do, Violet? Fuck you on the couch? We were just making out, it wasn't a big deal. Maybe I wanted to get you off—Jesus, I'm able to *control* myself."

"I know that!"

"Then why did you stop us?" I start to yank open the front door, pausing when she gives a diminutive shrug. "Are you afraid of one goddamn orgasm or are you just afraid of *me*?"

"I-I was trying to gather my wits!"

"What are you talking about?"

"We both know you have more experience than I do; maybe I wanted five seconds before letting you stick your hand inside my pants."

I stab my finger toward the ground. "This is the reason I don't do relationships. This. Right here."

"That's not a nice thing to say." She scowls as I step onto the front porch. "Did it ever occur to you not to react like I just rejected you? This isn't about *you*, Zeke, it's about *me*. We could have just stopped and cooled off for a minute."

Her voice gets louder with each word that comes pouring, crystal clear, out of her mouth, hands balled up into little fists.

Her frustration wins out a breath later.

"I-It's embarrassing enough t-telling you I have less experience. My track record is two guys! Two. And then you *throw* it back at me by being an insensitive jerk! Sex isn't a big deal to you, but it's a big deal to me—it's for *relationships*." She's stabbing herself in the chest with her thumb. "I don't know if you've noticed, Zeke Daniels, but I'm not the kind of girl you just sleep with. I-I'm the kind you *keep*."

She's glaring knives and daggers.

"Do you care? *No!* God no! You have your head stuck so far up your own ass, you probably haven't noticed that guys aren't exactly *lining* up to date me!"

What the hell? I'm the one getting rejected here, so what is *she* so upset about?

"You're taking this the wrong way. I just wanted to take a quick step back before we crossed the line." Violet's hand grips the door handle. "So go. Go on. Leave if you're going to be a big baby."

Then, just as I'm about to open my mouth and, I don't know, *apologize*, Violet does the *last* thing I expect her to do.

She slams the fucking door in my face.

Zeke: *You should know—I don't apologize to people.*

Violet: *Then don't.*

Zeke: *But I feel goddamn guilty about leaving.*

Violet: *You didn't have to text me to tell me that. I don't feel bad about kicking you out.*

Zeke: *You didn't kick me out, I left.*

Violet: *Remember that part where I slammed the door in your face.*

Zeke: *LOL right ... but not until I got up to leave.*

Violet: *Like a big baby.*

Zeke: *Sorry, what?*

Violet: *You heard me.*

Zeke: *You've called me that once already tonight, sure you don't want to take it back?*

Violet: *You have a lot to learn about relationships if you think getting huffy and walking out on someone is mature.*

Zeke: *Relationship? What relationship.*

Violet: *Our friendship. This relationship.*

Zeke: *Hate to break it to ya, but I walk out on my friends all the time*

Violet: *Your other friends might be okay with you treating them like that, but I am not.*

Violet: *I deserve more respect than that. Don't you think?*

Violet: *Don't you?*

Violet: *So now you're going to ignore me?*

Violet: *Hello? Are you there?*

Zeke: *Yes.*

Violet: *Yes ... what.*

Zeke: *Yes. You deserve more respect than that.*

Violet: *And you're sorry you walked out on me?*

Zeke: *Yes. I feel like a jackass for walking out on you, and it pissed me off when you ...*

Zeke: *Wait. Did you just use psychology bullshit on me to get me to apologize?*

Violet: *Maybe*

Zeke: *Please knock that shit off.*

Violet: *Maybe I will, maybe I won't. We'll see.*

"Fine, I'll cuddle you—but only if it's with the sole purpose of trying to survive."

Zeke

This place is such a dive. I can't believe we keep coming here.

An old-school biker bar turned college hangout, there's a jukebox hanging on the wall that has a catalogue of hair bands, 80s rock, Led Zeppelin, and any country music recorded before 1989.

Assholes and trouble can be found lurking in every dark corner of this hovel. Its parking lot. Its back alley. Its basement.

I would know—I've been in trouble in all three places.

When Violet walks through the big, busted up front door, I know it's her before I can even see her face.

She's not standing under a light, but her hair is so pale that it translucently shines from her spot near the bar, even though she's shrouded in semi-darkness. Braided around the crown of her head, the rest falls down her back in loose curls. Ethereal. Sweet, like she showers in flowers, rainbows, sunshine and shit.

I watch her profile when she nods, smiling up at her friend with the brunette hair, a tall, pretty girl with just as much laughter in her eyes as Violet.

They're out of place here, not fit for any of the assholes in here. Not a single one.

Including myself.

What the fuck are they doing here? What were her asshole friends thinking coming to this place? Despite being one of the most popular off-campus bars, Mad Dog Jacks is little more than a glorified biker bar. Loud, gloomy, and rough, the place has an odd cast of characters: drunk students, drunk locals, drunk bikers, and bartenders that pour heavy.

Violet breezes toward the bar with her three friends, so small and delicate, pale hair glowing under the lights like some kind of goddamn halo.

A pixie in a room full of dark, boorish giants with no manners.

Pixie.

I'm actually glad I texted her last night.

She's dancing now, spinning away from me, flowers at the knot in back of her hair. I can't tell what color the flowers are—probably some shade of purple—but they're stuck in the braid crowning her head. Jesus, seriously? Flowers in her hair at a biker bar?

They make her look youthful and naïve and vulnerable.

She is going to be eaten a-fucking-live.

Or worse.

I choke down the beer in the bottle I'm clutching. It's tepid at best, and barely tolerable.

Glaring, I turn my attention toward the cluster of preppy fraternity boys bearing down on her little group of friends, their pockets probably stuffed full of Rohypnol. The thought makes me queasy; Violet didn't come here to get pawed at or taken advantage of by a bunch of drunks.

After driving away from her last night, I realize I probably know her better than she realizes. I know she's a damn bleeding heart. I know she's selfless, but only to a point. Kindhearted. Quiet. Inexperienced.

Stronger than either of us recognize.

Too goddamn trusting.

Too goddamn sunny for my gloom and doom.

Too light for my dark.

Too good for my bad.

Too everything.

Not to mention, she's a horrible dancer.

I actually chuckle out loud at that last one as I watch her hopping around the dance floor, no rhythm. Taking another drag off my beer bottle, I drain it and set it on the round, bar-height table next to me, watching her from the corner of my eye. Violet's head tips back, the column of her slim neck visible under the lights as she sways to the music, laughing along with her friends.

I wonder if they're her roommates. I wonder which one of them brought her here.

"What the hell is Violet doing here," I finally wonder out loud to no one in particular.

Mostly to myself.

Only fucking Oz hears me, nudging me in the ribcage. "Dude, what is it with you accosting girls who go out to have fun?" He pesters on. "You did this shit to James when we started dating, remember? Every time we'd see her at a damn party, you had an issue with it."

I ignore him, gesturing instead to Violet and her friends, pointing like a dumbass. "Look how out of place she is."

Oz turns and regards me weirdly. Warily. "Dude, I think you're finally losing your grip on reality."

"Or maybe I'm just a concerned *citizen*."

He rolls his eyes. "Why don't you mind your own business and leave her alone. Stop fucking staring. We voted: you staring at her is weirding us out."

He's right, I should stop staring.

But I don't.

Because I can't.

Violet

The last person I expect to see at Mad Dog Jacks is Zeke—I've been here a few times in the past year and have never run into him and his wrestling buddies—but that's who is leaning in now, all lips and warm breath, murmuring into my ear from behind.

I shiver when his gruff voice inquires, "Vi, what the hell are you doing here?" The heat from his entire body presses into my backside.

I freeze when he rests those big hands of his on my hips.

"Same thing you are, I suspect."

"You suspect?" His hum vibrates.

"M-My friends love this place. Melinda's boyfriend works here, and I go where they go, so ..." I babble, pulling out of his embrace. Grasp? Hold?

I turn to face him. Give a helpless little shrug, giving his eyes permission to trail along the front of my dress. The long-sleeved baby blue tunic hits mid-thigh. The legs I spent ten minutes shaving and rubbing with moisturizer are silky smooth. The beige half boots add three inches to my petite frame.

The delicate silver *V* dangles between my breasts.

It's not the sexiest bar outfit—not by a long shot—but it's short and flirty, and I'm comfortable. Covered, really, since the only skin flashing is my legs.

Zeke drags his narrowed eyes up and down my torso, back to mine, leans forward, his palm grazing my forearm. "I still feel like a dick after last night."

"You acted like a d-dick." *Great, dick is the perfect word to stutter over, Violet. Real classy.*

"You look pretty."

"I do?" I mean, I do—I know I do, I'm not a fool. I know guys think I'm cute, know they like my pale wavy hair and weird hazel eyes.

But that's just it; I'm cute, not sexy. The good girl next door, not the polished sorority girl or outgoing flirt. The girls that show up at his wrestling meets all dolled up with half their clothes off.

Like the girls in this bar.

Like my own roommates, whose shirts are cropped. Whose pants are tight.

The music beats around us, bass pumping. It's dark and dingy and he has to move in even closer to hear me when I say, "You think I look pretty?"

He quirks one of those dark, somber eyebrows. "You know I do."

My head gives a little shake. "This isn't how you talk to me. You don't say things like that."

No, he normally growls words like a bear.

"Maybe I don't know how."

I tip my head to study him. "How many beers have you had?"

"Three."

"Three?"

"Yeah, three. But I'll stop if you want me to."

I giggle. "You're a big boy. I'm not going to tell you what to do."

He is laugh is sardonic. "Sometimes, Violet, I think I'd let you."

"Uh ..." It's the best I can come up with.

"Sometimes, Violet, I think I'd let you lead me around like a big, fucking dope."

"I-I ... wouldn't want to."

"No?" He's skeptical.

"No." My head dips shyly. "I wouldn't want to lead you around. I would never want you to feel like I was using you."

"Using me? *You?* Violet, look at me." He takes two fingers and tips my chin so I'm looking into his crystal-hued irises. His mesmerizing, weirdly colored eyes. Mouth now curved into a delicious smile.

A smirk.

"Use me *any* way you want."

I watch those full, sexy lips say the words and feel my entire body getting warm. Hot.

Oh. God. He isn't talking about me leading him around like a big fucking dope. He's talking about his body; I can tell by the way his pupils dilate under the light. The flaring from his nostrils.

Zeke Daniels isn't done with me.

We're not done with each other, not by a long shot.

Except I'm not a well-practiced flirt. I have no idea what to say or what to do with this strapping, broody boy in front of me who suddenly looks like his solemn self.

The boy who thinks too much and does everything with purpose.

I want to kiss that boy *so bad* my lips ache.

The music around us gets low, slow, and sentimental—I think it's a heavy metal hair band from the early 90s, but it's a ballad, and the dingy house lights get dimmer. Lights above the makeshift dance floor flicker, strobing. Biker couples and college students dance. Sway.

"I should probably get back to my friends. I'm sure they're looking for me."

His nose grazes my cheek when his lips find my ear. "You have to know this bar isn't *safe,* Violet. You have no business walking around, wandering off alone. You shouldn't even be in a place like this."

"Where *should* I be then?" My long lashes flutter. Lips tingle from our energy.

"Not here."

"*You're* here."

193

"True, but it would make me feel better if you were safe at home."

"I'm here with a group, so it's fine." To illustrate, I point to Melinda's boyfriend Derek, who's shaking a drink between two silver cups at one of the main bars. Mel and Winnie hover at his station, glancing my way.

"*Fine*? There are only three of you! You couldn't fight off any of the guys here if one was all up in your shit."

"All up in my shit." I laugh, crossing my arms and tapping my toe. "Stop being so bossy, Zeke."

His eyes go wide. "Bossy?"

I scoff. "N-No one has ever called you that before? I find that very hard to believe."

A snort comes out of his nose. "All I'm staying is, you could have picked a better place. Do not let your guard down, got it? Too much nasty shit goes down when no one is looking."

I cock my head, intrigued. "Yeah? Like what?"

"Like roofies and date rape and back-alley shit."

"Are you planning to roofie anyone tonight?"

For the first time since we met, Zeke appears absolutely horrified. "What? Jesus Christ, Violet, that's not even funny!"

No, it's not funny, not even a little bit, but a laugh squeaks out anyway. "Sorry, I can't help it. You should see the look on your face."

"I don't want to see the look on my face." He's snarling now, really getting worked up.

My palm finds his bicep, resting there, giving it a gentle pat. "I highly doubt I'm in any danger of unwanted attention, but you can keep an eye on me if it makes you feel better."

He silently stares down at me.

"Would it?" My lips are moving and he watches them intently. "Make you feel better to watch me, I mean?"

He nods. "Yes."

"You wanna know what I think?" My hand glides down his bicep, to his forearm, squeezing the tight muscles beneath my palm. "I-I think you care, Zeke. That's why you're so irritated with me all the time. I think you care a lot but you don't know how to say it."

His shoulders dip and he's leaning in again, driving me crazy with the smell of his aftershave. "Is that what you think? That I'm irritated all the time?"

"Aren't you?" I close my eyes when his warm breath lingers near my lobe, luxuriating in the closeness.

I long for it.

"No." His body presses into me; his hands slide up my neck, holding my face. Jawline. "I don't get irritated with you Violet, and I wasn't mad at you last night; I was mad at myself."

I inhale, holding my breath; *he's opening up to me.*

"I wish I could say I was going to try harder to not be such a dick, but this is who I am. I'm an ass and I've been like this a long time. But you're not jaded—not like me. I'm a beautiful mess." Rough thumbs tenderly stroke my cheeks. "You're just beautiful."

His words kiss my soul.

His lips kiss the exposed skin on my collarbone, up the side of my neck, gently.

My eyes close when he kisses the lids. The tip of my nose. The divot above my lips.

Tenderly, like we aren't in a biker bar, surrounded by people, in a room full of drunks and troublemakers.

I let my hands slide around his waist. Feel his intake of breath from the contact when I glide my hands up his chest, up his neck. Over the stubble to cradle his face like he's cradling mine.

I don't even care that he's probably kissing me because he's had three beers. That he might not be thinking straight. That in the morning he probably won't feel the same way I feel about him.

Because when our lips finally meet? It's magic. Tingling electricity all the way to my toes.

This kiss is music and moonlight and basking in possibility.

This kiss is …

A light tap hits my shoulder.

My roommate Melinda's voice somewhere behind me.

"Violet, please stop making out with the pissed off cheesy-looking bo-hunk. We said we'd stick together tonight, remember?"

I remember. We did say that.

But it's Zeke who pulls back first, dazed, hands still cradling my jawline. Mouth still inches from my lips.

It steals another kiss.

"Whoa. Jeez, you should see the look on your faces. You both look freaking drunk. Combustible."

Zeke releases me, hands sliding down my arms. "Did you just call me a cheesy bo-hunk?"

"Uh, *yeah*," my smart-mouthed roommate yells above the noise. "You're one step away from being oiled up and on the front page of a calendar. Dude, lay off the roids."

She grabs my hand, tugging.

I catch Zeke's toothy grin and my heart skips three beats.

He kisses me on the lips. "I'll be over there with a giant hard-on if you need me, Pix."

Zeke saunters off, leaving me rooted to the spot and staring off after him.

"Ugh, the guys that come to this place, I swear," Melinda quips, looping her arm through my useless one, and having never set eyes on him before, she gives Zeke Daniels a onceover. "What dark corner did you find him in?"

I lift two fingers, tracing my lips, and grin at him. Sigh.

"The library."

Zeke

As promised, I watch Violet from a distance the rest of the evening. Kind of like a stalker, but it's not nearly the same thing if she knows I'm doing it, right?

All I do all night is keep sentry as she dances, always with an ice water in her hand, always with those two other girls. Melinda and—what did she say the other one's name was? Wendy. Wanda? W something, shit, I don't remember.

The blonde, Melinda, continues running up to the bar, leaning in for quick kisses from the bartender. He's Hispanic, with a grin I can see from here. Every so often he strolls over and plants a kiss on the roommate, frequently wiping a glass or mixing a drink while he does it.

I stay with my friends, never leaving the confines of my group, shooting covert glances over at her every few minutes. She hasn't left my line of vision, and I've told myself over and over that it's for her own good; I'm watching out for her, not indulging myself.

Rex Gunderson is just setting another pitcher of beer on the high-top table when I trail Violet on her way to the bathroom in that sexy baby blue dress, stare at those pale legs, her heels clicking down the short, narrow hallway at the back of the bar.

I relax when she opens the door to the restroom, disappearing inside, but stiffen when I see some tall preppy dude waltz toward the bathrooms. Walk to the wall. Lean up against the black painted bricks like he's waiting for someone.

For Violet?

Hell no. *Fuck. That.*

"Hey Daniels, what was the name of that one chick you—"

I raise my hand to stop him from talking.

"No," I cut him off.

197

He looks confused. "Just real quick, I'm trying to win a bet here. What was the name of that girl you—"

"Shh!" *Jesus Christ.* "Shut the fuck *up* for a second, Gunderson."

I watch, transfixed, when the preppy guy pulls a phone out of his pocket and checks his screen while he waits. Slides it back into his pocket.

The women's bathroom door opens and Violet emerges, straightening the hemline of her pretty dress. She sees him, gives a start, expression friendly—she doesn't know he's been standing there waiting for her. There's also just enough light in the hallway for me to see her mouth move, lips forming the words, "Excuse me."

She attempts to sidestep around him.

He doesn't let her.

That stupid fuck.

I straighten, slamming my beer glass down on the table.

Arms drop to my side.

Flex my fingers.

"Daniels man, what's the name of—" Gunderson tries again. Oz grabs him by the arm, pulling him back, creating a wide berth; the parting of the crowd of friends affords me a better view of Violet and Preppy Fuck.

He blocks her retreat again, arm braced on the wall next to her head. Lowering my eyes, I see her slender fingers wringing nervously.

When he boxes her completely in? I've had more than enough.

He is a dead man.

I stride toward the bathrooms, eyes trained on one person only.

Violet.

It takes me thirty long-ass steps to reach her.

Fifteen long seconds to shove my way through this insanely packed bar.

I counted.

I don't mince words when I'm finally standing in front of them. Violet's narrow shoulders sag in relief at the sight of me, and I swear I get taller by a few inches.

Posture.

"This guy *bothering* you, Violet?" I look her dead in the eyes, not sparing the douchebag a single glance.

"I-I think I've g-got it handled, Zeke. I-It's f-fine." She lifts a trembling hand, running it down the back of her hair, but she can't hide the fact that her stutter is back and it's *bad*.

My guard goes up.

Everything is not *fine*, so why would she stand there and say it was?

"Yeah." The guy backing her into the corner smiles, his overly whitened teeth glowing under the hall lights. "She's got it handled bro. It's fine."

I want to yank the asshole by the collar of his pink polo shirt and sucker punch him in his arrogant fucking face.

"Things don't look fine, Violet. It looks like he has you pinned to the wall and is *harassing* you."

I dare them both to deny it.

Violet can't find the words, and the douche looks me up and down, lip curling, recognition drawing his face into a delighted grin. He obviously knows who I am—not hard when there's billboard of me plastered on the side of the university's field house.

"Hey, don't I know you?"

"No."

"Yeah, I'm pretty sure I do."

"Pretty sure you don't, but we're about to get to acquainted real quick if you don't back the fuck off and leave her alone."

"What are you, her boyfriend?"

My jaw clenches. "Does it matter?"

He raises his palms in a show of surrender, like he's the good guy here and I'm the piece of shit. "Look pal, why don't *you* back off. Violet and me? We're good. She's safe. You can leave the stuttering freak with me. I just wanna talk to her."

Um …

What?

"What the fuck did you just say?" I utter the words so quietly, so venomously and deliberately slow. Violet inches farther into the cinderblock wall behind her.

The preppy assfuck takes a step forward. "I said back off, *dude*."

I shake my head slowly. "No, no, the *other* part."

"You can leave her with me?"

"*No.*" I grind out between clenched teeth. "The *other* part. You know what I'm fucking talking about, so say it. Fucking. Say. It."

He smirks. "Stuttering *freak?*"

"Yeah." I rub my chin. "*That* part, you motherfucking piece of *shit*."

I lift my hands so they're illuminated under the dim light above us and he looks down, tracking my movements, staring at my open palms with wide eyes. "See these hands?" I ask, closing my palms into fists. "They are three seconds away from pounding the piss out of you."

"Zeke—" Violet tries to cut in, but I cut her off.

"What's it going to be asshole? Are you going to walk away, or am I going to take these fists and smash them into your face?"

"Zeke!" Violet gasps out a sob. "P-P-Please."

The guy looks back and forth between us, trying to decide what our relationship is, internally debating about how strong I actually am. If he can take me in a fight. How far he can push and push before I knock him on his ass.

If the stammering girl is worth getting his teeth knocked out.

The bag of crap decides she's not, rolling his eyes at us and shoving his hands into the pockets of his khakis. Khakis—who wears those to the fucking bar anyway?

Wisely, he takes a step back. "Whatever dude."

Then another, until he's backing away. Vanishing into the crowd, out of sight.

Violet turns to me. "I-I can't believe you almost hit him."

"He would have had it coming."

"I-I'm sorry you had to step in. Y-You know I-I didn't come back here to g-get accosted. I j-just had to p-pee."

Jesus. It sounds like her teeth are chattering, on top of her stutter.

I rest my hands on her slim shoulders. "Don't apologize, Violet—you did nothing wrong. I watched him waiting for you when you were in the bathroom."

She nods.

It's then that I take a really hard, piercing look at her. My palms look enormous splayed on her petite shoulders. I squat, bending at the knees so I can gaze into her eyes.

"Jesus, I thought he was hurting you. Did he touch you?"

A shake of the head. "No, he was harmless. Just a little … mean."

"Mean?" *I'm* mean. "What did he say to you, Vi?" I press, wanting to shake the words out of her. Rather than telling me, her lips press together in a thin line. "Violet, you can tell me. I'm mean, too, remember?"

I shoot her a wane smile.

"You're not mean, you're angry at the world. There's a difference," Violet reminds me softly. "He … he was making fun of me."

"Yet he wanted to get in your pants?" The question just slips out, bitter and cold.

"I guess." She shrugs, her shoulders moving up and down beneath my hands. "I don't want to repeat anything he just said. It's embarrassing."

She doesn't need to repeat a single thing that asshole said; I can use my imagination to figure that shit out on my own.

"I let that fucker off way too easy. No one talks to you that way, ever." I balance on my heels, still squatting, to meet her eyes. "No one. Not even me, you got that?"

When her bottom lip quivers, I stand. With instincts I didn't know I possessed, I tug her toward me, tucking her into my big body, wrapping my arms around her and resting my chin atop her pretty blonde head. Run my open palm down her back, stroking it gently.

Man, she's so tiny.

"It's okay Violet, it's okay," I'm murmuring into her hair. "I'm sorry."

"Sorry? Now you're starting to sound like me. It wasn't your fault," comes her muffled reply, her cheek pressed against my chest.

Her nearness feels ...

Good.

Really fucking good.

"Text your friends and tell them what happened. Let me take you home. Let me get you out of here. I don't trust any of the jackasses here."

Grappling for her, we head toward my friends so I can let them know I'm leaving. I brought them here, but doubt I'll be bringing them back—unless they all want to pile in my truck and leave with us *now*.

I don't make it all the way over.

Oz sees me weaving toward them through the crowd, Violet in tow, and gives me the nod.

I raise my hand in acknowledgement, shift gears, head toward the exit.

Violet

Zeke is hugging me again.

Zeke Daniels is hugging me on my front porch.

No, not a hug—an actual embrace.

I'm enveloped in his strong arms and can feel the dense muscles flexing as he reaches around me to run his hands up and down my back, comforting me.

I lean back to look up at him, the tips of his fingers finding purchase on my cheekbone, tracing my skin, the pads of his thumbs running under my eyes, wiping away whatever tears haven't been dried up by the cotton of his t-shirt.

Whisper-light touches. Soft.

"Zeke?"

"Hmm?"

"Why didn't you hit that guy?"

He strokes the top of my head, fingers doing this massaging thing to my scalp. "I didn't think you wanted me to."

"Does that mean you would have punched him if I hadn't been standing there?"

"Probably." His fingers stop for a few seconds. "I really wanted to knock him on his fucking ass."

His fingers resume their circular motions.

"W-what are you doing to my hair?" I sigh, voice wistful.

"Comforting you? I think. *Obviously* I'm drunk."

He doesn't seem drunk to me, not in the slightest, and if I'd thought for one second he was, I wouldn't have gotten in his truck.

"You are?"

"No. But I wish I was shitfaced. Hammered." He doesn't crack a smile. Not even the hint of one as his lips hover near my ear. "You always smell so good, Vi. Like sunshine and shampoo and flowers. Violets."

I take my own whiff of him, inhaling his masculinity. Inhaling the strength he exudes. It permeates, rolling off of him when he walks.

"Are you *sure* you're okay, Violet?"

I nod into his chest. "I am now."

Zeke pushes the hair out of my eyes, fingers the coronet braid cascading over my right shoulder. Rubbing the ends of it between the pads of his fingertips, he leans in and lifts it to his nose. Inhales.

"Violets," he says, repeating his earlier sentiment.

He's wrong though; it's cardamom and mimosa.

I don't correct him.

"Violet."

I stand feebly, awkwardly in the shadows of my front porch, letting this behemoth of a man sniff my hair for the second time tonight, the tip of his nose warm when it brushes my cheek. It trails its way to the crux just below my ear. His lips press on the tender skin of my temple.

One heartbeat.

Two.

I don't trust myself to speak.

To move.

To breathe.

I stand paralyzed, still as stone, rooted to the rough-hewn porch boards that should have been replaced years ago. Zeke's solid hands cup my elbows then glide up my arms. Land on my shoulders. Down again.

He's going to kiss me.

I'm going to let him.

My fingers rake through his hair, drawing his head down, meeting his eager, pliant mouth.

It settles on mine, lips pressing so tenderly there are no words to describe it—no one has ever kissed me this way. We kiss and kiss and kiss with no tongue, a union of lips and breath and skin. Tiny tastes of each other. Nips.

His mouth pulls at my bottom lip, gently sucking, before it opens, his tongue finally—*finally, thank GOD*—touching mine, almost timidly. Just enough to make my nerves quiver throughout my entire body.

We stand like this, kissing on my front porch in the cold, until my mouth is swollen—until he backs away, leaving my body instantly cold from the loss of his heat, regarding me in the porch light.

Acts like a gentleman.

"Goodnight, Violet." He swallows.

I have to force myself to speak. "Goodnight."

I won't lie, I'm disappointed when he steps away, backs himself down off the porch, and walks across my lawn, raking a hand through his hair. Yanks open the driver's side door with a grunt. Guns the engine and backs down out of my driveway, starts down the street.

I wanted him to stay with me.

Instead, I stand here alone, watching as his truck slows, pulls to the shoulder of the road. Flips on his hazards and … sits there, idling.

Very weird.

Curiously, I hold sentry as he does nothing but sit in that big black truck, folding my arms across my chest to ward off the chill, a thick billow of steam rising from my lips with every cold breath.

Inside the pocket of my thick winter jacket, my phone notification chimes.

I reach into my pocket. Slide open the lock screen.

Zeke: *Hey.*

I look up into the night. His bright red tail lights still glow eerily at the end of my street.

Violet: *Hey.*

Zeke: *How's it going?*

I laugh—what on earth is he doing?

Violet: *Good? You?*

Zeke: *I guess I just wanted to check in to see if you were okay after tonight. Because that's what friends do, right?*

I can't stop the smiling, and I bite down on my bottom lip.

Violet: *That's exactly what friends do. Thanks*

Zeke: *Hey Vi?*

Violet: *Hmm?*

Zeke: *So this is going to sound creepy, but I'm sitting at the end of your street like a damn stalker ... if I come back and get you, what are the odds you'll come to my place?*

I stare at that line, reread it twice, fingers hovering above the keypad of my cell. *What are the odds you'll come to my place?*

Would I go to his place?

Yes!

I want to do more than taste his lips.

I want to feel the heat from his body over mine. Feel him inside me. Know what his body feels like without the shirt, pants, and clothes.

Zeke: *Violet? You still there?*

Violet: *Yes.*

I suck in a deep breath, curls of excitement twisting my stomach into knots, and tap out a reply.

Violet: *Yes. If you come back and get me, I'll go to your place.*

Zeke shuts the front door behind him and suddenly, we're alone in the confines of his house. Standing together at the door, he crams his hands in the pockets of his coat, uneasily shifting his weight on the heels of his black boots. Removes his hands. Shrugs off his coat and hangs it on a hook before reaching to help me with mine.

Together, we slide it down my shoulders and he takes it. Hangs it. We both glance at our jackets, now hanging side by side.

It's an odd sensation, that. A new one I've never felt before, anticipation quaking in the pit of my stomach, sending butterflies flying. Fluttering.

Making me want to toss my cookies all over the leather boots he's bending to untie.

My knees feel wobbly. Weak. I can barely focus, bending to unbuckle the pretty little half boots I borrowed from Winnie and sliding them off my feet. Legs bare. Too exposed and open to his roaming, expressionless, pale eyes.

I know why I agreed to come here.

I like him; I'm probably half in love with him already. Enamored. *Charmed* by his rough edges and jagged lines. How we're opposites in every way that counts.

I know that's not a reason to fall into bed with someone, but I fell into my last boyfriend's bed for lesser reasons: loneliness. Out of curiosity. For the connection. Wanting to get the whole virgin thing over with.

I might not be completely in love with Zeke yet, but the stirrings are there, and that's enough.

I'm not asking for a commitment—not *yet* anyway.

As I stare at Zeke, filling the doorway of his quaint college house—he's huge and takes up the entire space—all my instincts tell me to trust myself on this decision.

Trust my heart for once, and not my head.

Trust that he has my best interests at heart, even if the words coming out of his mouth aren't eloquent. Far from it.

He swears too much.

He isn't nice.

He isn't sweet.

He isn't kind.

Or generous with words. Or affection.

But he's reliable. Dependable. And he was there for me tonight. I know he was watching out for me, or he wouldn't have seen that guy back me into a dark, back corner of the bar.

And thank god he was.

I don't know what I would have done.

Screamed bloody murder, maybe? Would anyone have heard me over the noise? The music? The packed crowd?

Winnie says Zeke is "a project", one that's probably more work than he's worth, with no guaranteeing the outcome. The thing is, I can't fool my heart into thinking he's not worth it, even when my head is telling me he isn't.

I know Zeke is an asshole.

I know he's crude and unsuitable.

Zeke might be brutal, but at least he's brutally honest, and the next thing I know, he's taking my hand, leading me down the hallway.

I let him lead me.

Floating down the hall to the bedroom, I'm light, a million worries lifting off my shoulders: self-doubt. Self-consciousness. The fear that he doesn't like me back. The desperation to be loveable that took root the day my parents died and further overtook me when my aunt and uncle moved away.

The fear that I'm not sexy because I stutter.

Zeke Daniels doesn't just want sex; he wants something more —I feel it in my heart. He's *seeking* something—the same thing I am.

Something permanent.

Constant and stable, and no one will convince me otherwise.

"Violet, I wouldn't—I don't want you to think I have any clue what I'm doing. Because I don't. I have no idea why the hell I stopped that car in the middle of the damn road, I just …" He releases my hand, closing the door to his bedroom.

Runs his fingers through his black hair.

"Do you know what I'm trying to tell you?"

"No." I give my head a little shake. "I have no idea what you're trying to tell me."

Zeke walks to the far side of the room, pacing back. And forth. Back. And forth. "Shit, I know I'm going to fuck this up."

"What are you going to fuck up?"

He laughs then, a loud, rumbling laugh. "It cracks me up when you say a swear word. It sounds so weird."

He stops pacing, stands in front of me. Reaches up and captures my face in the palms of his hands. Strokes my cheekbones with his thumbs. "God you're fucking adorable."

My lashes flutter. "Thank you."

"You're beautiful, Violet. I think you're beautiful." His head is lowered, our lips inches apart. "You're too sweet for me, you know that right? I'm such an asshole."

"I know." The whisper is more of a sigh.

His steely gaze studies me a few heartbeats, warm hands still caressing my face. "What are we doing?"

I can't answer; he's being way too nice. So unexpectedly tender.

"Do you respect me?" I ask quietly.

He nods, our foreheads touching. "More than anyone."

I believe him.

"Are we friends?" I ask, lifting my hands to grasp his wrists.

"Yes. You're one of my best friends."

I believe that, too.

"I am?"

"Yes," he whispers, voice gravely. "Even though I don't deserve it, you're one of the good ones, Violet DeLuca, and I don't have a clue what you're doing here in this room with me."

I swallow the lump forming in my throat, nose tingling from his words. His words.

His words, simple as they are, are *beautiful* words.

A tear escapes the corner of my eyes, but he catches it with his thumb. "Don't cry, Pix."

"I-I can't help it, you're being so sweet. It's so weird."

"You know I wouldn't be saying any of this to you if it wasn't true." His voice is raw with emotion, too, his lips brushing mine in a shocking jolt of heat. His breath is hot. He tastes like beer and peppermint gum. "Violet."

Zeke's hands don't leave my face, not until I release the hold I have on his wrists and touch his firm chest. His hard pecs. Drag my flattened palms along the planes of his shirt, letting the pads of my fingers memorize the lines.

His body is so strong. So impossibly unrelenting, in top physical form.

I release the top button of his shirt. Then another, and another, until his lips pull back, brows raised. "Are you undressing me?"

"Yes, I think so. Please stop talking—I don't want to l-lose my courage."

A chuckle. "Yes ma'am."

Closes in for another kiss.

Tongue.

My hands.

His body.

I just want to touch it.

See it.

All of it.

Insatiably curious, I part the collar of his shirt, sliding my hands inside, over his warm skin with a moan—is that his moan or mine? Zeke has hair on his chest, a light smattering on his pectoral muscles and sternum. Black and soft, I explore it, gently running my fingers across the sparse hair.

Finish unbuttoning the shirt. Spread it wide. Push it down over his broad shoulders. He shrugs out of it, watching it land on the hardwood floor at our feet in a heap.

His heated, liquid gaze is positively on fire, and it's directed at me.

I want to see every part of him, so I break our kiss, doing a short walk around him, eyes consuming the sight of his naked upper torso. Devour his graceful collarbone. His sinewy physique.

He has ink on his back.

I've never seen such a large tattoo in person; it's big and black, engulfing his entire muscular back, beginning at each shoulder blade, spanning down his deltoids and dipping low, disappearing down into the waistband of his dark denim jeans.

My fingers ache to touch it.

When I do, hesitantly at first, he shivers. A long tremor that ripples through his entire body when I caress the fine lines inked onto this beautiful, smooth skin. He's tense, but lets me trail my fingers across his ridged shoulder blades, along the intricate lines etched into his flesh.

I love this tattoo.

It's so perfect, angry and menacing and somewhat ominous in its design.

So him.

"Is this a phoenix?" Rising from the ashes, overcoming obstacles, wrapped in a map of the world rather than flames, its talons clutching a compass. Moving forward? Traveling the world?

His head dips. His skin breaks out in gooseflesh. "Yes."

I kiss his back, trailing my lips along his skin. His shoulder blades. The contours of his spine. "What does it mean?"

"I had it done when I was pissed at my parents."

"Why?"

"Because they're always gone. Traveling."

"Always leaving?"

"Yes."

"It's beautiful."

He watches me silently over his shoulder, eyes blazing, before deciding he's had enough of my feathery touches. Twisting his body around, Zeke pulls my hands to his chest, resting them on his firm pecs.

I've never touched someone with a body like this before; I can't believe I'm touching one now. He is tan, strong, well-defined—all rippling contours and bulging muscles.

Taut, tight perfection.

His low baritone interrupts my gawking. "My turn. Let's get you out of that dress."

I try to nod when he moves to stand behind me.

Zeke's fingers are clumsy, fiddling with the button at the back of my dress. "I have no idea how to be gentle with someone so delicate." His lips hover near my ear, warm breath caressing my neck. "Bear with me."

"Y-Yes you do. You've been doing it with me for weeks."

"I have?" He nuzzles my nape as he parts the zipper.

"Yes."

Now he's lowering the zipper, fingers skimming the newly exposed skin along the way. My eyelids slide closed when he pushes my hair aside, mouth brushing the skin under my ear. His lips are warm, gentle. Teasing.

I tip my head.

His lips find the pulse at the side of my throat.

I hum.

He groans.

Arms around my waist, his giant paws hug my hips, drawing me closer and pulling my butt snugly into his erection. Hands move lower. Fingers toy with the hemline of my pretty blue dress. Raise the fabric and skim my stomach, just above the elastic band of my white underwear.

His hands glide higher, dragging the dress along with them, skimming up my abs. Ribcage. The underside of my breasts.

The cool air hits my body at the same time his erection presses into my backside, straining against me. Zeke continues kissing my neck. Sucking. Licking.

Cups both my breasts in his giant hands, sliding them one at a time into the cups of my lacey white demi-bra. There are no wires and no padding; I don't need them.

"You feel so good, Vi. Better than I thought you would."

My head tips back, hitting his shoulder and resting there. "You've thought about how I'd feel?"

"Practically every night since the day we met."

Oh ...

Oh.

Oh! His fingers graze my hard nipples, back and forth, and I tip my head back, to the side so he can kiss me. Our tongues roll as he gently strokes my chest.

His calloused palms feel amazing against my smooth flesh.

Those huge hands travel back down my figure, gripping the material of my dress. I raise my arms when he raises the dress up, over my head, relieving me of it altogether, discarding it on his desk chair.

Turns me by the shoulders to face him.

Steely gaze raking me up and down, I stand before him, self-conscious in only my sheer, lacey bra and matching panties, half tempted to cover my small breasts with my hands.

But I don't.

I don't because if I can't stand naked in front of him without covering myself up, then I shouldn't be standing naked in front of him at all.

But I know the kind of women this guy has been with. Beautiful girls with incredible bodies. Great boobs. Big boobs. Fake boobs. Perfectly coifed hair. Sexy girls with hips and lips and bikini waxes.

I have none of those things.

I don't even shave down *there*. Not really. Sometimes I do a little trimming, but that's about as good as it gets—because really, who is going to be taking any peeks downtown?

I clear my throat to redirect his gaze, off my chest and back to my eyes.

It does.

Slowly.

Up over my lower abs. Flat stomach, ribcage, and breasts. Grazes over my collarbone.

Something in his look though …

It's tender and …

Kind of stupidly *goofy*.

Smitten.

His mouth is crooked, white teeth peeking out from between his lips before he bites down on his lower lip. Sucks on it.

Uh …

I take a step backward, legs hitting the back of the bed.

Crawling across the bedspread, I find my way under the covers.

Work the straps of my bra down and off my shoulders. Pull it up over my head and fold it into a square, resting it on his nightstand. Reaching under the covers, I peel my underwear down my legs.

"I cannot fucking believe you're getting naked in my bed." Zeke sounds giddy and excited while shucking his pants, fingers frantically working the zipper, pushing them down over his lean hips. His muscular thighs. He hops on one leg, kicking and shaking the offending jeans off and across the room toward his desk.

His body is a true work of art, flawless.

The mattress dips with his weight when he crawls toward me on all fours in nothing but his tight boxers. He seeks my mouth.

Our lips meet, but not in a frantic crush.

It's more of a slow burn.

Tongue. Lips. Pressing together, spreading apart. Sucking. Delectable, wet kisses. His mouth drifts down my neck, and I recline onto his stack of pillows, fingers threading through his hair. His thick, silky hair.

Zeke's nose nuzzles the curve of my neck, running the length of skin just under my ear. I can *hear* him breathing in the smell of my hair, my perfume, my collarbone, groaning like he's losing his mind.

I raise my arms so they're above my head, watching when his flat tongue glides up the underside of my bicep, back down again, palms pushing down the black sheets I've drawn up for modesty.

Drags the sheet down my thighs.

Digs his hands under my ass and lifts my hips, dragging me toward him so I'm lying horizontally on the bed. Inches over me, rising to his knees. One leg braced on either side of me, the massive, broody boy looks down at me.

I can't imagine what he sees, watching me with those insightful eyes. Long pale hair spread out on his black pillow. My slender, willowy figure lain out beneath him. My small, sun-deprived breasts.

"You should *see* yourself, Vi. Fucking hot."

He leans down for an open-mouthed kiss, all tongue and teeth. It's sloppy and delicious, and his lips begin a slow trail over my bare flesh, across my shoulders, over the curve of my breasts. His tongue doesn't stop until it reaches my nipples. He sucks gently, his palm drifting up my torso to cup the other breast.

His boxer brief-covered erection rubs my crotch and I lift my hips toward it, the throbbing between my legs getting more unbearable by the second. He's taking his time, planting indulgent kisses on my body—*all* over my body—the scruff of his five o'clock shadow leaving tiny beard rash as a delicious parting gift.

"I want to go down on you, Pixie. I've never seen a girl with hair on her pussy and it's driving me insane—will you let me?"

I just barely manage a nod, biting down on my bottom lip when he drags his hard length along my thigh, kisses creeping lower and lower.

Belly button. Abs.

Zeke's palms spread my legs farther apart. Head lowers between my open thighs, tongue licking my bikini line. His thumbs track together up the center of my slit, spreading me apart. Tongue flicks my—"Oh *shit!*" I gasp, breathless. "Oh my god, oh my *god!*"

He raises his head. "Not even close, baby."

There is no headboard to grab on to. No bedposts. No pillow or sheet to bite down on. "Oh god Zeke … oh *god* that feels so *gooood …*"

"What is this smell?"

"I-I …"

"Do you put perfume on this shit? It's like pussy crack."

Oh god, that horrible word is turning me on.

"It … it's b-baby pow … *derrrr*," I moan. My neck thrashes on the mattress, head thrown back, lips hissing when he finally stops licking long enough to suck my clit. "Baby powder."

"This baby powder-covered sweet spot is fucking amazing," he says, burying his face and sucking hard. "Mmm …"

His hand drifts, sinking into my pelvis, applying pressure.

My toes curl.

My spine tingles.

"Yes … *yes* … right there, oh yes …" I'm loud and I don't care.

Zeke hums into me as my legs instinctively spread farther apart.

The orgasm builds, starting in my ... *e-e-everywhere* ...

The orgasm is *everywhere*, every cell inside me shot up with sparks. My nerves buzz. Quiver. Ache.

Vibrate.

I moan and moan and moan until I'm finally, "C-Coming, oh god, I'm coming ..."

Zeke

Violet comes in my mouth—*hard*—swollen clit throbbing against my tongue as I suck it to a climax. She smells so good. So fucking good I could eat her out all night, over and over again, the amount of intensity I'm feeling indescribable. Surreal.

Having her in my bed, under me.

The taste of her cum, fresh on my mouth? Delicious.

Blonde hair spread across my pillows, she's pale on every part of her body, excluding the spots where she's blushing—those are rosy, pink, and ten different shades of peach.

The contrast of her porcelain flesh against my black bed sheets is stark; she looks like an angel lying here.

A pretty angel I want to stick my dick in and fuck.

I rise to my knees. Bend my head to suck on one of her tits, earning me a moan so throaty it gives me pause. Lips puffy from my mouth, eyes glazed over from her orgasm, I flick her nipple with my tongue and blow, the cool air making it pucker, stiff as my swollen cock.

She watches me stroke it, the widest eyes I've ever seen. I move to retrieve a condom from the bedside table.

I fucking hate these things.

Nonetheless, I tear it open, toss the wrapper over my shoulder, and slide that motherfucker on, teeth dragging across my bottom lip.

Her hazel eyes are glassed over and she nods, arching her back and rubbing her small breasts against my chest.

"Once we do this, you can't go back." *This is me you're about to sleep with,* I want to add. *Not some sensitive dude who's going to lavish affection on you afterward.* I sure as shit am not a cuddler.

"Stop talking," she demands. "Stop talking and *screw* me already."

Whoa. Holy shit.

"Do you like dirty talk, Violet?"

"I don't know," she blushes. "Say something dirty."

I hesitate and look down at her. Her giant hazel eyes regard me, so soft and pretty as my dick rubs against her slit, that halo of wholesomeness surrounding her head giving me pause.

Words lodge in my throat that won't come out.

Say something dirty, say something dirty, say something dirty ...

Shit, what the hell is wrong with me? Why aren't my lips moving?

"Zeke?"

Her hips wiggle beneath me, causing friction against my straining cock.

I'll give it to her dirty, all right, just not ...

Yet.

Not yet.

This is the first girl I've felt anything for, if you don't include the anger I feel toward my mother, and I don't want to ruin it by spewing any nasty shit.

What we're about to do feels so right and *wrong* at the same damn time, and yet here we are, about to cross this finish line. One I swore I would never cross, lest someone expect things I don't know *how* to give.

Violet stares up at me now, trusting. Aroused. Sated.

Sexy.

Ready.

I hover above her, bracing my forearms on the pillows. Slide forward. I'm going to push my dick forward and fuck her like the NCAA champion I am.

Skin against skin. Cock against clit.

219

I reach down and give it a few short strokes, run my hand down her hip. Between her legs.

She's wet, the soft curls between her legs making me harder than I was before. Jesus, the fucking curls—I haven't fucked anyone with hair on their pussy in years. It's a harsh reminder of how inexperienced she is.

I spread her with my thumb, rubbing my latex-covered cock up and down the slit in her pussy, pressing forward tentatively. I slide in a fraction at a time, a slow building moan rising inside my chest.

A test in self-control.

This slow burn is killing me; I want to plow into her so damn bad, it's physically painful.

She's so tight.

"You're not going to break me, Zeke. J-Just *do* it already."

I shake my head, sweat beading on my brow.

No.

No, I'm not just going to *do it already*.

Determined to take my time, I inhale a breath, counting like we do in wrestling. Counting like I do when I'm lifting. Counting like I do when—

"Don't move, *please*," I demand into her pouty pink mouth. "Please. Jesus, baby, don't move."

If she moves, I swear to God I will lose my shit and blow my load before I'm even all the way inside.

My lean hips push forward, instinctively wanting to thrust. And thrust, and thrust the *shit* out of her. I want to bang her into the headboard and *god this is torture*.

"Uhhh," Violet purrs, oblivious to my inner dialogue.

"You're only enjoying this because I haven't plowed you yet," I pant.

"Say that again," she moans.

"You want me to plow you, baby?"

"Oh you feel so *good* ..." Christ, she's moaning so loud and it's just the *tip*.

Her hands wander over my back, skimming and drifting over my taut muscles. Over my deltoids and down my spine toward my ass.

She needs to stop.

"You are going to come so hard when I'm inside you, I promise." I breathe into her ear. "But slow down Violet."

I'm so fucking afraid to hurt her.

"I can't! It feels ..."

"I know, I know," I chant into her hair, her gorgeous snowy hair.

My arms shake from their balancing act on either side of her head; not wanting to crush her under my weight, my dick presses into her slick heat. One inch. Then another, grinding my pelvis into hers. Not pushing, not thrusting—just grinding. The friction? Fucking combustible.

Violet gasps so loud I feel it in my cock and down to my toes.

Groaning, I slide my hand down her hip and under her ass. Spread flat, my palm slips under her butt cheeks, fingers finding their way to her crack, pulling me deeper inside her.

"Oh fuck," I blurt out because it feels so good my eyes roll back into my head.

My nostrils flare, and I inhale. Exhale.

"I-It's ... That ..." Violet breathes heavily, groaning. "That feels so ..."

"Say it feels good," I beg, needing to thrust. Pump into her. Something. *Anything.* "Please, baby, say it."

Her head tips back and I lick her throat. Suck and fuck. Bite on her earlobe.

Violet's hands snake down my lower back, grasping my ass. She squeezes. Tugs. "It feels amazing, amazing. If I spread my legs will it—"

I don't hear her finish her sentence; all I hear is *spread my legs, spread my legs, spread my legs* and I'm gone. I *feel* her spreading those fucking legs apart. Those porcelain, creamy white thighs I'm snuggly positioned between.

My dick pulses. Throbs.

"Did it just get *bigger*?" Her eyes are wide as saucers.

"*Yeah* it motherfuckin' did." I grind out through clenched teeth, unable to stop the dirty talk. "Do you like that?"

"Yes ..." Her mouth forms a tiny O, lips parting. "Yes, I-I love it."

I grind and grind my pelvis into her, my balls and her pussy pressed together so tight there's no room for even a finger to slide in.

"I need to fuck you, Pix, I have to ..."

I'm begging now, wanting to rail hard, no shame.

None.

"*Please*, Violet, fuck, please let me fuck you hard."

"Yes. *Yes*! Do it Zeke, *Zeke*, this is driving me crazy."

I pull out slow.

Thrust in fast.

Pull out slow.

Lips clamped shut, the anticipation and steady build are far more intoxicating than the quick, fast fucks I'm used to giving to nameless, faceless co-eds.

She's so blessedly tight. I'm not a religious man, but Jesus, she's so tight I throw up a prayer thanking my maker; I could die inside her and be in heaven.

The telltale sign of my balls tightening has me tensing up.

Oh shit, I'm going to come.

Shit, fuck, shit.

It's only been five fucking minutes, tops.

"Oh Christ," I curse. "Shit."

"Wha ...?" Violet is dazed, still holding on while I jerk my load inside the condom. "What was that?"

Oh my god.

My sweaty forehead hits the pillow over her shoulder. "My orgasm," I mumble into the mattress.

"You *came?*"

I grunt.

"Already?"

Seriously, does she have to say it out loud? It's emasculating.

"*Yes.*"

I don't wait around to make small talk.

Pulling out of her, I climb off, throw back the covers to hit the john, and toss the condom. Wash my hands.

Return to the bedroom and slide into bed, pulling the black sheets over us. Rest my arms behind my head while Violet watches me, uncertainly, from her side of the bed.

"Come here," I tell her, dragging her flush into my body so she can lean into me, resting her head on my shoulder. Reaching over, I stroke the silky strands of her blonde hair, letting the locks fall through my fingers.

Tentatively, she lays a hand on my chest, fingering the dark hair between my pecs, face tipped toward mine.

I kiss her nose.

"Are you sore?"

She wiggles her legs beneath the blankets, rubbing her knees together. "I don't think so? Maybe."

"I heard sometimes when it's rough, it burns when you pee afterward."

Why the hell did I just say that? Since when do I blurt out random shit? My body needs to do me a favor and chill itself the fuck out now that it dumped its load in under five minutes.

Vi doesn't reply, only traces my right nipple with the tip of her index finger, round and a round, in small circles. I know she's not doing it to be suggestive, so I take a few deep breaths, body beginning a slow buzz. Every little touch a spark to ignite me.

I fiddle with the single bracelet circling her wrist—the sunflower charm catching the light from my desk lamp.

She clears her throat delicately. "So, do you normally ... *you know* ... so fast?"

I grimace. "If you're asking if I normally *come* so soon, the answer is no."

She hums, finger moving from my pec to my clavicle, slowly dragging it along my skin.

"Did it hurt?" I find myself asking.

"A little, but it felt good, too. Real good." Her pretty face buries itself in my armpit, embarrassed. "It's been a while."

"How long?"

"I don't know."

"Come on, girls always know shit like this. You probably know down to the *day*."

"All right, fine. It's been fourteen months, ish."

"Fourteen months? That's over a year."

Wow. That sounded smart.

I plant a wet kiss on her parted lips, slipping my tongue inside, wanting to devour every inch of her.

"Is that a goodbye kiss? Is this the part of the program where you ask me to leave? Is that what usually happens with you? You kick people out after you've slept with them?"

She fires off a litany of questions, the answer to each one of them *yes*.

I try to make light of a conversation I don't want to have. "Yeah. It's what I would normally do."

"Do you want me to leave?"

I'm quiet then, because the actual truth is, while I was in the bathroom before, I considered how this would end for us if I kicked her out.

Thought about it while I was tossing the condom in the trash. Thought about how I could use a good night's sleep, alone in my own bed—considered it in the least douchey way possible.

But then I'd taken a long look at myself in the mirror, a good *hard* look at my reflection. The gray, lifeless eyes that normally stared back at me weren't lifeless at all; they were sparkling, which is the best goddamn way I can describe it without sounding cheesy.

And there was a fucking smile on my face. An actual smile, with teeth and everything—and that has to count for something, right?

So, like a good little boy scout, I pulled back the quilt and slipped back into bed beside her. Pulled her body close and thanked fuck she was still naked so I could fondle her tits without having to do it under her shirt.

"No, don't leave. I want you to stay."

Something—or someone—wakes me in the dead of the night.

A warm slumbering body pressed into my back. A willowy arm thrown across my waist, resting on my hip. A nose buried in the crux of my neck.

I scoot, giving myself room, then roll to my back.

Roll to face her.

Violet stirs, arm falling to the mattress.

The moon is bright outside my window, casting enough light into the room that I can study her sleeping form. She's so serene. Stroking the flat of my palm down the smooth skin of her shoulder, I skim it down her bicep.

Catch a satin blonde lock of hair between my fingertips, rubbing it, the silk fanning out on my pillow. No shame, I lean in, obsessed with the smell of her. Clean. Sweet.

Unassumingly sexy.

I scoot closer, head on my pillow, watching her doze.

Learn the contours of her face in the bright moonlight. The curve of her cheekbones and the bow of her lips.

Slowly, her eyes flutter open.

We regard each other, her lids heavy, eyes searching my face.

Wordlessly, the tips of her fingers extend to trace my heavy brow, down the bridge of my busted up nose. Trail along my cheekbone, thumb smoothing over my crow's feet.

I kiss the tip of her finger when it glides over my lips.

"I've always thought your eyes were incredible." Her husky voice is quiet, whispering, heavy with sleep. Has my black heart skipping a beat. Heat rises in my chest as she lavishes attention on me in the dark. "They're the best part of you."

"No. They're not," I whisper back, her fingers still bestowing tingles on my skin.

"They're not?"

"No." *Not even close.* "The best part of me is *you*, Violet."

Violet stills, her hand dropping to my chest. My pecs. Covering my heart, leaving tremors in its wake. "That's the nicest thing anyone has *ever* said to me."

"Then you've been hanging around a bunch of fucking idiots."

My dick twitches, jerking to life when she edges near—so near, her bare, naked skin presses against mine. Hand presses my shoulder blade forcefully, easing me onto the mattress until I'm flat on my back.

She lifts one leg, straddling me.

"Say something dirty." Her mouth finds mine. "Real dirty."

Oh Jesus Christ.

I grasp her lean hips, running my large hands along her thighs, the raging hard-on between my legs fucking with my head. "I don't know what to say."

"That's it? That's the best you've got?"

"No, but …" I inhale a sharp breath when her ass crack rubs my cock. "I don't want to be a pig."

Violet leans down, leaning in, her long hair dusting my chest. Tickling. Teasing. Her tongue flicks my earlobe.

"But I like it."

Her pussy is so close to my cock. So close. All I have to do is lift her, move her two inches to bury myself inside her.

I groan.

"T-Tell me what you want to do to me," she whispers in the shell of my ear. "I love your body, Zeke. I love how it feels naked, how big and strong. Your …"

"Giant cock?" I supply.

"Yes." She reaches behind her to latch on, giving it a few tugs. "It's so soft."

"I want you to fucking *ride* it. Climb on and fuck me, Violet."

She braces her arms on the headboard, placing her palms on the wall behind the bed. Lifts her rear and hovers above my thick boner.

My leg practically spasms from the anticipation as I brace her hips in my hands to steady her. Hold my fucking breath like an amateur when she sinks herself down, tilting her hips so it glides in almost effortlessly.

"Mother*fucker* that feels good … oh god, fuck." I utter out a string of curses when she slowly gyrates her hips, using the headboard as an anchor.

"Oh my *god* your dick feels good." Violet moans, rocking her hips on top of me.

"Jesus that was sexy." I give her ass a little slap. Reach with my mouth to suck one of her nipples into my mouth.

"I'm going to come if you do that," she warns me, arching her back and sitting up. Releasing the wall and leaning back, rocking and rocking and rocking her hips until my dick fucking throbs, hard.

On the other side of the room, someone bangs on the wall, three warning thumps.

Violet pauses, biting her lip.

Still grasping her hips, I push and pull her along my cock, the give and take working her pussy and, "Mmm, oh … uh … I'm trying to be quiet but I *can'ttttt* …" she whines.

Violet is a talker.

A dirty little talker.

"Fuck me, oh god Zeke …"

I jerk my hips.

"Oh! Ooohhhhhhh … yeah … I'm dying, I swear …"

"That's right Violet, fuck me, fuck it. You wanna get spanked?"

Her head lolls back and she gasps when I give her ass another tap. "Yeah spank me."

A loud thump interrupts.

"NO! SHUT THE FUCK UP! Some of us are trying to sleep!" More banging and Oz shouting from the other side of the wall. "No one is spanking anyone! GO THE FUCK TO SLEEP!"

A laugh brews, welling inside, beginning in my abs, working its way up and out of my mouth. Laughing while I impale her. I can't stop it.

Violet halts riding my dick to stare down at me.

"Why are you stopping?" I pull at her hips, tugging insatiably. I thrust up, greedy. "Keep going."

"Oh my god, Zeke, you're laughing." She leans down to press a kiss to my lips. "That was so sexy. You're so sexy."

My mouth latches on and I brush the hair out of her face to get a look at her beautiful eyes. Mouth. Lips. Nose. Chin. "You're fuckin sexy." Kiss. "Beautiful."

"I love this body, so much …" Her hands smooth along the planes of my pecs. Pinch my nipples. "I could stay here all night."

"Let's have a fuck fest all weekend."

The telltale sign of her pussy tightening has my eyes rolling to the back of my head. Clenching my cock. *Fuck it feels good, fuck it feels good, fuck it feels good …*

"Oh god Zeke, I'm gonna come, I-I'm gonna … I'm …"

Why does this feel so good? *Why* does this feel so good, *why* …

Violet's head tips back, mouth falling open when we come together—and I come hard.

Groan.

Groan so loud Oz starts thumping on the wall, banging loudly.

But the sound only makes me come harder.

#DOUCHEBAG

"What baked goods say,
Thanks for being a great tutor.
Let's have sex?"

Violet

"Those are some slick sneaks, Kyle."

It's Thursday and we're walking into the city's children's museum—Zeke, Summer, Kyle, and I— since the weather is too frigid for the park. The kids are skipping along when I notice Kyle's brand new shoes. I mean, the kid couldn't make it any more obvious, kicking his heels up every ten feet, stomping around noisily, bending to tie them near every bench.

He stops to tie them now for the third time since we've been here. "Zeke got 'em for me. I won a bet."

"You won a *bet*?" Whirling to him, I ask, "Dear lord, what kind of bets are you making with an eleven-year-old that require you to buy him new tennis shoes?"

He shrugs. "The normal kind."

"I beat him at hoops," Kyle brags, sprinting ahead to show off, jumping in the air and dunking an invisible basketball. His brand new navy and gray sneakers are high end and the latest style.

"The normal kind?" I turn toward Zeke, skeptically. "Is that so?"

I stop to tap the toe of my brown half boot on the marble floor impatiently.

"What's the big deal?" Zeke asks when both kids are out of earshot, studying a demonstration of weather patterns. I can see Summer pressing down on a lever, the display box in front of them flickering, lightning illuminating the exhibit.

"He needed new shoes."

"The big deal, Zeke, is those shoes are *expensive*. What if he had lost the bet?"

231

"You're so fucking cute." Zeke laughs, snorting through his nose. He grabs my hand and pulls me along. "He wasn't going to lose."

My brow furrows. "What do you mean, he wasn't going to lose?"

"Exactly what I'm saying. He wasn't going to lose the bet. The kid needed new shoes, his mom can't afford, he won the bet, end of story."

When he gives my hands a little squeeze, I yank his hand back, stopping us both in our tracks.

"Zeke Daniels. You big softie."

He laughs, beautiful mouth smiling, gently tugging me along. "Whatever, Pixie Dust, keep walking."

But I'm not giving up so easily. "Don't try to change the subject. I want you to admit you're not such a hard ass."

"Hard ass? You cursing today, Vi?"

"Knock it off! Don't change the subject!"

He heaves a hefty sigh, sounding put out. "All right. Maybe on occasion, I help people out."

"Why?"

"What do you mean, why? You just asked and I told you."

"I heard you, but if you like helping people, why do you always seem so, I don't know … pissed?"

"Long, drawn-out story you don't want to know."

"Of course I want to know—I want to get to know you, Zeke, especially if we're going to, you know …"

"Have fuck fest sex?"

I feel my cheeks burning. "Yes."

"There are a lot of things I want, too, Violet, but I don't bring them up just to make conversation." He looks off into the distance, at Kyle and Summer, squinting.

"Well I *want* a relationship," I announce loudly. "But I wouldn't want things to be awkward between us if you don't."

He stops in his tracks, my whole body lurching with the sudden inertia, regarding me warily.

"Violet …"

"No. I want to talk about this." I refuse to let him sidestep the conversation and tug his hand. "What are you like when you're in a relationship?"

His nose scrunches up and glances down like I've lost my mind, steely eyes skeptical. "I've never been in one. What about you?"

My chest swells, excited that he's cooperating and that we're talking.

"One or two. Nothing serious, obviously. Zeke, I … I-I can't sleep with you and spend *time* with you and not catch feelings."

"What do you mean, catch feelings?"

"The more we're together, the more I like you. Have you heard the phrase 'peeling back the layers'? You know, like an onion. I feel like I'm finally starting to see what's under that cool demeanor of yours, one layer at a time—and I'm starting to like the layers."

He grunts, still holding my hand. "Are you making it sound like a *bad* thing?"

"Do I have to spell it out for you?"

"Please." Zeke's nostrils flare.

"I'm just worried about myself. I've … been alone a long time if you don't count Mel and Winnie, and I've never depended on anyone to … gosh, th-this is going to sound really stupid."

"Violet, spit it out."

I take a deep breath and continue, releasing his hand to splay mine wide in front of me. "I-I basically raised myself. It's true that I lived in some really nice places—and some bad ones—but that's not the same as having security, or having my parents back."

I glance up, Summer and Kyle busy conducting electricity from a large round orb to their hair, which is now standing on end.

Cuties.

"Zeke, when we met, I didn't think you and I were going to get along. I was afraid of you—that's why I ditched our first appointment—but now I'm just afraid to like you. You're not the worst."

His large hand grapples for mine. Squeezes. "You're not the worst, either, Pix."

I give him a coy smile. "I know you like me, Zeke."

He rolls his eyes. "Obviously."

I yank his hand again so he looks as me. "No. I know you *like* me."

We regard one another in the dim lights of the museum, wordlessly sizing each other up. His cool gaze rakes me up and down, still holding my hand, a sliver of white from his perfectly straight teeth peeking through his lips.

He's smiling. "Prove it."

I narrow my eyes, biting back my silly grin. "*You* prove it."

"I thought I already did. I'm here, aren't I? Do you think I'd be caught dead in a fucking *kid's* museum if I didn't *like* you?" He says it low, dragging me against his body, angling my chin up with the tips of his fingers. Brushing his mouth against my lips.

Kisses me once before releasing me.

It's not exactly a declaration of love, not by a long shot.

But right now?

It's enough.

Zeke: *When you're done dropping Summer off at her mom's, you wanna study tonight at my place?*

Violet: *Will you be feeding me? I'm starving.*

Zeke: *Pizza?*

Violet: *Sounds delicious. No onion?*

Zeke: *Got it, no onion. My place at 8?*

Violet: *Your place at 8*

Zeke: *You need me to come grab you?*

Violet: *I can drive over, no biggie :)*

Zeke: *You sure? I can come get you.*

Violet: *It sounds like you WANT to come get me ...*

Zeke: *Shit. Here I thought I was being sneaky. And Violet?*

Violet: *Yeah?*

Zeke: *Bring a toothbrush.*

Zeke

"What do you suppose Elliot and Oz think of me being here?" Violet is lying across my bed, textbooks and laptop spread out in front of her.

"Who knows."

She considers this, pretty brow contorted. "It's just, Oz kept gawking at me in the kitchen when we were eating. Like I was an oddity."

"He's odd all right."

Violet rolls her eyes. "That's not what I meant. You would think your roommates haven't seen a girl in the kitchen. The whole thing was all kinds of weird. N-No offense."

"Oh trust me, none taken. Oz is a freak. Don't think I didn't catch him smiling at you like a big, dumb idiot."

I don't explain to Violet that the reason my roommates were acting like they've never seen a girl in the kitchen with me before is because they haven't. They've seen girls stumbling drunk down the hallway to my bedroom. They've heard girls mid-coitus through our thin walls. But they've never seen me *hanging out* with one.

Technically, this is Violet's third time here.

And technically, they did hear us mid-coitus through our thin walls.

But now I've started *feeding* her. My roommates watched me get plates and napkins and fucking cut her a slice of damn pizza—making meowing and whip-cracking sounds from the living room the whole time.

Ha fucking *ha*.

And when Oz and Elliot walked in to steal a few slices? They were elbowing each other in the ribcage like two juveniles and

236

giggling. Oz took it a step further when he coughed, "pussy whipped" into his hand not once, but four times.

Total and complete fucking morons. Kyle has more maturity than the two of them combined.

Vi chews the end of her pen. "They're goofy. What's Elliot's story?"

"Elliot's story?" I shrug, taking my iPod out of its sleeve and tossing it on the bed next to her. "Actually, he's a decent guy. Keeps to himself a lot, studies in his room. Doesn't go out much, kind of a loner, but not in a bad way. He has goals and is pretty tunnel-visioned."

"He sounds like my usual type." She laughs, eyes twinkling mischievously.

"Your type?" I narrow my eyes, moving toward the bed. "What is your type?"

"You know, serious. Quiet. Studious."

"Your type is boring."

She flops down on her back, long, wavy blonde hair fanning out over my bedspread. "Yes, probably."

"Well *I* can be quiet."

"Sometimes."

"And I can be serious." What am I doing? I have nothing to prove.

"Sometimes you're too serious, don't you think?"

"I'm studious."

"I know you *try* to be."

"That wasn't a nice thing to say," I chide flirtatiously, palms hitting the mattress and brushing the books and laptop and iPad out of my way. "If I had feelings, you might have bruised one of them."

I crawl up the bed, over the mattress, up her body, nudging her hair aside with my nose, lips brushing her ear. "You shouldn't tease me, it isn't nice."

"It got you over here, didn't it?"

I rear back, surprised. "Pixie, are you flirting with me?"

"Not on purpose." She licks her lips, and I lower my head to place a light kiss on her mouth, arms braced on either side of her head. "Yes."

My pecs graze her chest.

I drop my pelvis, the thickening erection between my legs brushing the apex between her thighs.

Kiss her jawline, from the tender spot below her ear to her chin … down the porcelain skin on her neck. Use my index finger to pull back the cotton of her t-shirt, leaving warm kisses in my wake. Pepper kisses on her collarbone. Glide my tongue down the vale of her breasts.

She sighs into my thick hair, fingernails stroking my scalp.

I let my hands wander.

Down the thin shirt better fit for my bedroom floor. Over her denim-clad hips. Across the belt loops of her jeans. Up and down her metal zipper.

She sighs again, her hot little palms running the length of my wide shoulder blades, fingertips pressing into each muscle. Branding them with her hot touch, learning every cord.

Our open mouths meet again in an unhurried dance—so fucking deliberate and intentional and *smooth* …

I'm dragging my tongue across her lips. It's sloppy, but the little shocks zipping up my spine have me shivering, dick stiffening in my pants.

My brows furrow from the friction, pained. From her tongue. Her smell, sounds, and gentle caresses.

I glide my hand under her t-shirt along her ribcage, cupping her right breast without preamble. She's wearing one of those little lacey bras again, the kind without wires or padding or pretense.

Just tits and lace.

I keep pushing the shirt up until together, we get it off and over her head.

The bra is lavender.

Violet.

Soft purple.

Delicate see-through lace just covering her nipples.

I can feel my pupils dilating at the sight of her small tits in the sexy miniscule bra that leaves nothing to the imagination. Her boobs might not be enough to fill the palm of my large hand, but they're perfect.

They're her.

I drag a strap across her shoulder, pushing the cup aside. Kiss my way down the side of her neck, dragging my nose against her skin. Lick and flick her peachy nipple, hand stroking the underside gently, teasing while I blow the wet tip. It's hard and just begging to be sucked.

My lips comply and latch on. Gently I draw it into my hot mouth, sucking.

"Oh *god*," she moans, fingernails digging into my shoulders. My scalp. "Ohhhh …"

I release the nipple, kiss the underside where my hand was, then lavish attention to the other one. Kiss up her bare shoulder, up the curve of her neck.

I nip and suck the entire way.

"Take your shirt off," she instructs. "I want to feel your skin."

I lean back, kneeling above her, yanking my shirt over my head then throwing it on the ground. Drag my naked torso up her body, firm pecs against her soft tits, the sensation indescribable.

Fucking amazing.

Fucking hot.

Fucking heaven.

She looks like a goddamn angel.

My fingers fiddle with the snap on her jeans, working the button free. Drag down the zipper, its metal teeth making the only sound in the room besides our heavy breathing.

Run my flattened palm over her stomach, dipping into the waistband of her underwear.

Her granny panties.

I chuckle; she's so fucking cute.

The differences between us are astounding; I almost pause to list them all, but abort when Violet shifts her hips to redirect my hand, squirming.

"You like that?" My voice is gruff, dirty thoughts taking root in my dirty mind.

"You feel so good." She gasps. "Your *hands* are *incredible* …"

Women have said this before, moaned into the air about how good I'm making them feel, but this is different. Nothing about Violet is rehearsed or dramatic. Everything is genuine.

So when she whispers that my hands are *incredible*, my chest swells with pleasure. Satisfaction and pride.

Lust.

I lick her earlobe. "You should see the things these hands can do. Want me to show you?"

A quick, fervent nod and another hum. "Mmm*hmm*."

We shuck our jeans enthusiastically, lying on top of the bed in nothing but our underwear.

Resting my head on her shoulder, I kiss the side of her neck, letting my flat, open palm float up her semi-nude figure, leaving a ripple of goose bumps in its wake across her skin. Beginning at her calf, my hand is so big it easily encircles her entire leg, flattening when I reach her knee.

Spans her thigh, stroking it leisurely. My thumb finds its way into the elastic band of her underwear, trailing up the leg hole toward her lean hips. Glides across her stomach, her abs, forefinger tracing around her belly button in slow steady loops.

She watches my hand the entire time, sucking in a breath when I walk my middle and index fingers up her delicate sternum.

Violet turns her face just then, our eyes connecting as I continue tenderly stroking her skin. Along the swell of her breasts, then down the smooth expanse of her shoulders. When I reach her wrist, our fingers entwine.

I kiss her nose.

She kisses mine.

I breathe her in—breathe in everything about this girl—from her scented shampoo to the smell of her clean, flawless skin.

They say not to judge a person by their appearances because looks can be deceiving, but there is nothing deceiving about this girl.

She is everything on the inside that she appears to be on the outside. Sweet. Compassionate. Kind. And beautiful—heart, body, and mind.

Violet DeLuca is my opposite in every sense of the word.

My finger travels the curve of her brow, trailing along to her temple. When her mouth tips into a shy smile and that pretty pink top lip bites down on the bottom … it's *agony*.

My eyes squeeze closed when I kiss her, dark brows creasing in concentration. I don't dare open them again.

Every part of me tingles during this kiss. The sensations are ones I won't surely forget any time soon, ones I can't even describe without sounding like a fucking pansy.

Shit, I already do sound like one.

Violet rolls into me, our fronts pressed together, perfectly aligned until I shift, my stiff dick snuggly tucked between her legs. Right where it fucking should be.

I wrap my arms around her, hands running down her spine, down her ass, squeezing both cheeks and pulling her toward me, the pressure in my balls so fucking satisfying, I groan.

Her hips gyrate slightly when my thumb hooks her underwear, dragging them down. She gropes at mine with fumbling fingers.

Together, we kick off our underwear, and, "Oh god, naked feels so good," she moans, tossing her head back when I suck on her neck. Drag my tongue down to her nipples and suck on those, too.

Her hand tentatively reaches between us and grabs my cock. Wraps around it tight, up and down. Up … and … down.

I stop moving. Stop breathing.

Hold my intake of breath, anticipation damn near killing me as my eyes roll to the back of my head from her enthusiastic ministrations.

"Yeah, stroke it," I groan into her hair, wanting to fist it but afraid I'll hurt her. "Shit."

"Am I doing this right?" Her hazel eyes are glassy, lips pink and pouty.

"God yes. All you have to do is touch me and I'd get off."

As she jerks my giant hard-on, I count to ten, not wanting to blow my load in her hand. I want to blow it inside her.

"Violet?"

She lifts her eyes.

"Bare back?"

We didn't use a condom last time and I never want to use them with her again.

Her mouth forms an O with a nod. "I'm on the pill."

I reach for her hips. Her lips.

Our mouths fuse like two lovers solely surviving on kisses. Wet. Sloppy. Exciting.

I reach between her legs, fingers dragging along her part.

Her head hits the bedspread, hair fanned out.

I lean down and cover her mouth with mine, drowning out her surprised yelp when my dick is buried to the hilt. A perfect fit. So fucking snug. Tight.

Using my muscular thighs, I slowly pump into her. Clench my ass cheeks from the effort. Violet's eyes soften, lids heavy. Mouth parts. Head tips back against the pillow.

Yeah, that's it Violet.

"Give in to the cock, baby."

My pelvis rocks, fueled by the sight of her aroused gaze.

I cannot stop kissing her lips.

Her pink, perfect lips.

This isn't a quick fuck; this is a slow sizzle, the build up crazy fucking good and *I can't even come up with the words.*

We barely make any noise; soft sighs and low, drawn-out moans are the only sounds filling my room, the bed scooting across the hardwood floor on its metal castors with every tender but forceful thrust.

I suck on her neck when my left hand digs under her ass to pull her in, binding us closer. Making me crazy.

God I love fucking. "Violet."

I love fucking *her*. "Violet."

She's so fucking sweet. "Violet."

I lick and suck and kiss her into a frenzy, her head lolling from side to side, mouth gaping open, arms thrown over her head.

"Does that hurt?" I demand, grinding her pelvis into my mattress. "Am I being too rough?"

A tortured whine. "N-Nooo, god no, it's perfect …"

"You fucking like it, don't you?"

"Y-Yesssss …" She's whining, hips raising, pelvis rolling. "God, yes."

Sweet, pretty little Violet doesn't mind a little dirty talk with her fucking.

"Say my fucking name."

Her glassy hazel gaze stares into me before her lips smirk, lust drunk. "Say *mine*."

"Violet."

"Ezekiel," she moans, stroking my cheeks. "*Zeke*."

They say you can spout off some crazy shit when you're in the middle of fucking, and I gasp out the words, "Where have you been all my life?" before I can stop them. They roll off my tongue like a plea, no taking them back.

Judging by the way her eyes soften, she's not hating them.

"Where the hell have you been?" I pant, pumping my hips, wishing I would just shut the fuck up already.

My sweaty forehead hits her shoulders and my hips pause.

"Oh fuck baby ... Violet ..." I thrust into her again, and again, so hard the headboard hits the wall with a satisfying bang. The lamp shakes. "Pix, I love being with you so much I don't know what's wrong with me."

I stop pumping. Stop thrusting.

Literally stop, mid fuck.

She strokes my hair as I lie still inside her, my dick pressed against her clit, all this honestly bullshit making it impossible for me to move.

Violet tests my resolves, squirming beneath me.

"I cannot stop thinking about you, Violet," I blurt out with a moan; she feels so goddamn good around me, so goddamn good. "I can't stop, I'm s-sorry."

Violet tips her head back, column of her neck exposed. "Now you're the one stuttering. You sound like me."

"God Violet, you're so ..." I drag my hand up her body, covering her breast, squeezing it gently. Pinching the nipple.

Endorphins are majorly fucking up my shit.

"I'm crazy about you." Shut the fuck up Zeke.

Stop talking and *fuck. Her. Already.*

"There is no one in my life like you, Violet. I ... I ..."

Don't say it.

Don't you dare fucking say it, you douchebag.

I gulp.

She stares up at me, half-lidded the way my friends look when they're stoned, waiting for the next words out of my mouth, fingers stroking my back.

"You ... what?" Her breathless whisper prompts me gently. "What do you want to say?"

I'm way too aware of her body beneath mine.

I don't trust myself to speak, so I cover her mouth with mine, putting all those unspoken words into that kiss. All the words I shouldn't or can't say. Pull back, balance myself on my elbows, and slowly pull in and out of her, my gray eyes meeting hers.

Powerful.

Intoxicating.

Exciting.

So intense that when we come, together, at the same damn time, Violet's low, pleading moans match mine.

Sebastian was right about one thing: the more time I spend with Violet, the deeper I fall, the more I lose my grip on reality.

#DOUCHEBAG

"I woke up next to her with an oven mitt taped to my cock. Dear god, I must have tried using it as a condom."

Zeke

"**Y**ou wanted to see me, Coach?"
I give the doorjamb of his office a few short
raps with my knuckles.

"Daniels, take a seat."

I enter the office, walking the few short steps to a chair, settling myself there. Spread my legs to get comfortable. Adjust the
brim of my Iowa baseball cap.

"So." Coach leans back in his seat, steepling his fingers and
leaning back to study me. "Tell me how it's been going."

My lips press together, my knee-jerk reaction to mumble
something evasive. But then, "It's been good."

He stares me down, letting silence fill the room—something
I've seen him do to guys a million times before. He's like a detec-
tive, using the tactic to pry information out of people, hoping
they'll want to fill the silence by talking.

It works on most people. But me?

I am not most people.

"Yeah, I'd heard that. Quite honestly, I'm surprised."

I raise my brows.

Coach leans back farther in his chair until the wooden legs
creak so loud I'm actually afraid the damn chair is going to snap in
half. Neither one of us wants to relent, but he's the one who called
me in here.

"Tell me more about your Little Brother, Kris."

"Kyle."

"Kyle then. Tell me more about him."

The question gives me pause, and I discover I actually know
the answer. I surprise us *both* when I say, "He is … a really quick,
uh, learner. He loves sports but his family doesn't have a lot of

247

money so he can't play at school. So, uh, I've been taking him and we've been brushing up on his basketball skills."

"Basketball?"

"Yes, sir."

"Why not wrestling?"

"I don't know, sir. I don't really want to push him into anything he doesn't seem interested in." I clear my throat. "He, uh ..." Jesus this is awkward. I'm singing like a damn canary. "We do his homework. He's a real freak about his grades."

Coach stares blankly, unimpressed by my choice of words.

"What I meant to say is, he's very vigilant about his grades. He starts middle school next year and wants to stay on top of things, especially math."

"You've been helping him with his homework?"

"Yes, sir."

He nods his approval.

Picks up a pencil, taps his desk a few times before tossing it aside. "Tell me about your girlfriend. She seems like a nice girl."

Girlfriend.

I have a suspicion he used that particular word on purpose, to get a reaction out of me.

Stiffly, I nod.

"Violet? We're just friends."

Friends who have slow-burning sex and spend a shit load of time together, sometimes doing nothing but lying around holding hands.

Yeah. Those kinds of friends.

"Does she know that?"

"Yeah she knows that."

"Do *you*?"

My lips press in a straight line when Coach's eyes roam my face.

"Why are you just friends?"

"What do you mean?"

"I mean, why are you just friends. Why isn't she your girl-friend? And don't give me the same bullshit excuse everyone else gives about time and practice. What's the *real* reason she's not your girlfriend?"

"Sir, with all due respect, is that the reason you called me in here? I don't see how this is any of your business."

He laughs, the old fuck, chuckling and coughing while I scowl. "It's my business because your personal life affects the team. When you're happy, your performance is better, dipshit."

Is it?

"You've been a real prick in the past, but since the fundraiser and those kids and that girl ..." He pushes a paperweight to the corner of his desk. "I'll admit you've been easier to handle."

I consider this; I guess it's true I haven't gotten into any arguments with anyone on the team since I started the Big Brothers program.

"Son, I'm going to ask you another personal question. You don't have to answer, but I want you to give my words some real consideration. Will you do that for me?"

What can I do but nod? I'm his captive audience.

He steeples his fingers again, resting his pointy, wrinkled elbows on the desk and leaning forward.

"Now, I don't want to sound preachy, but that little gal you're spending time with has had a difficult life. Anyone can see that. She worked tremendously hard to get to where she's at with all the hurdles she had to face."

How the fuck does he know all this?

"The last thing she needs is someone with a chip on his shoulder fucking it all up." Coach coughs into his closed fist. "I'm not telling you to break up with her, but I do want to tell you this: share your burdens with her, but don't weigh her down with them. I know you have a lot of anger because of your folks, but Zeke, you're a grown man. It's time to let that shit go.

SARA NEY

"More importantly"—his beady blue eyes pin me to the chair—"maybe it's time to relieve someone else of their burdens instead of worrying so much about your own."

I can't believe all the sensitive bullshit coming out of Coach's mouth; this is a man I've seen reduce grown men to tears, and now he's doling our relationship advice like he's ... like he's fucking Dr. Phil.

"Give it some thought," he concludes. "And close the door on your way out."

"Hey Zeke." Rex Gunderson, our team manager, nudges me in the arm with his boney elbow. I don't even know why the hell I let him and Oz follow me to the library tonight—neither of them ever shuts up long enough to let anyone study. "Isn't that your tutor?"

Gunderson's nasally voice breaks through my concentration, snakes through my cerebellum with alarming speed, and has me jerking my head up. Scanning the perimeter of the library. Skimming over the entrance. Glancing toward the back stacks, to the circulations desk.

Finding Violet.

Schooling my features into an expressionless mask of indifference so they don't start in with the questions, or give me a rash of shit.

"Yeah, that's my tutor." I lower my head, determined to keep my eyes glued to a term paper.

"She's not just his tutor," Oz says with authority. "Is she Daniels?"

"I don't want to talk about it."

"Why not?"

"He's why." I cast a glance toward Rex Gunderson, wide-eyed and curious, then back at my roommate. "Why are you even here?"

"Ozzy invited me."

"Of *course* he did." Because he knew it would irritate the piss out of me.

We collectively watch Violet round the circulation desk, bending at the waist to straighten a cart of books, pulling one out and moving it to the bottom rack. Stand. Straighten the hem of her dark gray shirt.

"Psst," Oz hisses loudly, cupping his large hands beside his mouth like a megaphone. "*Psst*, Violet."

"Dude, cut it out," I demand, smacking him in the tricep. "Knock it off."

He is the picture of innocence. "What? I want to say hi."

God he's so fucking annoying.

I suck in a breath when Violet glances up, eyes scanning the first floor of the library. Know the exact moment she spots us by her sweet smile. By the way she nervously smoothes down her hair and bites her lower lip.

Beside me, Oz seizes the opportunity of having her attention. Shoots his hand in the air when she glances over again, signaling her with a wave, wiggle, and shake of his meddling fingers. He waves and waves, tattooed arm flailing around as if independent from his body, causing a scene. She'd have to be blind not to notice him, especially with that bright yellow Iowa t-shirt he's sporting.

"I said knock it *off*." I'm gritting through my teeth.

I see her flaming red blush from here—a blush I've seen over her entire naked body half a dozen times—and want to fucking punch my roommate in the face for drawing attention to our table, and for making her uncomfortable.

"Put your damn arm down," I hiss, slapping at it.

"Dude, *chill*. I thought you'd want to say hi to your girl over there."

I do.

I don't.

I—not like this.

My face burns as red as hers, and I'm pretty sure the tips of my fucking ears are red, too.

"I do, but not right now."

Oz scrunches up his ugly ass mug. "Why not? I thought the two of you were a thing. Canoodling and shit."

"What's canoodling?" Gunderson asks.

"You know," Oz starts with an air of authority. "Snuggling and hanging out and shit."

I'm telling you, ever since he started dating Jameson, he thinks he fucking knows everything there is to know about relationships; I could do without his unsolicited advice.

"Why do they call it canoodling?" Gunderson just will not let it go.

Oz shrugs. "How the hell should I know?"

"It sounds awful."

"Well, Rexy, maybe that's why you're still single and Zekey and I are both in budding relationships." His thumb flicks between the two of us. "He's finally getting sex regularly, which is why he hasn't been such a bitch."

My response to them both is to glare down at my notebook and thump my pen on the table as Violet's jeans and white shirt appear in my peripheral view.

"Incoming! Look alive, old chap!" Oz declares merrily. "And try not to fuck this up by being your usual cheerful self. That was sarcasm in case you missed it …"

"Shut up, scrot."

"Why are you getting all defensive? I'm trying to help you charm the ladies."

"That's never going to happen," Gunderson chuckles.

They're the opposite of helpful, and they're grating on my last nerve. The tension in my hands, legs, and shoulders is insurmountable, my fingers tapping on the table anxiously like a fidgety crack whore.

Oz laughs, kicking me under the table. "Relax dude, or she'll think you have issues."

"I said. Shut. Up."

"Say shut up *please.*"

Oh my fucking god, seriously?

"Say it."

I clamp my lips together.

Oz raises his dark eyebrows. "Are you really not going to say please?"

I don't have to reply, because my eye roll speaks volumes. Crossing my arms, I glare.

"Your Darth Vader death stare doesn't intimidate me," he drones, unimpressed. "Just say please and we won't embarrass you when your girlfriend gets here."

My lips part, mouth clamps shut. Opens. Jaw clenches. Nostrils flare.

Violet zigzags her way across the room, sights set on me, timidly approaching with a warm smile on her lips.

"Shut up. *Please.*"

Ozzy and Rex Gunderson cackle like a pair of washwomen, Oz tipping back in his chair.

"Did you hear that Rexy? Daniels just said please! Holy shit, that's gotta be a record for *something.* Write that down somewhere. I—" His voice breaks off when Violet reaches the table.

"Hi guys. Zeke."

Oz and Rex wait for me to say something, one of them kicking my shin under the table.

I dig way down deep and come up with "Hey."

Violet shifts on her heels, lips rubbing together. "Hey." Her eyes twinkle, amused.

"How's it going, Violet? It's Violet, right?" Gunderson asks, his stupid face lit up with a stupid grin. The idiot is smiling ear to ear and gives me another kick under the table.

"Yes. Hi, we haven't met." She extends her hand and he takes it, first to shake it, and then to kiss her wrist.

"My cherie, a pleasure."

Violet giggles, taking back her hand, her light laugh indicating that she's entertained. "Very charming."

Oz groans. "Ignore him please; he's a moron, which explains why he can't make the wrestling team." He looks her up and down, smiling a crocodile smile that drops panties all over campus. "You working?"

"Yes, but only for another hour." She shoots me a sidelong glance. "No appointments today."

"Zeke says you're his tutor," Rex says. "What subjects do you tute?"

"A-All of them."

"All of them? Like—*all* of them?"

"I guess I shouldn't say all," she amends. "I should say, most."

"Maybe I should hire you." Gunderson waggles his brows at her, the little fucker. "I need serious help with chemistry."

"S-Sure," Violet stutters. "You can check the schedule at the circulation desk and arrange it."

"What if I pay you on the side? That's what Daniels does, isn't it?" The little asshole isn't talking about tutoring anymore, and everyone knows it. "Do you take side jobs?"

"Enough with the questions Rex. Jesus, give it a rest," I snap, ball cap coming off, fingers raking through my dark hair. "Leave her alone."

Oz clucks his tongue. "Now, now, don't be like that." He looks up at Violet. "He doesn't like sharing—not the keys to his truck, not his clothes, not his *tutor*."

He uses air quotes around the word tutor and winks.

If I thought Violet was red before, it's nothing compared to how bright her cheeks are now; the blush extends down into the neckline of her shirt, and I swear even the pale skin of her arms begins to color.

She's met him a few times when he's been on his best behavior, in the company of his new girlfriend; she doesn't know the idiot is a total pervert.

Oz looks at me. Looks at Violet. Looks at me, pencil limply flopping in the air to illustrate his point. "We have an away meet this week but our next match is home. You going to come cheer your boy on?"

Rex looks confused. "Why would your tutor come to our wrestling meets?"

Oz's sigh is so loud and drawn out, several people turn to stare at us. "Gunderson, try to keep up. They're dating."

"We're not dating." Not exactly. The hasty denial slips off my tongue. Out of my lips.

I sound petty and childish, and shift my gaze to the notebook in front of me, eyes trained on the paragraphs I wrote just hours ago. I refuse to meet Violet's hurt hazel eyes as she stands next to the table, spine ramrod straight, listening to the interaction intently. Waiting for me to say something to her.

Except now I'm too pissed to do anything but sit here, seething.

"Whoa." Rex shoots Violet a sidelong glance. "Is he this big a dick when you're studying?"

Why are they doing this to me?

Oh! I get it—this is because I'm such an asshole to Jameson. Well joke's on him, because I'm not giving in to his word bait. I'm not going to lose my cool. No fucking way. Let him poke the hornet's nest and see how well it ends.

I cross my arms, steaming.

"You, Violet, must be a saint," Oz teases her. "Even his friends can't stand him, yet you're voluntarily spending time with him."

Even his friends can't stand him?

"What the hell kind of dig is that?"

"It wasn't a dig," he deadpans. "It's a fact."

"You are such a dick."

"Maybe, but I'm not the one sitting here ignoring his girl that's a "friend" or *whatever* you want to call it. You are."

I realize I am, in fact, still ignoring Violet, who is standing at the table looking perplexed. Maybe even a little hurt.

God I'm a douchebag.

I know this.

But I can't stop. I can't take the words back—not in front of my friends. I'll be damned if I apologize to her in front of them. In fact, I can't remember a single time when I've apologized to *them* for my bad behavior. Not a single damn time.

Oz turns his attention to Violet, shooting her an apologetic smile. "Sorry."

Her hazel eyes regard me, unflinching. "Zeke, are we still doing something later?" Her voice is steady.

"Nah. We're good."

Her head bobs up and down unhurriedly, eyes narrowing in a decidedly un-Violet-like way. "I see."

No, she doesn't see.

It takes several seconds for Violet to collect her thoughts and speak again. When she does, the words come out halted and ineloquent.

"I-I …" Deep breath. "It was g-good seeing you guys. I-I have work to do, s-s … I sh-should should …"

"See ya." I force out those two words, affecting a bored tone but wanting to take those back, too. *Don't fucking listen me, please,* I want to shout. *I'm a clueless fucking moron!*

I should be ashamed of myself.

Shouldn't let her walk away when she spins on her heel, the soles of her worn brown boots needing replacing as much as Kyle's shoes did.

We watch her scurry away like a spooked rabbit. Her hip hits a table a few feet away and I wince as she rubs her side, rounding the corner, disappearing into a back room. I make note of it: private study room number four.

"Wow." Rex fills the silence. "Man ..."

"You really are a heartless prick," Oz finishes for him, pushing away from the table to stand. He shuffles his shit around, throwing his laptop and books in his backpack, the loud metal teeth zipping closed. His hand goes up, motioning toward study room number four. "Are you just going to sit there? Or are you going to follow her and beg her to overlook your stupidity?"

"Wait Ozzy, where are *you* goin?" Confusion fills Gunderson's voice.

"Leaving. I can't sit here and watch him self-destruct. Dude needs alone time to think about what a fucking bad move that was." He hefts his bag onto his broad shoulder. "You'd be wise to come with me, Rex. Leave him alone to his own miserable company. That's obviously what the poor sod wants."

Poor sod? Poor *sod*? What is he, British?

"What's a poor sod?" Rex rises, packing up his shit.

Good. Who needs them?

"It's another way to say sorry ass motherfucker."

"Really?" Rex sounds intrigued. "Where'd you hear that?"

I hear Oz shrug, their deep voices trailing off as they depart. "James and I were watching *Love Actually* last weekend ..."

I sit, gazing toward the study room Violet disappeared into, willing them both to hurry the fuck up and leave.

So I can finally follow her.

Violet

I manage to make it all the way to the study room before tears sting my eyes, flowing out like a dam that's been broken. I wipe them away with a trembling hand, swiping angrily at my own cheeks.

"Stupid, stupid, stupid," I repeat, cold hands bracing my cheeks to cool them off, to salvage whatever composure might be left inside my broken heart before heading back out and finishing my shift.

How embarrassing.

Why would he do that to me?

What is *wrong* with him?

I don't understand.

Of all the people in this world to develop feelings for, why did it have to be him and his foolish pride?

Suddenly I'm seeing what everybody already knew: Zeke Daniels is a heartless, cold-blooded jerk. Callous doesn't begin to describe his treatment of me just then. The cold, unreadable expression—he couldn't even look me in the eyes, the coward.

Well the joke is on me, because I thought …

I swipe another tear with my sleeve.

The bracelets circling my wrist jingle, an unfriendly reminder of an amazing evening we had. I do my best to tug the stupid sunflower bangle off my arm, yanking at it, tears still blinding me.

The jerk.

I tug.

Jerk.

Tug again and again.

Jerk, jerk, *jerk.*

A brisk knock at the door has my spine stiffening. Zeke's face appears in the narrow window of the study room, doorknob turns as he pushes his way into the small, square space, not waiting for me to invite him in.

Rude.

"What do *you* want? I'm b-busy."

Clearly I'm not busy doing anything but crying and pulling his stupid, beautiful bracelet off my wrist and he knows it. He enters cautiously, coming to a standstill on the other side of the long, wooden table. His thick arms fold across his chest.

"Violet."

My chin goes up haughtily, fingers swiping at my cheeks. "I said, what do you *want*, Zeke?"

"I … Fuck, I don't know."

"*Obviously.*" The sarcasm in my voice is hard to disguise.

For once in my life, I pull off a bitchy tone to perfection, secretly applauding myself with a mental pat on the back. I turn to the wall so I don't have to look at his handsome face—the one that not two minutes ago was so very unfeeling and dispassionate.

"We all know I'm an asshole, okay?"

"No. Actually, it's *not* okay."

Silence.

"What do you want from me, Violet?"

Is he serious?

With those words, I swing around to face him. "What do you mean, what do I want from you? I want nothing! Why can't we just *be*?"

What the hell is wrong with you! I long to shout at him, get up in his face, so he hears me. Really hears me.

I lower my voice instead, each word chosen carefully. "Why are you so angry all the time, Zeke?" I pause. "My god, you can't even handle your friends teasing you."

"I fucked up. What do you want me to say?"

"I want you to be a good friend, but you can't even do that, can you?"

"What do you mean?"

259

"I mean, was that necessary back there?" I gesture toward the door. "You could at least have told them we were friends; they kept calling me your tutor."

"I know."

"Then why didn't you say anything?"

"Because."

"That's not good enough."

"What do you expect? Jesus, how many times do I have to say, *I'm such an asshole!* before you start believing it? Everyone is not good and kind Violet. Some of us are mean. Some of us don't care enough to try. Stop the attempts to make me better!"

I'm ashamed to admit my shoulders sag, defeat pressing down on them. "You don't get it, do you Zeke?"

"No."

"You know that Zeke out there?" I point toward the door. "That Zeke treated me like a body for hire. That Zeke is not my friend. *That* Zeke can walk back out *that* door and out of my life for good." My arm remains raised, finger pointing. "I don't need him."

"Violet—"

"No! Be *quiet*! Stop saying my name! Oh my god, we were having *sex* last night and look how you treated me today. Y-You humiliated me by acting like I'm only your tutor!"

"Violet please, cal—"

"Don't tell me to calm down! You humiliated me out there. You're a *user* and everything my friends warned me about. Did I listen? No!"

His hands dig deep into his pockets. "I never said I was perfect."

"No, you said you were an asshole and a douchebag and a shitty boyfriend and I should have listened. *I'm* the idiot here for letting you lead me around. *Me.*"

"I'm glad you didn't listen."

A laugh begins in my abs, rises through my chest, and escapes my lips. "Oh, I'm sure! You're so *glad* I was dumb enough to ignore the warning signs!"

"Are you mocking me?" His eyes narrow. "I'm being serious."

"Oh please. If this is how you treat someone you're *glad* to have around, I shudder to know what you're like when you're not."

We stand warily regarding one another across the table; I seize the opportunity to size him up, drinking in the sight of him: tall, broody, and moody. So devastatingly handsome. Clear gray eyes. Heavy brows. Chiseled cheekbones and defined, masculine jaw covered in five o'clock shadow.

Beautiful. A poet's dream.

He might have acted like he didn't care but ...

It's his eyes that give him away. They're remarkable, yes, but forlorn. Serious but sad. Lonely.

That doesn't make it better, doesn't make his callous behavior *right*.

"What in the world do you have to be so mad about, Zeke?" I whisper into the room, more to the walls than to him, knowing he won't answer. "You're surrounded by amazing people. Why are you the only one that doesn't see that?"

He braces those giant palms on the table, leaning toward me. "You want to analyze me now? Go right ahead."

He's pushing back, and he's also giving me a small opening to talk—one I intend to seize.

"You have everything you could possibly want; why do you push people away?"

He scoffs, snorting through his nose. "I'm not getting into this with you—I hardly know you."

Yet his feet are rooted to the ground, hands anchored to the table.

"That's not true. You do know me," I whisper. "Sometimes I think you know me better than I know myself."

He's never had to say it with words; Zeke Daniels gets me. Looks past all my imperfections and sees that deep down inside, we're kindred.

We bear similar scars.

"Fine. Maybe I do," he concedes, one brick of his wall coming down. "You want to talk? We'll talk."

I suck in a breath, afraid to move lest I push him away, like spooking a wild animal I've finally convinced to eat from my palm.

"Everyone chooses to leave," he begins, the low baritone of his voice reverberating down my spine. "When my parents started their company, my mom's plan was to travel the world once they made their money. She wanted to 'see things', made list after list of places she wanted to go, things she wanted to see, and at first she would take me with her, right? I was only five when my dad sold his first software program. But you know, I was kind of a little asshole when I was little, so hauling me along became too difficult. It wasn't fun for her anymore. Having me along was work, because I didn't listen." He shrugs. "Because I was only fucking *five*."

"The more money they made, the higher maintenance and more demanding my mom became. Everything *had* to be perfect. Everything *had* to be expensive. When it wasn't convenient to drag me to France, they'd leave me with aunts and uncles and my dick of a cousin."

I listen silently as he begins opening up, words halted but constant. "My mom's sister was … not loving."

A stormy shadow crosses his eyes as he recalls his aunt from whatever memory category he's compartmentalized her in.

My heart skips a beat. "Did they hurt you, Zeke?"

A bitter laugh. "No. They did *nothing*."

"What do you mean they did *nothing*?"

I want to put my hands on him—touch him—but I don't. Can't.

The energy in the room grows.

"My aunt and uncle took me in for *money;* my parents sent them a shit ton every month so I was out of their way, so my mom could do whatever the fuck she wanted, when she wanted. It was all about *money*, a glorified foster care system."

It's starting to make sense.

The bets. The charity. Giving his parents' money away.

The anger and resentment.

Zeke Daniels feels abandoned by his family.

"My parents chose work and travel. My aunt and uncle chose money. Oz is choosing Jameson." His low voice rumbles, spitting the words out. "Everyone has a choice."

And no one chooses me.

The unspoken words hang between us, heavy and thick like a downdraft, like a noose around the column of his long, thick neck.

Slowly, I move around the table.

Slowly still, my fingers feel for his forearm, the tips brushing his wrist. "Zeke, I—"

His reflexes are quick, capturing my hand in his bear-like paw. "Don't, Violet. Don't try to make me feel better. Don't feel sorry for me."

"Maybe I don't feel sorry for you. Maybe I feel something else."

Compassion.

Empathy.

A connection.

Love.

"I can tell by the fucking expression on your face you feel sorry for me. Knock that shit off because this isn't a pity party, Violet. You know, when I came to college, I thought the team was going to be the family I needed. I couldn't *wait* to get out of my aunt's fucking house. Couldn't. Wait. If they had colleges on the moon, I would have applied there."

He continues on, oblivious to my concerned countenance, worried only about himself. His feelings. His childhood.

"Then Dorffman up and quits because he met his girlfriend Annabelle and wanted to transfer to Florida State. Pfft, *Florida* of all fucking places. Bryan Endleman used to hit and quit *everything*, including guys, until he met Rachel. Packed all his shit and moved out of the house and into her apartment just like that. We were like brothers." Zeke snaps his fingers in the air in front of his nose. "Two weeks and he split. Gone."

"But he was still on the team at that point, right?"

"His head wasn't in it. So what? We all moved on. Got along fine without him—he was a slob anyway and I didn't need his shit lying around. Oz moved in with us after that." He sounds bitter. "Then of course, here comes Jameson."

To ruin everything.

I hear the words as if he's speaking them out loud.

My head gives a little shake. "If you're thinking he chose Jameson over you, Zeke, *don't*. He's still your friend. You can't push him away because he's falling in love."

He snorts, crossing his arms. "Love. *Hilarious.*"

Love. Hilarious.

A little shimmer of hope dims inside me with his biting words.

"You don't think Oz is falling in love with Jameson?"

"I think he loves *fucking* her."

I pull away, his crude words startling. "*Fucking.*" I test the word out; it's one I rarely use. "Is that what we've been doing? F-Fucking? You know, since you obviously have no feelings for me other than physical."

His face is red. "Jesus Christ, Violet, stop twisting my words."

I tap my foot. "I'm not, I'm using deductive reasoning."

"That's not what this thing is and you know it. Stop putting words in my mouth."

I ignore him. "But the idea of romantic love is *hilarious*, right?"

Not surprisingly, he has nothing to say to that, so I ramble on.

"J-Just because Oz and James are sleeping together doesn't mean they're not in love and planning a *future* together. It doesn't mean he isn't still your friend."

"My friend? Bullshit. Those guys on the team aren't my friends. They don't give a shit about me."

Another shake of my head, this one woeful.

"I've never met anyone so self-deprecating in all my life," I all but whisper, just loud enough for him to hear across the room.

Zeke tilts his head and studies me, eyes thinning into slits. "*What* did you just say?"

"Y-You heard me." My chin tips up boldly, but I'm so *devastated* by this entire conversation my stutter decides to return in full force.

Zeke scratches his chin. "I don't think I did, because it sounded like you just called me a whiney baby."

"I-I didn't call y-you a whiney baby. I said you were self-deprecating."

"What the hell does that even mean?"

"It means ..." I start slow, choosing my words carefully and speaking them one at a time so I get them right. "That you're only seeing negative things about your life. Basically sabotaging your own happiness before you even know something is going to fail, before people leave. Because despite your tattoos and your devil-may-care attitude, you actually lack ..."

His nostrils flare. Gray eyes like gunmetal.

"Lack ... what? I lack *what*? Just fucking say it."

"Confidence!" There, I said it. "You lack confidence, okay?"

He laughs then, loudly tossing his head back, black hair tussling. "Oh okay. *I* lack confidence. Ha ha, good one, Violet." He moves back, pointing an accusatory finger in my direction. "*You* are out of your fucking mind. I'm the most ... the most ..."

He searches for the words but can't find them. "You know what, Violet? You're being a judgmental bitch. You don't know the life I've lived."

I stare are him incredulously.

The nerve of him. The *nerve*!

Blood rushes to my face and my fists clench at my sides.

"I don't know the life you've lived? *Me*? How ... how d-dare you!"

His lips begin to snarl. He opens that big insensitive mouth to speak, but I cut him off—something I've never done to anyone, ever. In my entire life, I've never interrupted anyone.

But my heart ... my heart won't let him speak.

"Be quiet! Shut up for once!"

Those stunning gray eyes widen with shock.

I've stunned him. *Good.*

"Oh my god, do you hear me talking about how shitty *my* life was growing up? Huh? Do you?"

Numbly, his head shakes back and forth, still stunned by my outburst.

"No, of course you don't. Do you know why? Because wallowing about how lonely it was would be pointless, wouldn't it? *Wouldn't it?*" This time I do shout, bracing my hands on two desk chairs for support.

"I didn't have rich parents. I didn't have *any* parents at all! They're dead, you selfish jerk. *Dead*! I had no one! Not even family, because no one could afford to keep me." The tears—all the hot tears—are rolling down my face, creating a path so wet I feel them dampening the collar of my shirt.

"No aunts and uncles to take me in like you had—there was no money to pay anyone off with. Poor as church mice, every last one of us. And my grandparents? They died before I was born. Yeah, poor Zeke, your parents travel." I roll my eyes toward the ceiling, staring into the fluorescent lights and swiping at another tear.

"Go see them! Go *do* something! My god! I-Instead of standing there in your two-hundred-dollar *jeans* and driving around in your expensive truck and whining about how *bad* you feel for yourself. Ha!" I laugh, the sound almost maniacal. "At least you *have* a family. I'm not acting like an asshole because I spent my childhood being ping-ponged around between strangers. Did you know I can't even go see my family because I can't afford a plane ticket."

My body is quaking.

And my hands?

I raise them up to stare at my fingers; I'm shaking so hard I can't even gather up my laptop.

Zeke takes a step forward.

"Don't come near me, I-I'm so done with you!" I'm shouting now and fighting to control my stutter, but it's hard. So damn hard my chin trembles. "A-All I wanted was someone to treat me with respect, but you couldn't even do *that*."

His mouth drops open to argue.

"I-I'm done listening to you cut people down instead of building them up. I'm d-done listening to you condescend to your roommates and to Jameson. She is amazing! Did you know that? And you won't even try to befriend her. You treat her like shit! Why Zeke? *Why*? What has she ever done to you but date your friend?"

My hands are balled into angry fists and I can feel my face burning up, to the roots of my blonde hair, and curse my pale skin.

Curse it.

Curse this whole miserable day.

"She's going to fall in love with him. Watch, Ezekiel. *Love*! Love, love, *love*," I repeat like a song, spreading my arms wide. "It's wonderful and I'm sorry you don't know what it feels like."

His face … it's hard to describe what it looks like in this moment as my words pour out on a wave of tears. Crestfallen and devastated. Furrowed black brows, heavy, but not from annoyance. Mouth downturned and sad.

Eyes?

I swear those sullen gray eyes are damp in the corners.

So achingly beautiful and heartbreaking and *devastated …*

Those eyes will haunt my dreams.

"You can't let yourself *feel* it, can you?" I whisper.

A shake of his head.

No.

I nod, understanding. "Well then, you're missing it, Zeke. You're missing out on your own life, one that could be filled with happiness instead of resentment. Or do you just resent those of us who are happy?"

The path is blurry, the tears clouding my vision as I stalk to the door, but I find my way, yanking my arm away from his when he tries to take hold.

He lets me go.

His tortured, *"Violet, Jesus,"* might have given me pause any other day of the week, but today? This? What I'm feeling right now is too raw and real to give me pause.

I inhale a breath then draw it out. "You … y-you're *not* a nice person Zeke Daniels." I look him up and down, starting with the tips of his black running shoes. Black. Dark. Like him.

"I thought I saw some redeemable qualities in you, but I guess I was wrong. You are blind and I can't make you *see.*"

"Violet, *please.*"

"No." I shove through the door instead, lingering briefly, glancing over my shoulder at him, allowing myself one last look. "They say the bigger the man, the harder they fall. Well this is me letting you fall, Zeke. I can't be there to catch you; I'm not strong enough to catch us both."

His barely perceivable, choked out *"I-I'm sorry,"* is the last thing I hear as the door closes behind me.

"When I said I wanted you
to make noises during sex,
I didn't mean mocking ones."

Zeke

"**S**o dumbass, how'd it go?"

Unfortunately for me, Oz is snacking at the kitchen table when I come crashing through the front door, so I have no privacy. No time to brood. I do my best to bypass him, but he's cunning and annoying, blocks the hallway with a formidable, boxed-out stance he probably learned in sixth grade basketball.

He leans against the doorjamb to the hall when I try to wedge past.

"So?"

"I have nothing to say to you."

"*Zeke.*" His tone demands attention, so I lift my head to look at him, his entire demeanor changing when he sees my face.

"Jeez, man. What happened with Violet after I left?"

I meet his eyes, swallowing the lump in my dry throat. "She doesn't think I'm a nice person."

Shit. It's one thing for her to say it, but it's another entirely repeating those fucking words out loud myself.

It actually hurts.

Sebastian Osborne's insightful gaze roams to the pile of Violet's things that I collected from Barbara, her boss, after she fled the library an entire twenty minutes before her shift was over. The crap I dumped next to the front door.

"What's all that stuff?" Oz meanders over to the purple stack, giving Violet's lavender laptop a poke and fingering a notebook that's sticking out of her backpack.

The backpack she left at the library when she ran out in a fit of tears.

I might be an insensitive prick, but I will never forget the look on her face. The devastation. The sheer and utter—

"Stop *touching* it," I snap at my roommate, who's pulling a notebook out of the backpack.

"Whose shit is it? Did you bring someone home?"

"No, of course I didn't bring anyone home."

"Then whose shit is it?" Hungry, he abandons Vi's stuff in pursuit of food, dumps his empty plate in the sink so he can rifle through the kitchen cabinets with two empty hands like a scavenger, even though he's going to pull the same damn shit out of the fridge he eats every damn afternoon: bagel, butter, and cream cheese—the only bready carb he allows himself to eat in a day.

He plugs in the toaster. "Humor me with an answer."

"No one."

"Is it Violet's?" He pins me down with a stare. "Just admit it. All that shit is purple for fuck's sake."

I hesitate, using the long stretch of silence to prepare oatmeal. I'm starving too and could go for a snack, so I add a cup of steel-cut oats and water to a bowl, pop it in the microwave. Let us sit in silence for the two minutes it takes for the water to boil.

"Yes, it's Violet's."

The microwave dings and I take the hot bowl out.

"What's going on with you two?" Oz asks innocently, yanking the fridge open with so much force the bottles in the door shake. He peers inside and asks, "Did she forgive you for being a giant prick?"

"No."

He raises his brows. "Really? I thought maybe—"

My head snaps in his direction, eyes glaring, and I snap, "What's with the twenty fucking questions!"

"Whoa, whoa, whoa. Parlay dude. Time the *fuck* out." He has his hands up in surrender. "I'm asking because you were a dick today, yet suddenly all her shit is by the front door. Christ almighty, give me a break."

Is what Violet meant when she said I don't let people in? Jesus, how did everything in my life get so fucking out of hand?

The steel-cut oats *barely* go down my throat when I swallow, so I take a chug of water. Count to five to gain back some of my self-control.

"Violet forgot her stuff at the library after ..." I force away the memory of finding her crying—no, *sobbing* in one of the library study rooms. It isn't something I'll soon forget, pushing through the door and having those joyful eyes turn on me with despair.

"After you treated her like she wasn't becoming the most important part of your life?"

"Yes."

After I did exactly what Jameson warned me not to do: ruin her.

I ruined Violet.

I put the tears in her eyes.

The tears in her eyes were *mine*.

Her bleeding heart was crying them *for* me, I goddamn know it.

Because she loves me.

Despite me.

Fuck.

As always, Oz's perceptive and shrewd observations are correct; I shouldn't have sat there today and treated her like she hasn't become the most important part of my life.

God dammit he's a fucking good friend; maybe he really does give a shit what happens in my life.

I stare down at the cold, hard Formica countertop, studying the pattern on its surface as Oz studies *me*, stuffing his face with the never-ending goddamn bagel. He stops chewing to swallow, then stuffs his face some more, earnest eyes silently watching me.

"Why ..." I start to ask. Stop to clear my throat. "Why are—"

He raises his brows when I cut myself off, unable to get the words out.

I try again. "Why are you friends with me?"

Wow. Asking that fucking sucked.

His brows are still stuck up in his hairline. "Are you being serious right now?"

"Yeah. We all know I'm an unrelenting asshole, so why the hell are you friends with me?"

That bagel is paused halfway to his lips. "You want me to be perfectly honest?"

It's on the tip of my tongue to say, *No, I want you to fucking lie*, but I don't.

I nod. "Yeah. Be honest."

"I don't know, Zeke." He sets the bagel down and walks to the fridge. Takes out two beers, pops the tops, then places one in my grip; it goes great with my oatmeal. "I don't know why I'm friends with you."

We stand in silence, him chewing on the bagel and swallowing his beer, me staring out the kitchen window, Violet's parting words rolling around my mind: *I'm done listening to you condescend to your roommates and to Jameson. She is amazing! Did you know that? And you won't even try to befriend her. You treat her like shit! Why Zeke? Why? What has she ever done to you but date your friend?*

"Since we're being honest, it's been hard being your friend since James and I started dating. We've—*I've* decided it might be best if …" Oz's voice trails off and he avoids finishing his sentence by taking a healthy swig of beer.

"Might be best if *what*. *What*? Just say it man."

A long, labored sigh. "It's gotten to the point where James doesn't feel comfortable coming over, all right? It's hostile territory in here man; I'm used to it, but she's not, and I don't like putting her in this position because I really fucking like her, so …" He shrugs and takes a deep, steadying breath. "So, I've been thinking I might move out at semester."

"*What*?"

"I'm sorry man, but I can't do this anymore. There's way too much tension around here to be healthy."

"So you're just going to move in with some girl you *just* met?"

"I didn't say that either, did I?" He sets the knife he'd been using to butter his bagel in the sink, wipes his hands on a dish rag, then turns back to face me, crossing his legs at the ankles and watching me. Gauging my reaction. "No. James and I aren't moving in together, but I have been thinking about moving."

"Then I don't get it."

He laughs, but it's an odd laugh. Kind of sad. "I didn't think you would."

"What the fuck is that supposed to mean? Cut the bullshit man. Please. Quit talking in riddles."

"You want me to spell it out for you? Fine. You're a shitty roommate dude, and I'm thinking about moving out. There. Happy? Now you can say and do what you want, be the huge fucking boner killer that you are, and it won't affect anyone else, least of all me and my girlfriend, who is the *shit*."

My jaw clenches when he shrugs again, almost carelessly.

"I don't know what Elliot's gonna do—probably stay because he can't really afford to move—but he's tired of the mood swings too, dude. We never know what we're getting with you."

My parents.

Violet.

Oz.

Jameson.

"The common denominator here is you. Get your shit together. We graduate next fall—what the fuck are you gonna do then? Are you going to act like a dick at your job?"

"How the hell am I supposed to change?"

His mouth is set in a grim line. "I don't know man. I've never really given anyone advice."

"Bullshit." I chuckle. "All you do is give unsolicited advice."

"Whoa, back the truck up." He points at my face. "What the hell was *that*?"

I play dumb. "What the hell was what?"

"Did you just laugh? That's the first time I've ever seen your fucking teeth."

"Whatever."

"Also, you're not half bad-looking when you smile. You're quite reasonably attractive."

I laugh again.

It feels good.

"See! That right there almost gave me a chubby down under," my roommate jokes. "Do not tell Jameson."

"I wouldn't dream of it." Since his girlfriend and I barely speak, it won't be a problem. "And you know smartass, I *laugh*. Just not—"

"Pfft, yeah right. Name the last time you laughed out loud at something."

"Last week when I was with—"

I stop. Frown.

"When you were with Violet?" he supplies.

"Yeah."

Oz's big hand clamps me on the shoulder and he squeezes. "You've got to *do* something man. She's one of the good ones—maybe too good considering how fucked you are in the head. You probably deserve someone more like that."

"Gee, thanks," I deadpan.

He ignores my sarcasm. "No, I'm being real here. You have some serious parent issues." Chuckle. "You also need to chill the fuck out, that's my advice—and smile more, chicks love that shit."

He's serious.

"Anything else?"

Oz rubs his chin, stroking the stubble along his jawline. "I think you're going to have to fight dirty to win this one. Violet doesn't seem like the type who's going to let this go; this blow was emotional. It's going to cut her deep and cost you. I'm glad she told you to fuck off."

"Violet did not tell me to fuck off."

"Basically she did …" he mumbles into his beer bottle.

"Um, no, she said I wasn't a nice person and she wanted nothing more to do with me."

"So in other words, fuck off." His middle finger salutes the air.

"Dude, seriously?"

"Yeah. That was her way of breaking up with you."

I roll my eyes toward the ceiling. "We weren't going out."

"Okay, well now you're *really* not going out, sooo …" Oz emits a low whistle, studying his fingernails. "Fuck off."

Is he always this impossible? "Is this how you argue with James?"

Shrug. "Yes."

He has no shame.

"It's really fucking annoying."

"But effective."

"Knock it off and help me." I sound complain-y but refuse to beg.

"*I* can't help you. You have to want to help yourself."

"I'm not looking for a twelve-step program, dipshit, I'm trying to …" I search for the words. "I'm trying to …"

"Win back the girl?"

I scowl. "When you put it that way it sounds so fucking dumb."

The bastard smirks and crosses his arms, leaning against the kitchen counter. "Only if you're an asshole. And you are, sooo …"

Good point. "All right, so what the hell do I do?"

"Depends. How serious are you? I mean, you can't go through all this effort to apologize and shit and then not do anything with it."

"What do you mean?"

"I mean, you better fucking pony up if you're going to grovel. And obviously give back all her shit, her backpack and stuff. Date her and commit and whatever."

I can do that.

I can date her and commit.

I think.

I mean, I've never done it before, but how hard can it be? "What if I'm bad at it?"

"Dude, let's be honest, you're going to be a horrible boy-friend. Like, the fucking worst. You're already off to a shitty start."

"What the hell, Osborne."

His hands go up in surrender. "Hey! You said you wanted me to be honest, I'm being honest."

"You're enjoying this aren't you?"

"*Immensely.*"

"Where are Violet and Summer? I thought they were coming with us?" Kyle buckles his seat belt.

"Not today, buddy, sorry."

"Why not?"

I sit quietly, debating between lying and telling him the truth. It's my fault his little friend isn't here and the poor freaking kid is going to be bummed. And pissed. "They're not coming with us to the batting cages because I'm an asshole."

He shoots me a sidelong, judgey glance, narrowing his beady little eyes. "You know you're not supposed to be swearing. It's in the rulebook."

The one I still haven't read.

"I know, I know, but sometimes there aren't any words but curse words to get a point across."

He commiserates with a rub to his chin like he's rubbing a beard. "True."

"Anyway, Violet's pissed. I hurt her feelings 'cause I'm a dumbass, so I don't think we'll be seeing her or Summer for a while. Not until I can figure something out."

"What happened?"

"I, uh, wasn't nice to her in front of my friends. It made her feel sad."

He scrunches up his face distastefully. "Why'd you do that? I thought you were friends."

"I don't know, because I'm an idiot, remember? I think I freaked."

Admitting that out loud makes it that much worse, because clearly, the more self-reflection I engage in, the more I'm convinced I'm actually just a giant pussy, not the badass I originally thought.

It's sobering.

"My mom says you clearly have abandonment issues," Kyle says so casually I have no idea how to respond. "Hey Zeke?"

"Yeah buddy?"

"What are abandonment issues?"

My hands tighten on the steering wheel as I consider my answer. "It means … a person thinks if they keep their heart *closed*, then no one in their life can abandon or reject them."

I rattle off a definition I read on Wikipedia just last night, after my little girl talk in the kitchen with Oz when he told me I had issues.

The problems associated with abandonment are typically wrong, one article read. *Abandonment, in simple terms, is essentially a heart that's been closed off.*

A broken heart.

"What does a heart closed mean?" Kyle innocently wants to know, and now I'm sorry I started this fucking conversation.

"It means …" I pause to think. "It means not letting people in your life—like not telling them shit. Not getting to know people even if you're hanging out with them."

"Do you do that?"

Do I? Uh, *yeah.*

"Yes."

"Why? Is it because of your parents sucking?"

I laugh at his unexpected choice of verbiage. "Yeah, I think so. Remember how I told you they were never around? Still aren't?"

He nods.

"Well, I really missed them when I was little. I cried a lot, and the people taking care of me used to get really mad and yell a lot, which just made me cry more, and all I wanted was for my mom and dad to come home."

But they rarely did.

"Did you have a home?"

"Lots of them," I admit. "But I lived with aunts and uncles. Once my parents were home for Easter. We took a trip down to Florida and I played in the ocean while they sat on the beach."

I remember it like it was yesterday; I was twelve. My parents had been in Greece for a month and thought it would be charming to celebrate Easter as a family. While I blissfully swam in the ocean, my dad spent most of his time on his laptop, and my mom drank wine while supervising a photographer for a magazine, sent to photograph the beach house.

The real reason they'd come home.

So her fucking beach house could be in a damn magazine. She squeezed it in before moving on to the next city on her world tour. City, town, island—wherever the hell they went next, they sure as shit couldn't be bothered to take their son.

"I guess you could say I was inconsolable, you know? Cried a lot. That sadness turned to anger, because by the time I was in middle school, I couldn't tell people how I felt. I couldn't put a label my own emotions because I was so young." I glance over to find him watching me rapidly. "We call that articulating our feelings."

He's soaking up every word like a sponge.

"Do you think I'm going to be like you when I grow up since my dad's not around?"

My throat contracts and I find it hard to swallow. "What do you mean, be like me?"

"You know, mad and stuff." He turns his head and stares out the window, watching the buildings and houses and trees roll by. People on their way home to their families. On their way home from work or running errands.

I slow for a woman in the crosswalk.

"I don't think I'm mad and stuff—not all of the time."

Kyle glances over. "Just most of the time?"

Am I?

"Is that what you think? That I'm mad most of the time?"

His slight shoulders give a shrug, and now he's looking down at his sneakers. "I think it would be cool to be like you when I grow up."

"Why?"

My blinker goes on, and I hang a left at the stop sign, racking my brain for a way to respond without sounding callous and bitter.

"Because you're big and good at wrestling and nobody tells you what to do."

"Violet tells me what to do sometimes," I point out.

"True." His head bobs up and down. "Why do you let her?"

"Why do I let Violet tell me what to do?" I clarify the question.

"Yeah," he says with a comical scowl. "You're always letting her boss you around."

"Well … I definitely wouldn't say she was bossy—she's too sweet." Suddenly it's hard to swallow. "But I guess I let her tell me what to do because I *like* her."

"Like boyfriend girlfriend?"

"Uh … sure."

Kyle's head hits the headrest and he quirks one of his puny little eyebrows, giving me a look I myself have made at him a thousand times.

Shit. The scrappy turd is mimicking my behavior.

"What do you mean *sure*. You either do or you don't."

"*Uh …*"

He taps his fingers on the center console. "It's not a difficult question you know."

"Yeah, but now you're confusing me because you're eleven and you sound twenty-four."

"I've had a rough life; I've picked up a thing or two."

"You know Kyle, you might have had a rough life, but there's always someone who's worse off than you—remember that."

"Okay, I will."

"I mean it, kid. If there's one thing I've learned through all this bullshit with having to hang out with you—"

"Hey!"

Now we're both rolling our eyes. "You know what I meant— no offense." I continue, "Anyway, if there's one thing I've learned being your Big, it's that even if the things you have are shitty— your clothes suck or you have to eat peanut butter and fucking jelly for every meal, there's a kid out there starving."

I cannot believe I'm giving him a pep talk. What do chicks call this? A life chat?

"It took me a long time to figure it out. I think I'm starting to be a better person. Maybe."

Jesus Christ I sound like a sap; thank god no one else can hear me but the kid.

"Do you think it's because you met Violet?" He wants to know, and I turn my head slightly to get as good a look at him as I can while driving. A good, long look at the kid.

281

His hair is shaggy and still needs a cut. His t-shirt is wrinkled and needs to be washed. His shoes are new but need to be cleaned. He's a mess, but an honest, hopeful one.

"No. I think it's because I met *you*."

"*Me?*" His voice is full of wonder.

"Yeah kid. You."

Kyle has nothing to say to that, so we sit in silence, the radio playing soft rock in the background. Finally, a smile lights up his scrubby face, and he's grinning from ear to ear.

"Cool."

Zeke: *Hey Vi, just making sure you got your backpack and laptop? Barbara from the library was worried and knew we hung out, so she asked me to bring it to you.*

Violet: *Yes, she texted me. Thank you for bringing it home.*

Zeke: *Your roommate Mel threatened to chop my nuts off when she came to the door.*

Violet: *Yes, she told me the whole story.*

Zeke: *Um, did she give you the message that I stopped by hoping to talk?*

Violet: *Yes.*

Zeke: *Well can we? Yes or no.*

Zeke: *Sorry. That came our harsher than I wanted it to. What I meant was, can we please talk?*

Violet: *I realize you're trying, and that's a big step for you on a personal level, but I'm not ready to sit down and listen to excuses. Not even close.*

Violet: *And the only reason I'm texting you back is because I felt it would be rude to ignore your messages. That is the only reason I'm replying.*

Zeke: *Please, Violet, I fucked up—I know that. There's some shit I need to say and I don't want to do it in a text.*

Zeke: *Please.*

Zeke: *Over the past few days, I was tempted a few times to come into the library, but didn't want to come off as a fucking stalker.*

Violet: *Thanks for the texts, really. I'll think about it and let you know.*

Zeke: *All right. Let me know—I can wait.*

Zeke: *How long do you think you'll need?*

Violet: *I don't know, Zeke. I guess when I decide what I want for myself and how I'll allow myself to be treated by you. That's how long I think I'll need.*

Zeke: *Violet ...*

Don't do this, I want to beg. *Don't make me wait.*

I can't. It's going to fucking kill me, this uncertainty, the doubt I already have about myself and my ability to be in a relationship with anyone other than myself.

I've never been a patient person, not even when I was younger. Add to that my competitive nature, and taking no for an answer just isn't in my vocabulary, even though technically that's not what Violet is saying.

She wants me to give her time, wants me to wait. She wants more for herself than a selfish, contemptuous asshole ... but there's so damn much I have to say. If I don't get this shit off my chest, eventually I'll say fuck it and I'll bottle it up inside like I do with everything else in my life.

The rejection will be unbearable.

So I go to my desk, pull out the chair, and root around for a pen. Paper.

Bow my head and do something I've never done in my entire fucking life:

Write a letter.

~~Dear Violet~~
~~I know you didn't want to talk, but~~
~~I'm an idiot~~
~~Fuck~~
~~If it were anyone but you ignoring me I wouldn't give a fuck~~
~~I cannot handle the silence.~~
~~Please talk to me.~~

Violet.

By now we all know I'm ~~a fuck up~~ an idiot when it comes to basically every single relationship I've ever had with anyone. My friends can't stand me, my parents think I'm a handful, my teachers tolerate me.

I won't admit outright to being a shitty human being, but I come close. I know what they say about me. That I'm unfeeling. Cold. A dick. Insensitive. All these words have been used to describe me by those I've pissed off in the past, including women I've slept with. Sorry, but it's true.

I'm wasn't sure how to start this letter—I've started it at least seven times, and nothing about it is right. I realize that if I ~~wasn't such a callous dick~~ had stepped up and ~~been the guy~~ said what I was feeling when you walked up to our table in the library, I wouldn't be groveling right now.

I've stared at this fucking sheet of paper for the past fifteen minutes knowing that nothing I write is going to undo the damage I've done to us.

I've never handwritten a letter before in my entire fucking life, and here I am writing one for all the wrong fucking reasons, pardon my French.

There is no excuse for how I behave.

No excuse for how I acted in the library, except the truth: I spooked when you came over. I'm such a dumbass, I get that now, and my ~~immature~~ sophomoric response to the situation is as embarrassing for me as it was for you. It even embarrassed my friends, and that's saying a lot, because they're mostly ~~imbiciles~~ imbeciles, too.

I am an asshole.

I am a prick.

I am a douchebag.

These are not badges of honor and I'm a dick for having ever worn these labels. A total and complete dick.

If you would have told me two months ago that I'd be hanging out with kids every week and having fun, I would have laughed in your face and called you a liar. The only person I thought about was myself, because growing up I had no one to tell me not to be a selfish prick. When you called me self-deprecating, you were right.

I am.

I had to google what it meant, but you were right. There are no other words for it. I don't know what to fucking say to you right now other than I'm sorry. So fucking sorry.

I am a soulless asshole who doesn't deserve to have you as a friend. Jesus Christ Violet, I wasn't thinking of you at all when you walked up and I just sat there. Fuck! I know you're hurting and upset but I was too worried about myself to see what was right in front of me. When even YOU won't talk to me—one of the nicest people I KNOW won't talk to me—that's how I know I've got a fucking problem. Pardon my French.

I'll be gone this week—we have a wrestling meet in Indiana at Purdue, and won't be back until late on Friday—but if it's okay, I'm going to try texting you from the bus. I miss you. I really freaking miss you.

Even if you aren't ready to see me, I had to try.

I might be a douchebag, but I'm not a quitter.

~~Yours~~
~~Sincerely~~
~~Fuck~~
~~Talk soon,~~

Zeke.

Violet

On Friday night, I've sequestered myself in my bedroom. Mel and Winnie are both getting ready to hit the bars since it's the weekend, but I've been in no mood to socialize.

With them, or anyone else.

My door is ajar, so I can hear them both laughing, and occasionally they stick their heads in to make sure I haven't changed my mind about going out. Getting dressed up. Getting drunk.

Or, *Zeke Wasted* as Winnie so eloquently put it.

I know waiting around for a guy to text you is a dumb thing to do—sadistic, really, and a little pathetic—but unlike a lot of guys, he isn't playing games. He said he's going to text me and I believe him.

I think.

I showed his letter to my roommates—a huge mistake, because obviously they're both outraged on my behalf, having found me crying in the living room the night I blindly walked myself home from the library, too upset and blinded by tears and mascara to drive.

The letter sits on my desk.

I've read it at least fifty times, fingers running over the hurried lines. The messy, hurried scrawl. Black ink. Black mood.

For him to write that?

My stomach flutters thinking about it, thinking about those words. All the words, spewed onto that abused sheet of paper, ineloquent and unplanned.

The least I can do is be present when he texts, and I can't do that unless I'm home.

I *want* to be home when he texts.

So I lie in my room on a Friday night, googling *televised college wrestling*. Find the schedule for Iowa. Find the network. Sprawled across my bed, remote in hand, flip through the TV menu until I find what I'm looking for.

Iowa versus Purdue.

I study the screen, transfixed. Study the sidelines and wrestlers as the camera pans the stadium.

I've never seen wrestling before, not in person and not on TV. Didn't realize it was even a big deal until coming to Iowa, where wrestling reigns and the boys here are bred for it.

The stadium is massive; I don't know what I was expecting, probably something comparable to a high school gym. This? Whole different level. The arena is massive.

The blue mats are huge.

There are wrestlers on my screen who are fast on their feet, stalking each other in the center of the mat, grappling for the upper hand. The guy in black suddenly has his opponent in a headlock, and I realize with a gasp that I recognize him.

Sebastian Osborne, Zeke's roommate. It takes him two rounds to win his match.

The next Iowa wrestler is Patrick Pitwell; he wins as well.

Followed by Jonathon Powell, who takes three rounds.

Sophomore Diego Rodriguez takes just one—and loses.

Zeke Daniels walks onto the screen, his stats displayed on the bottom of the screen. He begins stretching his thick quads on the sidelines, removes his pants, sliding them down over his muscular thighs.

I feel my cheeks turn bright red, furiously blushing crimson despite being in the house alone. Those thighs in his wrestling uniform are firm and hard.

His very visible bulge lies flat against his lower stomach.

I know what *both* feel like between my legs; that spot gets hot and wet and blushes, too.

Overheated, I whip off my bedspread, flipping onto my back, staring at the ceiling. Catching my breath. Salvaging what's left of my composure when it comes to this boy. Trying to get my temperature to drop and get a grip on the reality of what's happening with us here.

Trying to focus on my screen.

I've never paid attention to wrestling, have no idea what those leotards they're wearing are called. Leotards? No, that can't be right.

I grab my laptop, flip it open, and search *wrestling one-piece*.

Wrestling singlet, noun. The uniform is tight-fitting so as not to get grasped by one's opponent, allowing referees to see each wrestler's body clearly when awarding points. Underneath the singlet, wrestlers can choose to wear nothing.

I get it now; I get why the girls on campus go crazy for these guys. Even jerks like Zeke Daniels.

Strong, powerful, and larger than life, he moves into the center of the ring. Grips his opponent's hand to shake it. His pouty lips are set in a grim line, eyes bearing down on the wrestler from Purdue.

I've seen that look of determination in person. That formidable, unsmiling face. Felt his potency firsthand.

The announcer begins his commentary; the two wrestlers circle and lower their levels, blocking each other. Zeke's opponent—a junior named Hassan—circles away, removing his hands so Zeke can't get control of them.

Both wrestlers are grappling, bodies hunched, hands extended, both immobile for only a split second before Zeke makes his move. Striking fast.

He flies into action, grabbing Hassan by the inner thighs, hauling him up. Lifting. Hefting him up and over his shoulder like a sack of flour. Hassan is suspended in the air while Zeke gets into position to drop him to the mat so he's flat on his back.

Zeke's biceps and thighs ripple. Glisten.

Oh my god, oh my god, oh my god, he's going to drop him and break the poor kid's back!

I can't watch. I'm horrified.

I hold my breath, covering my gasp with the palm of my hand. Release it when Zeke slowly lowers his torso and adversary with steady, skilled precision to the mat without hurting him or losing control. Unbelievable strength.

The tattoo on his back strains with every shift, every calculated movement of his muscular, tight body. Sweat dampens his furrowed brow. His black hair. Perspiration beads on his back and chest.

Within seconds, he has Hassan pinned to that blue mat.

Seconds.

I stare, eyes wide when the referee counts out the win. Pounds the mat. Watch when both wrestlers rise to their feet, the referee taking Zeke's wrist and raising it above his head, declaring him the victor of that match.

His chest heaves from the exertion he made look so effortless.

I'm trying to reconcile this sweating, aggressive Adonis with the one who's been so gentle with me. Tender. Loving and kind with me in bed—not like the one in front of me now, hefting a two-hundred-pound human in the air like he's weightless.

In front of an entire stadium full of spectators. In front of a nation of people.

My mouth gapes, and I lean toward my monitor, enthralled.

He is larger than life, this boy.

This *man.*

Zeke: *It's me. You have time to talk?*

Violet: *Yes.*

Zeke: *How was your week?*

Violet: *Okay. Yours?*

Zeke: *I've had better—I miss you Violet. I really fucking miss you.*

Violet: *It's only been a few days.*

Zeke: *It doesn't matter. I feel sick to my fucking stomach every time I think about this whole damn mess.*

Violet: *I honestly still don't know what to say about it, Zeke.*

Zeke: *Did you at least get my letter?*

Violet: *Yes, I got your letter.*

Zeke: *What did you think?*

Violet: *I think it was your truth, and I know it took a lot of effort for you to say all those things*

Zeke: *I hear a but coming.*

Violet: *But actions speak louder than words, Zeke.*

Zeke: *Then help me Violet. I don't know what I'm doing.*

Violet: *I know you don't. I wish I knew what to say. I wish you hadn't ... made me feel what I felt, good and bad. In a matter of weeks, you've managed to make me feel both.*

Zeke: *Pix, please. I am sitting on a bus in the middle of fucking nowhere, unable to do anything but text you, and it's going to take at least another two hours before I'm home. So PLEASE just don't tell me no. Not yet.*

Violet: *Are you sure you're not feeling this way because you're not getting what you want? Is it because you care, or because you're being stubborn?*

Zeke: *Probably both, but that doesn't mean I don't care about you. I care a lot—more than I've ever cared about ANYTHING. I can't even believe I'm having a conversation like this. Do you realize that? This is insane. I'm texting about my FEELINGS.*

Violet: *It's nice.*

Zeke: *It's nice? That's all you have to say? Because I'm skittish as hell and kind of want to puke my guts out.*

Violet: *YES ZEKE. That's all I have to say. Because it's really nice to hear, and maybe someday you'll get to the point when you can SHOW it.*

Zeke: *I know I deserve that.*

Violet: *I hear a but coming.*

Zeke: *But it still fucking sucks.*

Violet: *They're just words, right?*

Zeke: *No. They're not just words and we both know it, and I'm sorry I didn't realize it until now.*

Violet: *Can I tell you something?*

Zeke: *Of course.*

Violet: *I watched your match against Hassan tonight on ESPN.*

Zeke: *You did???? Wow. Seriously? I'm typing so fast right now, LOL*

Violet: *Yeah. I googled it and hunted down the channel.*

Zeke: *Well—what did you think???*

Violet: *I thought it was amazing—YOU were amazing. Everything about it was incredible. You're so strong. I am so in awe of you.*

Zeke: *No one is more in awe of someone than I am of you, Violet. And no one is stronger. And when I get home and you're ready, I'm going to come see you. There's so much shit I want to say that makes being on this bus a fucking nightmare.*

Violet: *Hey Zeke?*

Zeke: *Yeah?*

Violet: *I'm ready.*

Zeke

I sat on that damn bus for *four* hours and fifty-eight goddamn minutes with nothing to do but think. And think some more.

So when I step onto Violet's front porch and give the wooden door a few short raps with my knuckles, I'm a ball of energy, body buzzing—not just from my win tonight, but from my text conversation with Violet.

I bounce on the balls of my feet nervously, hands stuffed into the pockets of my gray sweatpants. In a mad dash to get here, I didn't bother to change into something decent, like jeans or whatever. Sweatpants and hoodie are as good as it gets and I make no apologies for it.

The door swings open.

Vi's roommate Winnie glares at me through the storm door, scowling. "Can I help you?"

I scowl back, tempted to roll my eyes. "Is Violet home?"

"Why should I let you in?" She folds her arms, looking me up and down through the glass. "You look like a murderer."

What the fuck. I sigh. "What would make me look like *less* of a murderer? So you let me in." It's fucking cold.

She taps her chin, thinking. Smiles.

"Well, you can start by taking your hood down. And take your hands out of your pockets where I can see them. You look shady."

"You know damn well I'm not shady."

Her pleasant smile turns into an evil grin. "Yeah, but I know you're going to listen because you want me to let you inside the house. Am I right?"

I nod.

Remove my hands from the pockets of my sweats, reach up, push the hood of my sweatshirt down.

"Satisfied?"

"Almost." She stares through the glass, crossing her arms. "I just want you to know, just because you think you're hot shit doesn't mean the rest of us approve of you."

I cross my arms, mimicking her stance. "Is this where you threaten to kick my ass?"

"No. This is where I tell you ..." She inhales. "This is where I say ... I hope you know what you're doing. Do you? Have *any* idea what you're doing?"

"No. I don't have a fucking clue what I'm doing."

"Hmmm." She regards me through the window. "At least you're honest. I can't say much for your foul mouth though. You should work on not being such a total dick."

"Yeah, that's what I've been hearing."

"So, just so you know, if you hurt her—"

"You'll kick my ass?"

Winnie stares me down until I clamp my lips shut and listen.

"Just so you know, if you hurt her, you're hurting all of us. We're friends, and we do this together."

What the fuck does that mean? "Like, I have to date all *three* of you?"

She rolls her eyes. "Oh my god, no. I mean, Violet is our best friend. If you hurt her, we're all going to be hurt. Her pain is our pain. Do you want to make all *three* of us hate you?"

"No." I shake my head.

"Good, because Melinda and I will kick your ass if you do."

I knew it, *knew* she was going to threaten to kick my ass!

"Uh ... so ..." I try glancing around her into the living room for any sign of Violet. "Can I come in?"

Her eyebrows rise. Chin tips up defiantly.

"Please Winnie, can I please come inside?" Jesus Christ, I cannot believe I'm begging to be let into a girl's house, but desperation does some fucked up shit to a guy.

"Hold on a second. Let me check with Violet." With another scowl, Winnie shuts the door in my face, disappears into the house.

A minute passes. Then another.

Then five.

Then ten, until I'm freezing my balls off.

Then.

The door finally opens, and Violet is standing on the opposite side of it, looking ...

Like a breath of fucking fresh air, light shining from behind her, pale hair glowing ethereally. Long and wavy and I want to bury my fingers in it, breathe her in and sleep beside her.

Bare feet, jeans, and a faded yellow sweatshirt, Violet is the picture of light and sunlight and everything I've been missing for the past few days.

She unlatches the door.

Steps forward, pushing on the glass, so it opens all the way.

"I missed you." That's the first thing I say when she gives me room to step up into the house. I stop in front of her, gazing down into the hazel eyes that have been haunting my damn dreams for the past few days. "I really missed you." My hands reach for her face, cupping her jaw, thumbs tracing her cheekbones.

"You smell good," her pink lips reply.

"Oh yeah? Like what?" I lean forward so we're close enough to kiss. So close I can taste it.

"Like ..." She sniffs. "Shower and sweat. Strong."

"I smell *strong*?"

"Yes."

I bend, brushing my mouth across her lips. "I missed you so much."

Somewhere from within the room, a feminine throat clears.

"Please go do that in her *room*."

Winnie.

The plain girl with the death glowers.

Violet blushes, pulling on my wrists so my hands release her face. "S-sorry Win."

"I do not want to hear you having sex," her roommate makes a *hmph* sound. "Make him *beg*, Vi."

"I will."

Violet takes my hand, leading me through the living room to the hallway. To her bedroom door.

Leads me over the threshold.

I pause in the doorway, hesitating.

"What's wrong?"

"Nothing. I'm just … looking." The room isn't what I pictured in my mind; I'd imagined something more flowery and froofy. Fussy with knickknacks and posters and shit. Like, unicorns and crap.

This room is nothing like that. One double bed with no headboard, there's a light gray comforter pulled over the top. Three white pillows stacked, one on top of the other. White blinds on the windows for privacy, no curtains. A wooden desk that probably came off the curb at the end of the spring semester. Small desk lamp. Chair. School supplies neat and methodically arranged into rows. Above that, a corkboard with small, instant camera film. Several movie tickets stubs. A red ribbon—from what victory, I can't tell from here.

On the far wall is a narrow rack with some shirts I recognize, pants folded neatly and stacked on top. I make a quick count of the four pair of shoes lining the bottom. One pair of boots.

It's plain and simple, and bare.

Confused, my brow wrinkles. "Where's all your stuff?"

Her face turns pink, but she laughs. "I don't *have* any stuff. I'm an orphan, remember?"

Oh fuck. Shit.

"It's okay, don't feel bad." She pats my arm, and I tense up from the contact. "It works because I drew the short straw; no closet, no clothes. I borrow a lot from Mel and Winnie."

She bumps my hip, shooing me from the door so she can close us in. Locks the door.

I shrug out of my jacket, hanging it on the chair. "Where do you want me to sit?"

"On the chair I guess. I'll take the bed."

I straddle it, throwing a leg over each side. Rest my hands on the back, leaning forward. Violet is sitting cross-legged in the center of her bed, positive and pretty radiating off of her like sunlight.

"Winnie is a good little guard dog," I begin, chagrined.

"I-Is she?" Violet demurs, studying her fingernails, peeking at me from under her lashes. "I hadn't noticed."

Smartass.

"Yeah. I was outside freezing my ass off for almost fifteen minutes before you came outside."

If Violet is surprised by this news, she doesn't show it. "She's my people."

My people. My friend. My family.

"You won big today. I can't believe you picked that guy up from a standstill—I was scared to *death*. How did it feel?"

"Heavy." I roll my shoulders, listing my head from side to side, knots burning from the inside out. "I'm the last wrestler on the roster. The sooner I win, the sooner we can leave, and honestly, I wanted to get it over with so I could come home."

"What was the rush?"

I meet her eyes; they sparkle naïvely into mine.

"You know what the rush was." She can't be that oblivious.

"You picked a guy up off the *ground*, slung him on your shoulder, dumped him onto the mat, and pinned him in under a minute so you could get home sooner?"

"Home to *you*," I clarify.

"To *me*?"

A nonchalant shrug. "Basically."

She considers this quietly, biting down on her bottom lip in concentration. Then, "Do you think you could you lift *me* onto your shoulder?"

My eyes start at the top of her pale white hair, trail down her chest. Stomach. Waist. Thighs, legs, and feet, weighing her in at one twenty-five soaking wet.

"Easily."

"Hmmm," she hums, all twinkling and mischievous, like she suddenly wants to play and get sweaty with me.

My dick twitches.

We haven't had sex in days, and I'm getting turned on by the mere sight of her. By the smell of her clean room and the exposed skin of her stomach whenever she moves around on the bed.

"Do you *want* me to pick you up and lift you over my shoulder?"

Naked.

Just the thought turns my twitching dick into a semi-boner.

Violet leans back, foot dangling off the bed. She jiggles it up and down, drawing attention to her cute little toenails. Light purple.

"I don't know; maybe. We'll see after we've had our talk, won't we?"

Fair enough.

I sit up straight, arching my spine, stretching. Put my hands on the small of my back, press down, and groan.

Her smile is slight. Soft and sweet.

"Here, come sit on the bed; it's probably more comfortable than that chair I found at a garage sale. I trust you'll keep your hands to yourself."

She pats the spot next to her, scooting over to provide more space.

I stand. Kick off my shoes. Crawl across her bed.

Seat myself in the center.

Instead of sitting next to me, Violet lies down on the bed, curls her body, and rests her head in my lap. For a second I just sit there, frozen, unsure of what to do—I've never had anyone curled up on me before. Never had anyone's head in my lap.

My hands poise above her relaxing figure, suspended in mid-air. Gradually I lower them to her face, touching tentatively, my rough, calloused hand seeking the silk of her hairline with a caress.

Gently.

Fingertips trail her forehead and down the bridge of her pert nose. Trace the cupid's bow of her top lip.

She looks up at me, speaking softly. "We're a lot alike, you and I."

Stated so simply, as fact.

I swallow the lump in my throat that has me choking down a hoarse reply. "Yeah."

"Tell me why you were so upset in the library."

Her eyes flutter closed when I stroke her widow's peak, down her temple to touch her cheek.

"I understand if you're angry with your parents, Zeke, but that doesn't give you the right to be angry with everyone else, least of all me. It hurts."

"I know." I lean down to kiss her forehead, sweeping her long hair away. "I'm … I can't explain why I acted like an ass, and I feel like a bigger asshole apologizing; it makes me feel like one of those pricks who treat woman like shit. I'm not that guy."

Her hazel eyes regard me thoughtfully. "If you're not careful, you could be."

It's a sobering thought that gives me pause.

She's right; I could end up as one of those guys. The dickhead who's always making his girlfriend feel like a useless piece of shit. Demeaning her. Belittling. Apologizing until it becomes a cycle neither of them can climb out of.

I've seen athletes—who I spend most of my time with—do it all the time. Athletes with way too much testosterone and adrenaline pumping through their bodies, taking their restlessness out on the woman they're dating—or screwing.

Witnessed plenty of public fights. Girls crying in corners, consoled by their friends. Football players hurling beer, picking fights. Posturing to their girlfriends.

It's fucked up.

A sense of embarrassment and shame washes over me, knowing I've done it. Picked arguments with Jameson. Her roommate Allison at a party.

Because of my damn pride.

"I never thought I'd ever have a girlfriend—never. So I guess I wouldn't know how to treat one."

"How would you *want* to treat one?"

"I don't fucking know. Like ..."

This.

I run a hand through her hair, letting the long, silky strands thread through my fingers. "Like this."

"And how does *this* feel?"

Awesome. It feels fucking amazing.

"Zeke?"

I still don't respond.

"If you ever do anything like what you did to me in the library the other day, I will not see you again. This is your chance to redeem yourself. You get one."

"But what if I do something stupid?"

Her eyes smile. "Well *that's* a given; you won't be able to stop yourself from some things, will you? It's just who you are. I'm talking about embarrassing me in public, treating me like crap because of your pride." Violet raises her palm, running it along my unshaven jaw. "And I-I want you to be faithful."

"All right."

"Not just physically, Zeke. Anyone can keep it in their pants if they try hard enough. I'm talking about being respectful of me even when we're not together."

"Are you talking about not letting chicks grab my junk?"

"Girls do that?"

Is she for real? How did she not know this? "Uh, yeah."

She scowls up at me.

"Violet, you do realize I'm a *conquest* to most girls who flirt with me, not an actual candidate for a relationship, right?"

"G-Girls seriously grab your ... you know?"

"Dick? Yeah. At parties and shit—it's the wrestling singlets. Obviously you can see the whole full frontal, and some girls consider that an invitation to get handsy. I don't know why anyone considers grabbing a dude's nuts through his jeans sexy." I blink down at her. "Unless it was you. You can grab them any time you want."

She snickers. "I will *not* be grabbing your nuts."

"Hey, hey, hey now, don't be so hasty," I tease, grinning.

Violet stops smiling, suddenly serious. The tips of her fingers lovingly cross my lips. "Has anyone ever told you how beautiful you are?"

No.

I get told I'm hot by random girls. I get told I'm pretty by my teammates when they're fucking with me, handsome by my mother on those rare occasions she hosts a holiday and demands I come home.

Beautiful? That's a first.

Beautiful sounds like *more*.

More of everything.

She's not just calling me beautiful, she's ...

Shit, I don't know what the hell I'm saying; Violet is turning me into a fucking pansy. I used to be a hard ass, and now I'm talking about feelings and all that other bullshit. Soon she's going to have me holding babies and volunteering with old people, I just fucking know it.

Whatever.

I'd do it.

I'd do it just to see those eyes of hers light up. I'd do it because when her small, slender body is pressed against mine, mine lights on fire. I could get used to these feelings, could get high now that I know how fast my heart beats when she's near.

"Violet," I say, almost breathlessly.

"Yes?"

I let the open flat of my hand graze her shoulder, down her arm, over the sleeve of her sweatshirt. Take her hand, dragging it to my chest. Flatten her palm against my violently pounding heart.

Wordlessly.

Violet shifts, drawing away. Sitting up, she climbs in my lap, facing me, and settles down, one leg on either side of my hips. Slides her palms up my hard pec muscles, then down my torso, grasping the hem of my hooded sweatshirt. Burying her hands inside. Hauling the hem up my abs. We pull it off together. I'm wearing a cutoff shirt underneath, and in short time, we remove that, too.

Together.

Moments later, I watch her hands disappear between us to drag her yellow sweatshirt up, over her head, and toss it to the floor.

Except for her sheer, lacey bra, we're both naked from the waist up.

Those delicate hands of hers glide slowly along my bare shoulders. Down my deltoids. Over the smooth expanse of my clavicle, index finger drawing along the planes of my naked torso, committing every inch to memory.

Her palms brace the column of my corded neck. Drift slowly behind to my nape, thumbs fiddling with the hair that could probably use a trim. Back down my chest, sliding through the hair on my sternum. Traces my nipples.

It gives me goose bumps.

Gets me hard.

She leans in close, so close her small breasts press against my chest, and rains kisses on my neck. Along my collarbone.

It feels so fucking good.

Enveloping her tiny waist with my arms, I drag her close, positioning us so all our best parts are aligned.

Skin on skin, my hands skim her spine.

My neck bends forward and I drop my forehead so ours touch. Our noses. Our *breaths*.

"Violet?" I whisper.

"Yes?" she whispers back.

"I love you."

It's a confession.

Closing my eyes, I say it again. "I love you Violet."

A prayer.

Seconds pass. Stretch out.

Moments of silence.

Then, "I love you, too."

She draws back to look at me, heavy lidded eyes softening, dampening at the corners, bottom lip trembling. When she squeezes her eyes shut and a tear slips down her cheek, I take her face in my hands, cupping her chin in my hardened, massive palms.

Kiss her mouth. "I'm in love with you."

I don't know what else to say, want to keep repeating the words. Suddenly, all these emotions and shit I've kept to myself are emerging as heart emojis, sappy love songs, and chick flicks. I look at Violet and all I want to do is spout mamby pamby love bullshit. Roll around on the bed and cuddle with her and crap.

She's so cute.

So fucking gorgeous.

So sexy.

I love her.

How many times am I allowed to say it before sounding like a douchebag? I'll have to ask Oz.

"You make me ..." There's that lump in my throat making it almost impossible to get the words out. "I want to make you happy."

Oh my god, listen to me.

"You do."

When our tongues meet, my lips tingle, dick twitches. Everything about this feels ... new. Different somehow.

Violet's hands reach for my sweatpants, disappearing into the elastic waistband. Tugging. Pulling. Without breaking our kiss, I shove them down my hips. Kick them off and onto the floor, along with my boxers.

Her jeans and plain white underwear follow.

Violet pulls back the coverlet on her bed, spreading back the quilt and crawling underneath. Pats the space beside her. Drags the covers waist high when I'm settled.

She lies flat in the center, wearing nothing but her dainty little bra, rosy nipples displayed through its sheer white lace. I rub one of the straps between my fingers. Trail my pinky inside the fabric, over the shallow swell of her breasts.

"I hate this bra," she groans.

"Why?" I lean in, kissing her flesh near the tantalizing lace.

Violet shivers.

"It's not sexy."

"It's not?" Kiss.

"You're saying it like you don't agree."

I trace the sateen strap, the edge of the cup. "I don't agree. I can see through this to your skin; how is that not sexy?"

She says nothing more after that, resumes silently observing me drawing on her skin with my fingers.

Violet

I believe him.

I believe he thinks I'm sexy. Me. The bra. My body.

What I *can't* believe is that he said he loves me.

He said it and he said it first.

Zeke gazes down at me, propped up by an elbow, his mammoth upper body a wall of steel. Imposing. Strong. Unyielding.

His fingers linger on my bra strap, make their way up the column of my neck. Bury themselves in my hair. I want to touch him, long for it, but he's so content to lie here touching *me*.

So I watch.

Could lie here *forever*.

He's ridiculously attractive.

Zeke's bulging biceps flex with every movement of his arm, muscles corded … tan skin … tight six-pack … the V of his pelvis dipping into the waistband of his jeans.

He's running his big hand up my thigh, stroking my hip, a relaxed smile playing at his lips.

He's tired.

"A-Are you spending the night?" I try to inquire as nonchalantly as I can, but my stomach and tongue are doing somersaults.

"I can if you want me to. I can grab my overnight bag—it's in the truck from our match at Purdue."

"All right then, it's settled. You're sleeping over."

"I'm sleeping over," he parrots, testing out the words with an amused expression. "Shit, those are three words I've never said to anyone."

And they're for me.

"Don't look so smug," he teases, reaching for me under the blankets, hauling me closer, snug into his body.

He draws down the strap of my bra, kissing my shoulder blade. Kissing the curve of my neck. Pulls back the lace and kisses my nipple, licks it.

An excited gasp of eagerness escapes my lips.

"Shh." He silences me with a quick kiss on the mouth. "We have to be quiet. Winnie doesn't want to hear us having S-E-X."

S-E-X. He spells it out like it's naughty.

"I love your pretty little tits." He sucks gently until my head hits the pillow and I'm clutching my bed sheets. "I could suck your nipples all night."

Oh god, I would let you.

He lifts his eyes, nuzzling the underside of my boob with his nose. "Shh, that was out loud."

Oh god.

"That too."

I don't know how long we stay like this, him exploring my body with softly roaming hands—seconds, minutes maybe?—but when my eyes get heavy, his palm slides behind my neck.

He cradles my head in one hand, the other tracing the curve of my waist, up and down my ribcage. It takes a trip over my stomach, over my belly button, finger circling the small indentation there.

His mouth soundlessly forms the words, "I love you."

Lips meet my mouth.

Tongue dips inside.

Slower than he's ever kissed me before.

Wide, open-mouthed kisses. Slow, delicious tongue.

Wet.

Zeke repositions himself, his knee inserting itself between my legs, gradually nudging them apart. Firm, hot thighs. Tight ass. Chiseled, sexy body.

Mine, all mine.

When his hard, sinewy biceps brace themselves on either side of my head, our lips meet again.

He pushes in effortlessly. Slowly.

Magnificently *stiff*.

Gloriously long.

We moan in tandem, his face buried in my shoulder, nipping.

I cradle his head, spreading my legs farther when he begins a slow, steady rhythm, grunting with each thrust.

"*Uhh* ..." My eyes roll toward the ceiling, vision blurry. I can't focus. "*Uhh* ..."

When his mouth muffles my moans, my brows furrow, almost painfully. It feels so "*Mm* ... mmmph ..." I break the contact. "*Oh god* ..." I pant. "Oh Zeke, *yes* ... I love you ..."

"I love you, Violet. I fucking love you ..."

Our kisses are frenzied. Frantic. Desperate.

Wet.

Panting.

Moaning.

"You feel so good, *oh god*, deeper ..."

His pelvis rotates, controlled, pushing deep. Grabbing my ass and pulling me in, sinking into me as far as he can go. So thick. So hard. So ... so ...

I want to cry good. Painful good.

Mouthwatering.

Eye rolling.

Hot.

My toes curl.

The pumping becomes excruciatingly slow, our heads thrown back. He leans in to suck on my neck, my breasts.

When his tongue latches onto a nipple, "*Ffff* ... uck ... that's gonna make me come ... *push* Zeke, *harder* ... oh god, *yeah* ... yesssss ... oh god, *yes yes* ..."

Then my mouth is open, but no sound comes out. Stars shine behind my eyelids, and—my own name? Violet *who*?

"Violet, Violet ..." he chants, remembering it for me, all attempts at silent sex long forgotten as Zeke comes, entire body jerking. Grips my hips with his fingers, releasing inside me with tiny spasms.

Shudders.

I can feel it—every bit of it—warm and hot.

#DOUCHEBAG

"I might have pulled a muscle
in my back masturbating
this morning. I feel like that
really set the tone for
my shitty day."

Zeke

"**I** feel like a circus freak. Everyone's staring like I'm a sideshow."

Violet pats my hand. "They're not staring at you; they're staring at *us*."

"No, babe. They're definitely staring at me."

We're at the movies.

On—get this—a *group date*.

My personal hell has officially frozen over with rapid-fire speed.

This group date shit is just so fucking *weird*. Strange.

But I'm doing it for *Violet*, and at least it's not one of those hideous canvas-and-wine parties I've heard about from other guys, which Jameson originally planned for this date night. "Unfortunately" the place was booked solid.

Dodged a bullet with that one.

In front of us, a two-story projection screen runs a reel of movie trivia while the audience waits for the movie to start—trivia questions Oz and Jameson keep obnoxiously shouting out the answers to.

Fortunately, there are people sandwiched between us, so I don't have to sit next to my irritating roommate. It's me, Violet, Rex Gunderson, his date (some chick named Megan? Teagan?), Oz, Jameson, and then Elliot, odd numbering out the cluster to make it even *more* of a fuck.

I glance down the row—because I'm a sadist—to find Oz watching me. He wiggles his fingers in a cheeky wave then winks. Tips his head back on the seat when I scowl, laughing.

James kisses his neck, his lips before settling back in her seat, tossing a kernel of popcorn into the air and catching it with her mouth. She catches me watching and smiles, holding the tub forward in the universal sign of an offering: *You want some?*

I glower in her direction.

Turn to find Violet staring at me.

Even in the dim theater, I feel my face get red, embarrassed at having been caught shooting unfriendly faces at my roommate's girlfriend by my … by kindhearted Violet.

I reluctantly raise my hand toward Jameson in a friendlier gesture. Mouth *No thanks,* and want to fucking *disappear* into the plush movie recliner beneath my ass.

I pull the black ball cap lower over my eyes.

Lift the center console between Violet and me, satisfied when she inches closer. I slide my open palm over her thighs, my palm so big it covers most of her lap, resting it on her dark denim jeans. Squeeze.

Leaning into me, Violet slides her hand over mine, her thumb stroking back and forth across my rough skin, and I stare at it. Stare at how right our hands look together.

"Oh my god," I hear Oz say in a staged whisper. "Look how cute the kids are; they're holding hands."

From Jameson, "Stop teasing Sebastian, you're going to make him mad."

Oz snorts. "He's always mad."

Rex, peering down the row, "He can hear you, you know."

Oz, stuffing a handful of popcorn down his gullet, "Yeah, I figured, but he deserves it. Just like he deserves a swift kick to the ball sack."

Rex's date, WhatsHerFace, "Shhh."

Oz, to Rex's date, "Who even *are* you?"

Rex's date, "My *name* is *Mon*ica."

Oz, using air quotes, "Okay, *Monica,* whom I have never met before tonight, I'll *shhh.*"

Monica, "You know, I heard you were a jerk."

Oz, "Douchebag."

Jameson, laughing, "Okay guys, knock it off."

Rex, "Yeah, knock it off, the movie's starting."

And on and on and on.

Violet chuckles beside me. I squeeze her thigh. Manage to steal a few covert kisses in the dark. The entire movie flies by in less than two painless hours.

All in all, not the best night out I've ever had with my friends. But it's a start.

"Dammit! I knew she was here to stay the minute I met her."

My body jerks when the voice arises out of semidarkness, shrouded and scaring the living *shit* right out of me.

"Jesus Christ James—do you have to keep doing that?"

"Doing what?"

"Scaring the shit out of me in the dark."

"Sorry?"

She's in my kitchen, with only the microwave light on, scooping ice cream out of the container like it's the middle of a heat wave in July. Leaning against the counter, not a care in the world, Jameson's pajamas are an asexual two-piece flannel set that look like they're for men, but come in patterns for women.

Hers are pink with yellow rubber ducks—not even remotely sexy—and I briefly contemplate how Oz manages to maintain a stiffy while his girlfriend wears fuck-a-duck pajamas.

Then I picture *Violet* in them, maybe lying on my bed in *just* the button-down shirt ... something cute printed on them, like hearts or flowers or some shit. I could easily unbutton and slide my hands into them ...

Maybe I should buy her a pair.

"Hello?" James says to get my attention.

I quit gawking at her ducking pajamas long enough to shake the vision of Violet from my head, pad barefoot to a cabinet for a glass, and fill it with water.

Chug the entire ten ounces.

Set it on the counter near the sink.

"As I was saying," James starts, spoon suspended near her lips. "I knew Violet would be back. I'm glad I was right ... but I really wish I had taken that bet with Oz. I would have won."

I'm not sure how to respond to that, but I know if I don't say *something*, she's going to keep rambling. I attempt conversation, going with a cool, "Uh, yeah."

"I *really* like her."

Me too. "What are you doing up? It's one o'clock."

She shrugs with a sigh. "Your roommate woke me up with his roaming hands. Couldn't get back to sleep after that. What about you?"

"Your boyfriend woke me up with his roaming hands. We share a wall."

Jameson giggles. "Good one."

I kind of smile. "Thanks. I try."

"*Do* you?" Her question is full of skepticism.

"No. But I'm going to."

She laughs at that too. "Ahh, *I* see how it is."

I roll my eyes, playing along. "What is it you *think* you *see*?"

James is silent for all of ten seconds. "You love her, don't you?"

We have a reckoning then, she and I, and judging by the firm set of her mouth, this question is a test. Jameson Clark is testing me, daring me to answer with the truth.

Patient, I know she'll wait me out until I'm the first to speak.

My choices are simple. I can lie and be the guy Violet warned me *not* to be, *or* I can suck up my pride and choke out the truth, despite myself. Despite wanting my private life to be private and wanting to keep the details to myself.

Shit.

I nod. "Yes."

Jameson's mouth falls open. Hangs there.

"Have I stunned you into silence?"

"You might have." Her spoon digs deep into the ice cream. "I mean, wow. This is great. I'm happy for you. I'm happy for me—another girl around the house? This is going to be *great*."

Oh Jeez, she's going to make this weird. "Please don't."

"Don't what?"

"Don't get all …" I wave my hand in circles in front of me. "Girly. Stop planning dates and shit in your head."

Another laugh. "Too late for that, my friend. The damage is done."

"You realize you're beginning to sound and act just like Oz? Always trying to give advice and meddling in my life."

"I do? I am?" Her eyes crinkle at the corners, pleased. "Aww! You are too sweet, because I think he's the *best*."

Such a smartass, even at one in the morning.

"Did I-I miss the party invitation?"

James and I both jump, startled, turning at the sound of shuffling in the doorway. Violet enters the kitchen in one of my wrestling t-shirts, rubbing the sleep from her eyes with a yawn.

Her pale blonde hair falls in a long braid over her shoulder.

I slide my arm around her waist and squeeze, dropping a kiss on the top of her sleepy head. "Hey babe, what are you doing up?"

Violet nests into my side, fits perfectly against my ribcage, like the missing piece of a puzzle.

"The sound of laughing from the kitchen woke me up." Yawns.

"Sorry. I was thirsty, and *apparently*, this one night binges on mint chocolate chip."

Jameson taps the spoon on the container in her hands, looking *way* too awake. "Guilty."

"Well on that note, Pix and I are going back to bed."

James rolls her eyes. "Night guys."

I lead Violet down the hall, climb into bed behind her, wrap my arms around her waist.

"Goodnight," she whispers in the dark, cuddling her backside into my junk—which never bodes well for my ability to sleep.

"Night," I mumble, burying my face in her hair. "Love you, baby."

So fucking much.

"I love you, too."

Violet

"Pix, I wrote you a poem, wanna hear it?"
"Uh, *yeah*."
"Roses are red, Violet is blue—"
"Hey! I am not."
"Okay, okay, let me try again."

Zeke clears his throat dramatically, leaning into me from across the table.

"Roses are red, Violet is pretty, I wanna lay her."
I scrunch up my nose. "Is that the entire poem?"
"Uh ... something ... something city?"
Giggle. "Just stop."
He leans closer.
"Just kidding, that poem's not your real gift." Zeke clears his throat. "I have something for you."
My real gift? What in the world ...
I blink, confused. "For what?"
He shrugs. "I mean, it's been like, six months. Don't people give gifts and shit?"
Six months?
I have *no* idea what he's talking about. "Give gifts for *what*?"
Zeke picks the menu up from the center of the table—the one that's been obstructing our view—and sets it off to the side.
"Are you being serious right now? You really don't know what I'm talking about?"
My head shakes slowly. "Sorry."
"Oh my *fucking* god—I am going to kill him when I get home."
"Who?"

318

"Oz." He lets out a breath. "I am such … I am an *idiot*. God damn him, this is his fault. No, it's mine. I shouldn't have listened."

"*Now* what did he tell you to do?"

"He said to get you a gift for our anniversary, a really nice one, but obviously people don't do that."

Our *anniversary*?

"It's our anniversary?"

Is that what this fancy dinner is all about? The dressy clothes and expensive restaurant? I thought we were just having dinner.

Zeke's Adam's apple bobs when he swallows, face turning red with embarrassment. "Shit."

"I'm sorry. I knew by looking at the calendar we've been together that long, I just didn't realize you'd want to celebrate it."

"What do you mean you didn't realize I'd want to celebrate? You're my *girl*friend."

He's looking at me like *I'm* the weirdo here.

Oh my god, it's so sweet.

"So … can I have my gift?"

"Yes," he grumbles. "But I feel like such an asshole."

"You feel like an asshole for buying me a gift?"

"Nooo, I feel like an asshole because—well … don't feel bad, okay? I know you didn't get me anything." If sullen eyes can pout, his are doing it right now.

"Don't mope. I would have gotten you something if I'd known this was a celebratory dinner."

Zeke lifts his hips off the seat, digging in his back pocket. Produces a narrow envelope and sets it in the middle of the table.

I stare at it.

He prods me. "Go ahead. Take it."

My fingers deftly pluck it up. Examine it.

His beautiful lips curl into a smile. "Any guesses?"

It could only be … "Concert tickets?"

SARANEY

"Nope." He casually reaches for a water glass, takes a sip, cool as can be. Sets it down and says, "Just open it. You'll never guess."

My thumb cuts through the envelope, revealing the paper folded inside. I unfold it, bringing it closer to my face, studying the printed details. "It's airline vouchers."

He's smug. "Yup."

"For Colorado."

"Right." He straightens his utensils.

"I don't understand."

His brow furrows. "Isn't that where your aunt and uncle and cousins live?"

"Yes." I drag the word out slowly, still staring hard at the black ink printed on the paper. I lower it after a few more seconds, my heart …

Swells.

"Zeke." I finally raise my misty eyes to look at him. "Did you buy me tickets so I could see my *family*?"

"No, I bought *us* tickets so we could see your family." He says it nonchalantly, like it's no big deal, taking a piece of bread from the basket on the table and tearing off a chunk. "I was thinking June, but …" He shrugs. "Whenever."

My fingertips trail over my name on the plane voucher. The departure and destination airports listed at the top.

"Why would you do this?"

"Because you deserve it."

I bite down on my trembling lower lip. Give my head a shake. "I don't remember even mentioning this."

"Sure you did, remember? In the library that day when we got into our first fight. You were yelling about how they moved and you couldn't afford plane tickets."

"That was months ago, and I yelled a lot of things at you that day—how did you pick that out of everything I said?

His gray eyes soften. "I hear everything you've ever said to me Pix."

The tears start falling hot and fast; I can't swipe them away quick enough. "Th-This means everything to me Zeke—*you* mean everything to me. I love you—s-so much."

He tries to smile at me, tries to be tough, but there's no hiding the slight quiver of his bottom lip as he speaks. "You deserve to see your family, baby. They deserve to see *you*."

My head bows, shoulders hunched. I take deep, steadying breaths, trying not to cry at the dinner table. Wipe my nose with a white linen napkin.

My heart is bursting with so much joy I don't know what to do with it all. Pride that he's mine to keep. That I was smart enough to take a chance on him despite my friends. Despite his manners and bad attitude.

He's amazing.

He doesn't realize it, but he is.

He stands then, coming around to my side of the table, wrapping his arms around my shoulders from behind. Kisses my jaw and the corner of my lips. Kneels beside my chair and hugs me.

I lay my forehead against his shoulder.

"I can't believe you did this for me." I quietly weep.

"Of course I did this for you," his deep, unsteady voice rasps into my ear. "I love you. You're my family Violet, and if I have to buy a ticket, hop on a plane, and take you to see yours, then I'm going to do it. I love you." His voice cracks, barely above a whisper. "I would do anything for you. I want to take care of you."

I lift my face, tears dampening my cheeks. Zeke's hands wipe them away.

"I don't want you to take care of me."

"Then what do you want?"

"I want *us* to take care of each *other*."

He kisses me firmly on the lips, like we're the only two people in the room, mouth lingering.

"I want to go home," I mutter against his warm lips.

"Okay," he says slowly. "My place or yours?"

"It doesn't matter, I just want to climb into bed and cuddle you."

He raises his arm, signaling to the waiter to bring the check with a brief nod of the chin. When he's taken care of that, he stands, helping me to my feet. Helps me slide into my jacket.

People are staring at us, the big, angry-looking boy and the crying girl—I can only imagine what they're thinking.

"You know, just now I was reminded of something."

"What?"

He turns me to face him, reaching for the collar of my coat and pulling me close. Kisses the tip of my nose. "I loved you first."

My brows rise. "You did?"

"Yeah."

"I'm not sure about that, but I'll take the bait. When did you know?"

"Remember that time I came into the library and rang that little bell on the desk? It was really obnoxious but you were really polite. The look on your fucking face though ... I loved that face."

"That's really mushy coming from you." I roll my eyes, which are still damp. "I thought you were the most handsome guy I'd ever seen."

"When?"

"At the grocery store, when you got those ice cream cones down off the shelf for Summer."

"Really? I was a huge dick that day." He leads me to the front of the restaurant toward the exit, hand at the small of my back.

"I know, but you made my heart leap, and it hasn't stopped since."

He stops walking. Turns to stare at me. "That was so fucking cute."

"We're disgusting."

"Fuck yeah we are, but you know what they say."

"No, what do they say?"

"The bigger they are, the harder they fall."

The End

Acknowledgements

My brother thinks he is a douchebag ...

Seriously. He fancies himself THE Douchebag (he's really not). I'm racking my brain for some examples of his douchiness, but the only thing I can come up with is the time he got up to pee in the middle of the night, and ended up peeing in a cabinet in my room. So there is that ... But I'd like to thank him for answering my calls when I have questions or need advice about what a "real guy" would do.

My husband and daughter, Merrit, for their patience every time I write a book. Especially this one, because there were a lot of missed meals and long nights when my nose was stuck in the computer. Fine. A few missed showers, too.

A huge, massive thank you to my Beta Readers: Author Andrea Johnston, Author SJ Sawyer, Christine Kuttnauer, Melinda Lazar, and Laurie Darter. Without your feedback and critiques, Zeke wouldn't be the douchebag he is today.

We are all kindred, you and I—each of us having something in common; books. Reading. Imagination. Thank you to my book friends; you are truly family. There aren't enough words to describe what our community means to us—so I want to thank *Ney's Little Liars* and the *Nerdy Little Book Herd* for being a part of my daily.

My friends are my family, and one of them also happens to be my right hand. I message her every single day—all day, every day—and could not have finished this book without her patience and feedback. Christine Kuttnauer, you are my jinx for life. I heart you. Thank you for loving this process as much as I do—and thank you to your family for sharing you (Sue Hodge, I'm looking at you …)

Christine, along with Laurie Darter, also helps with my social media, posting giveaways and threads when I'm knee-deep in my writing cave. They keep me organized and on track, despite myself. And they do it asking nothing in return.

Thank you to Caitlin Nelson (Editing by C Marie) for her edits. Julie Titus, (JT Formatting) the most talented Formatter, and Okay Creations for the gorgeous covers; I'm glad I was able to keep this one on schedule. Thank you for taking it from a manuscript, to an actual book.

To my Swag Hags: Book Boyfriend Candles (candles), and Mockingbird Apparel (shirts and decals) for the kick-ass swag. Seriously the best hags a gal could ask for.

Thank you to ALL THE BLOGGERS and Reviewers; there are too many of you to name, but I appreciate all the time you put in to posting, reading, and writing reviews for not just my book— but all books.

My Nerdy Little Book Herders … ME Carter, Andrea Johnston, Shirl Rickman, Jessica Hollyfield, Rachel Schneider, Andee Michelle and Emma Hart. Big hearts, no drama, and lots of laughs.

For more information about Sara Ney and her books, visit:

Facebook
https://www.facebook.com/saraneyauthor/

Twitter
https://twitter.com/saraney

Goodreads
https://www.goodreads.com/author/show/9884194.Sara_H_Ney

Website
http://kissingincars.weebly.com/

Instagram
https://www.instagram.com/saraneyauthor/?hl=en

Facebook Reader Group: *Nerdy Little Book Herd*
https://www.facebook.com/groups/NerdyLittleBookHerd/

Don't forget to join the official *Ney's Little Liars*
https://www.facebook.com/groups/1065756456778840/